From MARRIED BUT STILL LOOKING
by Travis Hunter

Genesis Styles is a conflicted man. . . .
"Genesis stood there for a moment, still unable to bring himself to touch that towel. Guilt came from both directions. Here he was, in another man's house, naked. Then there was his fiancée, Terri. In his mind, it seemed the more he messed up, the sweeter she became. Even when he knew she'd had enough of his antics, she would always surprise him with her forgiveness. Every time he cheated on her, he told himself it was the last time. . . ."

Praise for MARRIED BUT STILL LOOKING

"Travis Hunter offers insight into the male psyche in ways that will captivate the reader, with stories that are both entertaining and compelling. There is a truth and boldness to his words that make him a noteworthy force in a new generation of fiction writers."
—LOLITA FILES, bestselling author of *Child of God*

"Despite its title, *Married but Still Looking* is about the sanctity of marriage, accepting responsibility for one's actions and understanding the consequences of bad choices. . . . [Hunter is] a good storyteller . . . readers are given solid, positive messages. . . . There's a lifetime of lessons in these pages."
—*The Dallas Morning News*

"The novel brings [Genesis Styles] and a handful of other characters . . . to understand that they can accept responsibility as lovers and parents only when they have worked through the consequences of their parents' failings. Gr⬚⬚⬚⬚ having the faith, and the conviction, to be better ⬚⬚⬚⬚ ext generation."
Post

"Hunter's writing is fluid a⬚⬚⬚ ⬚⬚⬚ and gritty yet comical."
eview

Praise for THE HEARTS OF MEN

"Entertaining yet enlightening . . . Travis Hunter holds the reader hostage in his thought-provoking debut. Be prepared to laugh and cry as you examine *The Hearts of Men*." —E. LYNN HARRIS, author of *A Love of My Own*

"Travis Hunter takes us into the lives, the thoughts, and straight into the hearts of men. His work reflects the voice that is often missing—the voice of a brother who loves, listens, and tells his own truth." —BERTICE BERRY, author of *Jim and Louella's Homemade Heart-Fix Remedy*

"A book I'll share with my sons for years to come." —CARL WEBER, author of *Baby Momma Drama*

"This moving novel . . . is insightful, sensitive and impressively real." —*Essence*

"True-to-life debut novel. Tough lessons and father-wit loom large in this story about men staying the course and stumbling along the way." —*Black Issues Book Review*

"[An] interesting and revealing look into the male psyche." —*Today's Black Woman*

"Even cynical readers may be won over by his relentless positive message and push for African-American communities built on respect and love." —*Publishers Weekly*

"Hunter is a fresh new talent and his book *The Hearts of Men* gives us a glimpse into the mysterious void where black men hide their expectations, inspirations, disappointments and dreams—a place they rarely share with anyone." —*St. Louis American*

STRIVERS ROW

During the 1920s and 1930s, around the time of the Harlem Renaissance, more than a quarter of a million African-Americans settled in Harlem, creating what was described at the time as "a cosmopolitan Negro capital which exert[ed] an influence over Negroes everywhere."

Nowhere was this more evident than on West 138th and 139th Streets between what are now Adam Clayton Powell and Frederick Douglass Boulevards, two blocks that came to be known as Strivers Row. These blocks attracted many of Harlem's African-American doctors, lawyers, and entertainers, among them Eubie Blake, Noble Sissle, and W. C. Handy, who were themselves striving to achieve America's middle-class dream.

With its mission of publishing quality African-American literature, Strivers Row emulates those "strivers," capturing that same spirit of hope, creativity, and promise.

MARRIED
BUT STILL
LOOKING

MARRIED BUT STILL LOOKING

a novel

TRAVIS HUNTER

Villard • New York

2003 Strivers Row Trade Paperback Edition

Copyright © 2002 by Travis Hunter
Reader's guide copyright © 2003 by Random House, Inc.
Excerpt from *Trouble Man* copyright © 2003 by Travis Hunter

This work was originally published in hardcover by Villard Books, an imprint of The Random House Ballantine Publishing Group, a division of Random House, Inc., New York, in 2002.

This book contains an excerpt from the forthcoming edition of *Trouble Man* by Travis Hunter. This excerpt has been set for this edition only and may not reflect the final content of the forthcoming edition.

Library of Congress Cataloging-in-Publication Data
Hunter, Travis.
    Married but still looking : a novel / Travis Hunter.
      p.   cm.
    ISBN 0-8129-6838-7
    1. African American men—Fiction.   I. Title.

PS3558.U497 M37 2001
813'.6—dc21

                                        2001055932

Villard Books website address: www.villard.com
Printed in the United States of America

9 8 7 6 5 4 3 2 1

Book design by Joseph Rutt

To my wonderful mother, Linda Hunter:
You are a true survivor, and for that I love you unconditionally.

MARRIED
BUT STILL
LOOKING

one

DOING WRONG!

I*t's hard to make a woman your wife when you've been sexin' married women for most of your life,* Genesis Styles thought to himself as he lay on his back, breathing hard after an exhausting session with his workout buddy, Sheila. They had been going at it for more than an hour, and now that it was finally over Genesis swore to himself that this was the last time he'd ever see Sheila. But that was a promise he made after all of their workouts. She was too aggressive, too pushy, and did too much yelling.

Genesis pulled his lanky six-foot-four-inch body up from the floor and headed for the shower. As the hot water and Camay cleansed his skin, he looked up into the steamy shaving mirror and smiled at himself. The power that he had over the women he dealt with was invigorating.

He preferred to deal with married women simply because they couldn't rightfully ask for him to commit to them totally. And, for the most part, they were always easy. It was either/or with them. Either they were happy with their husbands and wouldn't mess around, or they were unhappy and his for the taking. Every now and then he would run across a selfish one who had a good man at home but didn't give a damn. Those were the ones he really didn't respect and he made it a point to dog them out until they felt like their husbands were the best thing since K-Y jelly. But things in his life were changing, and as those changes came into view, his smile turned upside-down. Now the face he saw in the mirror didn't seem all that grand.

For the last six months Sheila had been grooming Genesis to become a personal trainer, but for the last three, when they got together, exercise was the last thing on either of their minds.

As Genesis stepped out of the shower onto the cold tile floor, he reached for the towel Sheila had placed on the countertop, but stopped in his tracks. As he stared at the towel, he frowned and took a deep breath, but still was unable to bring himself to touch the sheet of cotton. *TLG!* It was as if the fancy three-letter monogram held venom within its fibers. As Genesis stood naked in the steamy bathroom, dripping water onto the floor, he shook his head to relieve himself of this self-imposed trance, but to no avail. Something was wrong. He had been in this house with Sheila countless times before, but never had he felt like this.

This kind of thing had been happening ever since he got down on one knee and proposed to Terri. He convinced himself then that he was ready to settle down and leave all the other women alone. On the one hand, he loved Terri with all he had to offer, but on the other, he lacked the willpower and discipline to say no to a fat butt and a pretty smile.

Genesis stood there for a moment, still unable to bring himself to touch that towel. Guilt came from both directions. Here he was, in another man's house, naked. Then there was his fiancée, Terri. In his mind, it seemed the more he messed up, the sweeter she became. Even when he knew she'd had enough of his antics, she would always surprise him with her forgiveness. Every time he cheated on her, he told himself that it was the last time. Then Genesis thought about the possibility of another man standing in his bathroom naked after he'd just finished sexing Terri and his heart skipped a beat.

"Ain't this a bitch! Gon' disrespect her husband like that. I should leave my drawers in her hamper so he'll beat her ass," Genesis said to himself as he wiped the steam from the mirror with his bare hand. "Sheila," he called out.

"Yeah, babe!" The tall, bronze beauty appeared in the bathroom doorway wearing only a white silk robe.

"I need another towel," Genesis said as he pointed at the initials on the towel. "How you gon' give me your husband's personal towel to dry off with?"

"What difference does it make?" Sheila said, unaware of her transgression.

"What makes you think I wanna use that man's towel?" Genesis snapped.

"Who are you yelling at? In here tripping over a damn towel! Whatever, man! Got-damn hypocrite," Sheila said in disbelief.

"Just get me another towel!"

"Is this more to your liking?" Sheila said sarcastically as she handed Genesis a plain white towel. "And since when did you start caring about my husband's things? You drive his car, eat his food, and sex me up at least twice a week. You know what you're full of, don't you?"

Genesis took the towel without response. He dried himself and threw on his basketball shorts and plain white tank top, slipped his feet into his Adidas flip-flops, and walked out the door without saying good-bye.

Damn, is it just me or are women getting out of hand? Genesis wondered before hopping into his black Chevrolet Blazer.

Life had been a constant roller-coaster ride for Genesis since he asked Terri to marry him. It had been a daily struggle to be faithful. Every time he was faced with a chance to do right by his fiancée, he failed. In the two years they had been dating, the longest he managed to remain faithful was three weeks. And that was torture.

After his failed attempt at monogamy he understood how a drug addict felt. He really wanted to kick his sex habit but something stronger than his will kept forcing him to give in to his temptation.

But life as a good-looking brother in Atlanta was unfair, Genesis thought. It seemed like someone had gotten on a loudspeaker and told the female population that one more single man was about to be taken away. Ever since he popped the question, it seemed women were coming out of the woodwork, making his quest to be monogamous an impossible task. The women he was already dealing with became more demanding. Sheila was the worst. She acted like Genesis was *her* man. He remembered the look on her face and the questions she asked when he informed her of his engagement. The look was one of pure confusion and her questions confused the hell out of him. "How could you do this to me? What about us? What did I do wrong?" *I ain't did a damn thing to you, there is no us, and what you did wrong was get married in the first place if you still had some outside freaking to do.* But those answers never left his mouth. Instead he assured her that nothing was going to change between them, kissed her lips, and got ready for a long workout.

Women like Sheila made him nervous. Her type made it hard for him to trust people like Terri, who in his heart he knew deserved his complete trust. But then again, how could he expect Sheila to respect his engagement when she didn't even respect her own marriage? Sheila's mentality came into play with most, if not all, of the other married women he had shared a bed with—they played the role of the faithful wife in public, but behind closed doors they were freaks of the week. Now that he was about to jump the broom, his past indiscretions with married women were ever so haunting. Yet something kept telling him it was time to settle down, and after two years of Terri's unconditional love, he knew she was the one to do it with.

As Genesis strapped himself into his seat he noticed the red message light on his cell phone flashing. He pressed the mailbox icon and found he had two messages. The first one was Terri's angelic voice.

"Hi, honey. I know you're probably still at the gym but you promised you'd paint today. It's Friday. If you have any suggestions for dinner tonight, give me a call ASAP, otherwise it's pizza. I'm gonna try to get outta this store a little early. Love ya, kiss kiss."

"Damn," Genesis said to himself. Hearing Terri's sweetness only made his unfaithfulness that much harder to bear. This new feeling was totally confusing—he'd been unfaithful from day one. Why all the guilt now? Maybe it was the fact that he had spent damn near all of his savings on her ring.

The second message was from his favorite sister, Grace, who lived in New York. "Hi, sweetie pie. It's me. Call me when you get a moment. I love ya."

Genesis smiled at hearing his sister's voice. He really missed spending time with her and often tried to persuade her to move back home, but he knew he had to respect her decision to live elsewhere, especially when he understood why she'd felt a need to leave. They were always so close. As a matter of fact, there were times when he felt she was the only family he had. Even though he had a mother, a brother, and another sister, it was Grace with whom he shared a special bond.

Genesis pulled himself together and headed to Home Depot to pick up the paint that Terri had preselected. As he waited for the paint to be mixed, he roamed around the huge warehouse looking at all of the things he would use one day to remodel his house. He noticed a sale on the electric drill his nephew had been hinting for him to buy since he started taking wood shop at his junior high school. He decided to spend the forty-nine dollars in hopes of getting the little fellow to loosen up and have some fun. Every time Genesis thought about his nephew, he became sad. Jalen had been through way too much for one so young, so Genesis made it a point to brighten his day whenever possible. He smiled as he thought of how happy Jalen would be when he received his gift.

Jalen was always happy to spend any time with his uncle G. Even though he never came out and said it, when his eyes lit up, that said enough. Genesis had always wanted kids, and since his brother, Grover, was such a horrible dad, Jalen somewhat filled that void. He paid for his items and decided he'd stop by his mother's house to pick up Jalen and let him help out with the painting. As he placed the bags and cans in the back of his truck, he heard his cell phone ringing. He slammed the back hatch and ran to catch the call.

"Talk to me," Genesis said after checking the caller ID.

"Yo. What's the deal, dog?"

"P-man, what's up? Where you at?" Genesis said to his best friend.

"Headed to your spot. My wife and your future wife got a wedding to plan. I guess I'll watch you paint. Where are you?"

"Just leaving Home Depot. I'm about to run by my mom's and pick up Jalen. You got Blake with you?"

"Yeah, he's here but we're about to drop him off at basketball practice. So it's just me and the wifey."

"Okay, tell him I said what's up and work on that left hand. Blake got game, P!"

"Come on, dog. Who's his teacher?"

"I see he's picking up all your bad habits. Why you teaching him all that nonsense?"

"It ain't me, it's them damn And One tapes. But wait a minute, who died and made you Lenny Wilkens? Plus I got drama. I need to holla at you without the kids around."

"Say no more. I'll get Jalen tomorrow. Peace." Genesis hung up the phone wondering what kind of drama Prodigy had.

Genesis jumped in his truck and headed straight to his house.

He walked in and smiled at the place he called home. The three-bedroom ranch-style home wasn't the biggest or fanciest one in the world, but it was his, and since Terri had moved in last month everything had changed. The hardest part was getting used to sharing his space with someone else.

Genesis placed his bags and cans on the living room floor and walked into the kitchen where Terri was sitting at the table reading a wedding magazine. He walked over to her and gave her a peck on her forehead.

"How long you been home?"

"About ten minutes ago. How was your workout?"

"The same as always. Exhausting," Genesis said as he walked back into his bedroom to check the messages. Grace, Prodigy, and a few bill collectors.

He grabbed a pair of underwear, a T-shirt, and some nylon sweatpants out of the drawer and headed into the bathroom for another shower. He wanted to give the appearance that he had just finished working out.

Terri walked into the bedroom and caught him just as he closed the bathroom door.

"Genesis."

"Just a second, baby. I must've eaten something bad."

"Are you okay?"

"My stomach has been killing me. Do we have any of the pink stuff?"

"Let me check," Terri said as she retreated into the kitchen. She returned and knocked lightly on the bathroom door.

"Come in," Genesis said as he sat on the toilet making faces like he was really sick. "Just set it on the counter. Thank you, baby."

Terri held her breath, set the Pepto-Bismol on the counter, and closed the door behind her.

Genesis smiled to himself as he sat on the toilet doing nothing.

A few minutes later he stood and flushed the toilet. He turned the shower on until it reached the temperature that he liked and stepped in. Five minutes later he was dressed and smelling like the soap Terri was used to smelling. Before he walked out of the bathroom, he took a swig of the pink stuff to complete the lie. He walked out into the hallway and was met by Terri's concerned eyes.

"Is everything okay?" Terri asked.

"Yeah, I'm straight. That Nutrabar didn't seem to be all that nutritious," Genesis said, rubbing his stomach.

Terri reached up as far as her five-foot frame would allow her and gave her fiancé an I-missed-you hug. She seemed truly happy with the man who stood before her. He wasn't perfect, but he was the most gentle and attentive man she'd ever met.

"Other than that tummyache, how was your day, baby?" Terri asked in her soft voice, which still held a hint of her Caribbean accent.

"It was fine. What about yours?" Genesis replied, smiling at the woman who would soon walk down the aisle to meet his smiling face.

"Fine until some little floozy called here asking who I was and demanding to speak with you. Now, I'm not jumping to any conclusions, Genesis, but I suggest that you handle your past before it starts affecting our future," Terri said softly before walking back into the kitchen.

Terri was a petite woman but she carried herself with such class and dignity that she demanded the respect of a person ten feet tall. She was a true sister who pulled no punches. Her take-no-crap attitude and work ethic was what attracted Genesis to her in the first place. That and the fact that she had more curves than a San Francisco freeway.

Terri wasn't afraid to take chances. She'd left a good-paying job at a bank to open a small bookstore, even though everyone told her she couldn't compete with the large chains. She was determined to be successful, so every morning at nine o'clock her doors would open and her customers were greeted by a smiling, cocoa-brown sister with a tiny diamond stud in her nose, saying "Good morning, brother" or "Good morning, sister."

The African-American Book Nook was the place to be. Her book-of-the-month selections were always the talk of book clubs throughout Atlanta and Terri had this uncanny ability to bring in authors who were mainstays on the best-seller list. Three years after opening the African-American Book Nook for business, she was operating in the black, all because she'd figured out a way to make reading cool. Now she was in the process of adding a coffee and bagel shop to the premises to give her shop a more family-oriented flavor.

GENESIS STOOD THERE wondering which one of his chicken heads could be threatening his future. More important, what the hell did she say? Terri wasn't one for drama, so she was known to leave out some details just to keep the peace.

"Who was it?" Genesis asked Terri, following her into the kitchen.

"I don't know. All she said was, 'Tell Genesis to call me. He knows the number.' Then she hung up."

"Well, baby, you know there are women from my past who don't wanna see us happy and will do anything to break us up, so don't pay that any mind."

"Yeah, yeah, yeah. I've heard it all before. It's already forgotten." Terri was an eternal optimist, sometimes to a fault, but that was how she'd been raised. She was a very spiritual woman and took people at their word. She was well aware of Genesis's player lifestyle and trusted him when he said those days were behind him. But she wasn't stupid or gullible.

Genesis walked over to Terri and brushed his fingers through her soft, short hair. He kissed her forehead, then the tip of her nose, and then he slid his tongue between her mocha-covered lips. Terri's eyes closed, and her heart seemed to beat a little faster. She loved it when he touched her.

"What are you doing?" Terri moaned.

"I'll tell you what I'm not doing. I'm not about to let the best thing that ever happened to me slip away," Genesis said, sliding his hand down the front of Terri's white stretch pants. Terri took a deep breath. When she exhaled, the doorbell rang.

Terri shook off the erotic trance she was in and smiled at Genesis. She whispered, "Go and wash your hands."

"I ain't," Genesis said as he licked his fingers.

Terri waved him off, laughing, and walked to the front door. She looked through the peephole and saw a tall, baldheaded, dark-skinned man and a fair-skinned lady with jet-black hair and dark eyes. She opened the door, and Prodigy and Nina Banks walked in carrying boxes.

"Girl, you moving in?" Terri asked, jokingly.

"Whew, I didn't know I had this much wedding stuff. But you'll need it, trust me," Nina said, smiling.

"Hi, Prodigy," Terri said, smiling at the "I can't believe y'all" expression on her best friend's husband's face. "You wanna help us plan the wedding?"

"Terri, I'd rather have a root canal. Where's ya big head man? And what was y'all doing in here that had us standing outside so long?" Prodigy asked, setting the boxes down on the kitchen table.

"Mind your business. Genesis just ran out back to get some throw covers for the painting. But wait, what do you mean you'd rather have a root canal? Didn't you have fun helping Nina plan that beautiful wedding extravaganza that y'all had, or did she do all of that on her own?" Terri teased, knowing Prodigy would always play-fully take credit for all the good stuff and blame Nina for the bad.

"Oh, I didn't do that much when we got married. I just picked out her dress, my tux, the bridesmaids' dresses, the groomsmen's tuxedos, the church, the pastor, wrote the vows, and sent out all of the invitations—but she did everything else," Prodigy lied with a straight face.

"Is that all?" Terri played along. "After all that you should still be tired, so why don't you go on in the living room and rest up. That other liar should be in here in a minute. You want something to drink?"

"What y'all got in here?" Prodigy opened the refrigerator and took a peek inside.

"Will you get out of their refrigerator?" Nina said as she took a seat at the table.

"Oh girl, you know he thinks he lives here. Go on and get what you want," Terri said, joining her friend at the kitchen table.

"Thank you, Terri, and I would help but y'all need to learn how to function without me." Prodigy twisted the top off a German beer bottle and tossed it in the trash can. "If y'all get stuck on something I'll help, but try to handle it on your own." Prodigy walked over to kiss Nina on the forehead, but she turned around in her chair and gave him the "talk to the hand" sign.

" 'Bye, Prodigy. We have work to do. I have to try and duplicate all the work *you* did for our wedding," Nina said, playing into his game. Everyone was well aware that all Prodigy had done was name his groomsmen and show up at the church thirty minutes late.

PRODIGY WALKED INTO the living room, took a seat, and picked up an old photo album. The first picture he saw was of their old Philly crew. He chuckled at how corny they once were. Genesis had an Afro and some tight jeans on. The rest of the crew had flat tops and an assortment of colorful Adidas warm-ups.

Prodigy and Genesis were childhood friends. Prodigy grew up in Philadelphia and Genesis was raised in Atlanta, but every summer,

Genesis would visit his uncle, who lived right next door to Prodigy in Philly. With a shared love for basketball, the two tall boys became good friends.

Every summer they would play Little League basketball for the Police Athletic League, exchange southern and northern ways of life, and chase girls. Prodigy would tease Genesis about his country accent but use his influence to keep the neighborhood thugs from robbing the country boy named after the first book in the Bible. A few more summers would go by before they would go their separate ways. Not because of any animosity between the two; they just started running with different crews. Prodigy started hanging with the thug element that had once threatened to rob Genesis, while Genesis stayed on the basketball courts and continued chasing girls. His years on the court had paid off, but his appetite for women had him paying.

After two years of college, Genesis signed a lucrative contract to play in the European Basketball League. On the last game of his fourth professional season, he tore his Achilles tendon. Then news came from the States that his mother needed his help with his eight-year-old nephew, Jalen, who was born addicted to cocaine. Genesis had been hearing stories of his older brother's battle with drugs and how he wasn't doing anything to help in raising his own son. So Genesis cut his rehabilitation short and returned home to help his mother take care of his nephew.

Prodigy moved to Atlanta from Philadelphia and renewed his criminal ties with an uncle already living in Atlanta. But after a divine encounter with a man he affectionately called Poppa Doc, Prodigy left the criminal faction. He got a legitimate job and finished up his bachelor's degree in psychology. Now he was passing what he had learned in the streets and in the classroom to the younger generation as executive director of the Atlanta Youth Center.

Genesis had heard through the grapevine that Prodigy was living in Atlanta and looked him up just before he and Nina got married. Genesis was surprised to hear that Prodigy had changed his player ways. Prodigy asked Genesis if he would stand as one of his grooms-men and they had been tighter than dreadlocks ever since.

"WHAT'S UP, DOG?" Genesis said as he walked into the den and bumped fists with Prodigy. "Where's the wife?"

"She's in the kitchen with your happy-ass wife-to-be."

"Hey, Nina," Genesis yelled into the kitchen, taking a seat across from Prodigy.

"Hey, Genesis. Come here for a second," Nina yelled from the kitchen.

Genesis got up, walked into the kitchen, and returned with his lip turned up.

"I don't give a damn what the tux looks like," Genesis said under his breath. "They getting on my nerves."

"Just go with the flow, my man. It's easier on the blood pressure."

"I can't believe how they're tripping over this thing." Genesis shook his head, annoyed.

"Women like weddings. Let Terri have her day. Calm the hell down. Terri's probably been dreaming of this day since she was old enough to know what a wedding was. You got to relax, dog," Prodigy said.

"How can I relax? Whenever I walk in the house a damn wed-ding magazine is thrown in my face," Genesis said, getting even more agitated.

Prodigy laughed. He'd been through the same thing. As he looked a little closer at Genesis he sensed the intensive wedding planning wasn't really the issue. "Let's take a ride. I need to talk, and you do too."

They got up and headed into the kitchen.

"Where y'all going?" Terri asked.

"We gotta run to Home Depot to get some more throw covers. The ones in the shed done dry-rotted. Y'all need anything?" Genesis asked.

"Nah, just don't get lost. You've been putting off painting for three weeks now."

"We'll be right back, Terri. Stop stressing the man out," Prodigy said.

"Nina, tell your husband to stay outta grown folks' business," Terri said.

"Prodigy, stay out of grown folks' business. And bring me some butter pecan Häagen-Dazs while you're out."

"Your ass gonna get fat eating all that junk," Genesis said.

"Terri, tell your man to mind his business," Nina said.

"As long as she doesn't work out like you she'll be all right," Terri shot at Genesis.

"What's that suppose to mean?" Genesis said innocently.

Terri flipped the page of the magazine and ignored him.

"We'll be right back," Prodigy said as he ushered Genesis out, closing the door on the two wedding planners.

BLACK LIKE ME

P hyllis slipped her feet into her black mules and pulled herself out of the overstuffed leather chair at her favorite hangout, Spa Sydell. After a long week of locking up some of Georgia's worst criminals, helping Zachary with everything that went on in the life of a seven-year-old, shopping, cooking, and dealing with her husband, Carl, this trip to the spa was exactly what the doctor ordered. Two hours of manicures, pedicures, and massages lessened the stress in her life and gave her the energy needed to fight through another week. After saying good-bye to the staff and setting up her appointment for next week, she headed out the front exit and back to reality.

Phyllis opened the door of her white Mercedes C class, slid into the driver's seat, and pulled her to-do list from her purse. First she had to pick up Carl's tux from the cleaner's, then pick up her laptop from the repair shop, and pick up her dress for tonight from her tailor, then it was off to pick up Zach from his basketball camp. There never seemed to be enough hours in her day.

As she pulled out of the parking lot, her thoughts drifted to the awards banquet taking place that evening. How would everything turn out? Nights like tonight always made her nervous. She would be meeting with some of the top law professionals from all over the country, and she needed to look and feel her best. Then her cell phone rang.

"Hello?"

"Hello, darling," Barbara said in a playful British accent—even though she was from southwest Atlanta.

"Hello yourself. I missed you today at the spa. What happened to you?"

"I'm just trying to get myself together for tonight. There's going to be too many single and available men for me to even think about half-stepping. Did you forget how fine the selection was last year?"

"Girl, I'm married. But no, I didn't forget. I'm headed to pick up my dress right now."

"Well, don't you sound excited?" Barbara said. "Aren't you getting an award tonight?"

"Yes, but I'm a little nervous."

"Nervous? Oh, my goodness, whatever for?"

"Carl!"

"Carl?" Barbara asked, confused.

"Yes, Carl. He can be a handful at times."

"Oh, darling, I'm sure he'll be on his best behavior tonight. I mean, this is your profession and I'm sure he wouldn't want to jeopardize that."

"Don't count on it. Carl is just . . . ugh . . . he's so unenlightened. And he doesn't seem to care."

"Well, enlighten him. You know why they call men dogs?"

"I sure do, but let me hear your version."

"Because they need to be trained. You have to train him, girl. Sex is a treat. You play your hand right and you can get Carl to sit and stay on command."

Phyllis chuckled. "Girl, I wish it was that easy. That man is so against me being me that he's not open to anything I have to say. If I tell him something, he thinks I'm trying to change him or I'm putting him down. Oh, he drives me up a wall."

"Oh well, that's your husband."

"Don't remind me."

PHYLLIS WAS A true professional in every respect. She wanted everything in her life to be first class, and she almost had everything the way she wanted it—except for her husband. Carl's physical appearance wasn't in question. He was a strikingly handsome man. He had that George Clooney thing going for him. He was in the best shape and was totally at ease in a room full of African-Americans. But for some strange reason he had this thing against intellectuals. He would fiercely argue that a degree didn't make a person any better than anyone else, while Phyllis's opinion was that a degree stood as your credentials and should be respected.

Placing Carl in a room full of juris doctors, PhDs, a few MDs, and alcohol was a recipe for disaster. Phyllis's nervousness stemmed from the way their relationship had been going for the last few years. The last thing Phyllis wanted this evening was for Carl to deliver one of his "all y'all bureaucrats can kiss my ass" speeches like he did the last time they went to a party for one of her co-workers.

Her thoughts drifted to when they first met, back when she always knew what to expect. Carl was quite the gentleman. Phyllis never thought much of the flirtatious comments he made every day when he saw her on the military post where they both worked, simply because he was white. But he persisted and slowly she started paying closer attention to the laid-back white man with the sparkling blue eyes.

Carl asked her out on a date, and she surprised herself when she said yes. She told herself it was just a movie and a dinner, but she couldn't deny her attraction. She kicked herself for even considering turning her back on black men, but then she thought back to the worst day of her life and remembered that a black man was to blame.

One dinner date turned into two and then came the feelings.

Once the feelings arrived, the expectations soon followed. Thirteen months after their first date, they were married at a small military chapel in Fort Lewis, Washington. Once the new interracial couple got used to the stares and smirks of black men and women who disagreed with their crossing racial lines, they settled in for what they considered eternity.

In the beginning Carl seemed to be on a constant mission of self-improvement, which Phyllis admired. He worked on the military post during the day as an instructor and attended the post's university at night. He took her coat and was always there to pull her chair out before she took a seat. He would break his neck to open her door and always provided a shoulder to lean on when she needed one. Now it was a totally different story. Life as the wife of Carl Olsen was miserable.

"You know I don't miss going through that foolishness for one minute," Barbara said. "My ex-husband, Derrick, wanted me to apologize for being educated. Do you believe that? If his loving wasn't so good, I wouldn't have stayed as long as I did. Girl, every time I picked up to leave, I'd think about that long, black . . . oooh, let me shut up before I call that nut." Barbara laughed at her own comment.

"At least you were getting some good loving. My husband is white, if you know what I mean." Phyllis held her thumb and index finger about two inches apart and frowned for her own benefit. "If I would have known that I'd have to deal with all of this ignorance, I could've married a black man. At least I'd be getting some kind of satisfaction."

"Girl, you're too much," Barbara said as she let that bit of stereotyping slide without a comment. Barbara was Phyllis's paralegal, but she was working on obtaining her own law degree, and she felt that there would come a time when she would benefit from Phyllis's connections and knowledge. But her constant undercutting of black men got on Barbara's last nerve.

"I've been dealing with this man for the last ten years and—" Phyllis said before she was cut off.

"Phyllis? Phyllis, your phone is going in and out. I can't hear you, but if you can hear me, I'll see you tonight," Barbara said as she hung up the phone. She always found a way to leave Phyllis when she started one of her antiblack soliloquies. Barbara wondered how Phyllis could live in a black body every day and hate black men so much.

Phyllis looked at her phone, confused, before pushing the End button.

After running all her errands and dropping Zachary off at the baby-sitter's, she pulled up to her comfortable two-story home. As she got out of her car, she couldn't believe her eyes. A tall white man with long dark hair and a full beard was on the front lawn chipping golf balls into a net. She stopped in her tracks.

"What are you doing?" Phyllis asked as if she was about to scold a child.

"Practicing my short game. What does it look like I'm doing?" Carl responded like a child who was tired of his mother's nagging.

Phyllis was furious but she tried to control herself. "I can see what you're doing, but don't you think you should be getting ready for the banquet tonight?" Phyllis asked.

"Should I?" Carl said as he chipped another shot.

"Yes, you should. Didn't you get my message asking you to shave and get a haircut?"

"No, I got a message *telling* me to shave and get a haircut. How many kids do you have? One! And I'm not him. I don't know who you think you are but you better start talking to me a little nicer."

Phyllis recognized Carl's defiance and wondered what had gotten into him. She tried to soften her tone a bit. "Carl, will you please get dressed and shave?"

"No and no," Carl said.

"Why not?" Phyllis asked, exasperated.

"I'm not going, and I like my beard," Carl said as he squatted down and stared at the golf ball.

"What? What do you mean you're not going?"

"Just what I said—I'm staying home."

The soft tone wasn't working so Phyllis went back to her normal self and screamed, "Carl, this is a very important night for me, and I don't have time to play games with you. Now will you go in the house, shave, and put on this damn tux!" Phyllis threw the tuxedo at him.

"Nope, I said I wasn't going, and that's what I meant," Carl said as he stood and attempted to chip another ball, but the tuxedo hit his arm and slid to the ground just as he swung the club. "You're messing up my form."

"Fine, Carl. Stay here."

"That's the plan."

"You're such an ass," Phyllis said as she brushed past him.

"And you'll fit right in tonight with all those superficial, high-falutin, bourgeois-ass liars. I mean lawyers."

Phyllis ignored his last comment and stormed into the house, clicking her mules on the hardwood floors along the way. She stormed upstairs to get dressed. All kinds of negative thoughts ran through her mind as she showered, curled her hair, and applied makeup. What would everyone say when she showed up alone? How would she answer the "where is Carl" question? Then, as if a lightbulb went on, she realized that Carl staying home wasn't as bad as it appeared. She would have to arrive dateless, but she wouldn't have to worry about Carl pissing off one of her colleagues. She slipped into an elegant black evening gown, wrapped a string of pearls around her slender neck, and slid a set of matching pearl earrings into her lobes. She then placed her freshly pedicured feet into a pair of black silk pumps and headed down the stairs and out the door. Carl was still in the front yard chipping balls when she backed out of the driveway. The tuxedo was still on the ground where it had fallen.

AFTER PHYLLIS PULLED off, Carl tried to think back to when things became so bad between them. Things seemed to have gone downhill the night she told him that she was pregnant. Carl remembered being excited, but the look that Phyllis had on her face was far from what he was feeling. He remembered how she ranted and raved about how having a child would derail her career objectives and how she wasn't ready to have a baby. Then she cursed him out for wanting to have sex without a condom, but when Zachary Jonathan Olsen entered the world, her whole attitude changed. All of a sudden, Phyllis treated Carl as if he were in the way. He couldn't do anything right. He didn't hold the baby's head in the correct position, he didn't change Pampers the right way, and on and on. Carl often contemplated leaving, but then thought about his own father and decided that for the sake of their child, he would stay and hope for the best with Phyllis.

Carl kicked himself for marrying a woman who showed such blatant signs of the behavior that he despised. But he still couldn't put everything on Phyllis. He held his father responsible for the life he'd lived.

Carl's mother died while giving birth to him, and as he grew older, he realized that his alcoholic father blamed him for her death. Carl's father seemed to hate anything his son did or was associated with. When Carl was about ten years old, he became fast friends with a little boy at his school. They did everything together. One day Carl asked his father if he could attend a sleepover at the little boy's house. His father said he could and Carl was ecstatic about being able to spend extra time with his best buddy. The weekend finally arrived and his father drove him to his friend's house. The whole trip Carl babbled about how much fun they were going to have. When they arrived at the house and knocked on the door, a black woman answered with a smile. Carl remembered his father snatching his son's arm like he had seen a ghost.

"Ahh, I think we have the wrong house. Is this the Darby residence?" Carl's father asked.

"Yes, it is," the lady answered as her son ran up to the door and yelled in excitement to his schoolmate.

"Ahh, ma'am, we're sorry to bother you but we must be going." Carl's father grabbed his son's arm and pulled him back to his truck. The more Carl protested, the tighter his father squeezed his arm. He cried and turned around to see his friend being comforted by his own mother. He saw the confused look on his friend's face and the disgust in Mrs. Darby's eyes as she pulled her son in the house and closed the door.

Once inside the truck Carl chastised his son. "Why didn't you tell me that dat dar boy was a nigger?"

"What's a nigger?" Carl asked.

"Don't get smart. You know I don't socialize with niggers, and no son of mine bet' not be doing it either. I don't want you playing with that lil darky anymore, you hear me?"

"Why?"

"Cuz they're filthy and don't have no damn morals. Hell, they kill their own kind. Whaddaya think they'll do to your little narrow ass? You better learn to stay with your own. Now, if I come up to that school and hear 'bout you playing with him, I'll pull ya lil tail outta there and whip you good."

When Carl went to school that Monday, he was labeled a racist. He wasn't allowed to play with the black kids, and even if he could have, they rejected him. He would often get beat up at recess by the same people he used to call his friends. When he told his father what happened, all his father said was, "I told you those niggers don't know how to act. Stay away from 'em." But Carl never adopted his father's way of thinking and secretly made amends with the kids at school by convincing them that it wasn't him but his father who was the racist.

The day after he graduated from high school Carl was shipped off to the army, where he spent his time going out of his way to hang around blacks. And now he was married to a black woman with views similar to his father's—except she hated her own race.

Ain't that a bitch? Carl thought.

In most of Phyllis's and his discussions on race Carl found himself defending blacks more passionately than she did. He would usually shake his head and walk off. He never understood where all the hate came from.

Carl's father had a heart attack and died about a week after Carl's wedding. Carl thought it was because he didn't tell his father that Phyllis was black and when he showed up to celebrate his son's nuptials his old ticker couldn't take it. Carl paid for his father to have a proper burial, but he didn't shed a single tear. The tyrant was dead.

"Got-damn you, old man," Carl said out loud to no one in particular. "You never taught me a damn thing."

Carl's mind left his troubled past and found its way to the problems of the day. *Phyllis, our days are numbered. I'm only forty years old, and I'll be damned if I spend the rest of my days with your evil ass,* Carl thought.

PHYLLIS ARRIVED AT the elegant Fox Theater in downtown Atlanta just in time to walk in with her co-worker Darrin Harrington. Darrin was good-looking, tall, and well educated. And he made it no secret that he wanted to see a little more of Phyllis than he saw in the office. Phyllis acted as if he was just another office worker and mostly ignored his off-the-cuff comments. But there was no denying his charm, and even though she could never see herself stepping out on her marriage, she sort of looked forward to his compliments every day.

"Good evening, princess. You look exquisite," Darrin said, as he eyed Phyllis's slender yet curvaceous body.

"Good evening, Mr. Harrington."

"Congratulations. I hear you're getting an award tonight for saving the world or something like that."

"Thank you. I'll see you on the inside," Phyllis said, walking past her tall, dark, and handsome co-worker. Darrin was one of four black lawyers who worked with her in the DA's office. He was the only male and had a reputation for being a ladies' man, so the last thing she wanted was to be seen alone with him.

"Save a dance for me," Darrin said as Phyllis hurried into the dining area.

"She wants me. I can smell it," Darrin said to himself as he watched her sashay away.

ONCE INSIDE, PHYLLIS made her rounds to shake hands, smile, and mingle with her colleagues. She noticed Barbara holding court by the cocktail table with a good-looking olive-skinned man.

Phyllis decided to walk over and strike up a conversation. Barbara saw her coming.

"Hey, girl, where's Carl?"

"Home. Thank God for small favors."

"Is everything all right?"

"Yeah. Nothing major, just Carl being Carl. He started the minute I pulled in the driveway."

"Does Carl have a case of asshole-itis?"

"Have you always made up words?"

Barbara chuckled and turned to introduce her date. "Phyllis, this is Carlo."

"Nice to meet you, Carlo."

Carlo reached out and kissed Phyllis's outstretched hand. "The pleasure is all mine," he said in a practiced, suave voice with an Italian accent.

Phyllis turned to Barbara and nodded her approval.

Barbara frowned, swatted her comment down with her hand, and said, "Escort service. Carlo, will you be a doll and go and get us two glasses of wine?"

"White or red, my darling?"

"Doesn't matter, just go."

"No, you didn't go out and get an escort?" Phyllis asked, shocked.

"Yes, I did. It's slim pickings for a sister with standards."

"Damn. Is it that bad?"

"Hell, yeah! Why are brothers so intimidated by sisters with educations and expectations?"

"Because they're not used to having anything, don't want anything, and don't want you to have anything. Plus they have these uneducated, unsophisticated, uncouth hoochies they can control."

"How's that fine brother of yours doing?" Barbara asked.

"I have two brothers, but you're probably talking about Genesis. And he's engaged," Phyllis said, rolling her eyes at the thought of her brother settling down.

"Damn. You see what I mean. Somebody done snatched him up too. What's up with the other one?"

"Oh, I wouldn't wish Grover on my worst enemy."

"Why?"

"Because he has issues that no sane person can deal with and remain sane."

"We all have issues in one way or another. Give the brother a break."

"Girl, Grover is a drug addict, an alcoholic, and just plain trifling."

"Damn, what's up with my brothers?"

Barbara's three margaritas were starting to affect her judgment. But she caught herself. The last thing she wanted was to get into a conversation with Phyllis about black men. She was saved by the amplified sound of a fork hitting a wineglass, the cue for everyone to take their seats and let the ceremonies begin.

As Phyllis sat, she noticed Darrin eyeing her, and every time she looked his way, he would give her a lustful nod.

"Well, damn, don't be so discreet about it," Barbara said with her usual sarcasm, noticing the intense eye contact Darrin was giving Phyllis from across the table.

"He's so ignorant," Phyllis said.

"One day his penis is going to fall off. Damn freak," Barbara said.

Phyllis looked at Barbara and gave a smile that said she sensed something had transpired between the two.

"Did you know he was married?" Barbara said, pointing at him, then toward her wedding finger.

"Nah, I didn't know that."

"Well, he is, and he still has more women than any single man I know."

"Where does he hide his wife?"

"She's not hiding. You would never see her out at a place like this with him. They might bump into somebody that could ruin her career. She's a news anchor. But girl, she's just as freaky as her damn husband. They do the swinging thing."

"Swinging?"

"That's right, swinging. You know, switching partners, having sex with other couples, and crap like that."

"Oh, my God. You've got to be kidding me."

"If I'm lying, I'm flying, and I haven't left this chair."

"Wow," Phyllis said, speechless. "How do you know all that man's personal business?"

"Chile, I work out at the same gym as his wife and . . . anyway, to make a long story short, one day I was doing Rolanda's aerobics class, and we had to partner up to stretch. Well, I partnered with her, and she was just staring at my stuff. I'm like, *damn!* So anyway, after the class, she comes over and says she recognized me from her husband's job. After a little small talk, she seemed to be really nice, so I chalked up her little coochie-staring episode to my imagination. Anyway, we hung out a few times, and all was well until one Friday night she asked me to hang out with her and Darrin and one of his friends. Well, honey, we went to this club. The minute I walked in, something didn't feel right. The place was darker than your normal club would be. It had dark walls and blue lightbulbs in every damn socket. All the people were paired up. Now, this is Atlanta, women outnumber men ten to one, so my antenna went straight up." Barbara paused to take her drink from Carlos. She nodded for him to take his seat, then went back to her story.

"But I'm cool; I decided to play this out because the brother I was with was super fine. Well, all of a sudden, folks started taking off their clothes, kissing and feeling all over one another. Porno movies flashed up on the television screens hanging from the walls, and the dude that was with me started kissing Darrin's wife. I'm like, 'Oh hell no, let me out of this sin trap.' Darrin grabbed my hand and tried to place it on his crotch and got the shit slapped outta him."

"Girl, what did you do?" Phyllis said, holding her hand over her mouth.

"I marched my one-man-at-a-time, need-a-little-privacy, monogamous ass out of there and called a taxi."

"That was rude to just invite you to a place like that without telling you what was going on. You were recruited."

"I know—into a lifestyle of freaks and weirdos."

A TALL CAUCASIAN man who looked to be in his late fifties or early sixties took the podium, interrupting Phyllis's and Barbara's freaky tales. He was the City of Atlanta's district attorney. He went into a long-drawn-out soliloquy about how great he felt to be in the presence of such great legal minds. Then came time for the presentation of awards. The DA went through a list of high- and low-profile cases, presenting a host of awards. Then he cleared his throat and shook his head as if he were amazed.

"The final award tonight goes to a person whom the state of Georgia can truly be proud of. With a caseload of more than four hundred and the successful prosecution of several of this year's high-profile cases, the award for Prosecutor of the Year goes to none other than Phyllis Olsen," the DA said, beaming a broad smile at Phyllis's table.

Phyllis walked toward the stage and was handed a glass trophy of the scales of justice.

"Wow," Phyllis said, before pausing to hug the district attorney. "First I'd like to thank my distinguished colleagues. I have to thank my staff for working long hours and helping me do God's work. My reasoning for going into criminal law stemmed from a deep-rooted need for righteousness. I wanted to help the helpless. I wanted to put people who prey upon the weak away so they could never harm innocent people again. Nothing feels better than to look into a victim's eye after the jury hands down a guilty verdict. I wish there wasn't a need for people like us. I wish this world was a fair and honest place, but it's not. Therefore, without people like you and me, there would be total chaos. I'm an advocate for justice. I'm an advocate for law and order. So as long as there are people out there with hateful hearts and a need to do wrong, then I'll always join the fight for justice. Thank you for this award."

Phyllis made her way back to her chair to a standing ovation. As she sat down, her pager went off.

three

MAN TO MAN

Genesis held out his hands for the keys to Prodigy's black Range Rover and jumped in the driver's seat. They took the scenic route to Home Depot so they would have a little more time to talk.

"What took y'all so long to get over here?" Genesis asked as soon as the truck was moving.

"We had to stay at Blake's practice for a minute. You got him obsessed with a left-hand lay-up," Prodigy said.

"Good. He's gonna need that one day. I miss my little homie. How's he doing?"

"He's straight."

"I'mma have to come scoop him up one day and let him hang with a real ball player," Genesis said, steering with his leg as he shot an imaginary ball through an imaginary hoop.

"Air ball!" Prodigy said, his eyes following the imaginary ball.

"Whatchu do all day?"

"I went to the gym, heard you were there too. I must have missed ya," Prodigy said sarcastically.

"Oh, man, I was fucking with ol' trifling-ass Sheila. Man, that chick bad for my health."

"I know! If her husband finds out about you, he just might kill you."

"You know what she did today?" Genesis said, ignoring Prodigy's warning.

"What? Kicked you out?"

"Might as well had. Gon' give me her husband's personalized towel to dry off with. Ain't that some foul shit?"

"You're crazy. You know that, don't you?" Prodigy said, shaking his head.

"I feel like I'm going crazy. Something just didn't feel right. I couldn't even touch the damn thing. I just stood there like a damn fool." Genesis thought back to earlier that day.

"It's called a 'conscience.' And it catches up to you sometime. Whatchu trynna do, get all your creeping in before you get married?"

"Hell yeah. I ain't cheating after I hop the broom, baby. Genesis Styles's jimmy will officially be off the market," Genesis said proudly.

"G, do you really believe that you'll be faithful after you get married? I mean, you might at first, but once the routine sets in, yo ass will be right back out there sticking and moving."

"How you know? Is that what you did?"

"No sir. I stopped cheating way before I got married. And you know what? I got a conscience, too, and I hate lying to Terri all the damn time."

Genesis looked at Prodigy like a kid with his hand caught in the cookie jar. Prodigy was a year older and always acted like it. He had walked the road that Genesis was on and knew it didn't lead to anywhere fulfilling.

"Man, what kind of drama do you have?" Genesis asked, changing the subject. That simple comment from Prodigy let him know his days of using Prodigy as a cover were numbered—if not over.

"You're about to get married. Don't you think it's time to stop acting like a horny-ass little boy?" Prodigy said, sticking with the subject.

"You never cheated on Nina?" Genesis asked, with a look that said, "Don't lie."

"Didn't I just tell yo simple ass no?" Prodigy said with a straight face.

"Ever thought about it?" Genesis pressed on.

"Not seriously. I mean, I see good-looking women every now and then, and the mind wonders, but nothing more. But thinking is different from doing. Ya see, G, this might sound corny, but Nina's my friend, and I don't fuck over my friends."

"Yeah, but you slicker than that. What she don't know won't hurt her," Genesis replied.

"You're not hearing me. Okay, let me put it to you like this. You're my dog, right?" Prodigy said, shifting in his seat.

"Right, right."

"Now would I be your true dog if I did some sneaky, foul shit behind your back? Even if I knew you would never find out. I would know, and I could never look you in the eye again. You see, that's how I look at cheating. I made a promise before God to Nina, and ain't no way I'm breaking that. Plus, I'm satisfied. I've had my share of women and none of them can hold a candle to my wife, so why would I mess that up?"

Genesis nodded as the realness of what Prodigy had just said sunk in. It was a hard pill to swallow, especially since he and Prodigy were once considered the biggest womanizers in Philadelphia. Times were changing and he definitely noticed the growth in his longtime road dog. Genesis had always looked up to Prodigy, but this faithful man thing was something he had to conquer on his own.

"Cheating is the easiest thing in the world to do. Hell, you can always find somebody to sleep with you, but you gotta look at who you'll hurt in the midst of you getting your pleasure and is it worth it. And if you got a good lady, it ain't worth it."

Prodigy didn't like preaching to or judging Genesis, but he knew the true meaning of being a friend. And that was to give him the good and the bad.

Genesis sat, silently nodding. "How you do it, man? I mean, I know that wedding band don't stop women from coming on to you. Hell, it probably makes 'em want you more."

"You just gotta know where your priorities are. Like I said, it's about keeping it real with your lady."

Genesis sat lost in his own thoughts for a moment, staring straight ahead. He thought about how nice Prodigy and Nina's wedding had been. He thought about the blissfulness he saw on his best friend's face as his soul mate walked down the aisle to meet him at the altar. It was on that same occasion that he met Terri, Nina's sorority sister and one of her bridesmaids.

Genesis remembered being instantly attracted to Terri and practically begged Nina to let him escort Terri down the aisle at the rehearsal. She agreed, even though she thought he was too tall for Terri. Genesis remembered how, for the first time in his life, a woman intimidated him. Terri had her stuff together. After the rehearsal, Prodigy took the wedding party out to eat, and Genesis couldn't take his eyes off Terri. After Terri informed him that she didn't have a man, he knew that he would marry her someday. She was such a far cry from the women he normally dated. But he also knew if he got with Terri, he would have to step up his game.

"MAN, WHAT KIND of drama do you have?" Genesis asked as he snapped out of his thoughts.

"Blake's biological pop called Nina," Prodigy said as his jaws tightened.

"What!"

"Blake's bio—"

"I heard you! What he say? How did he find her? What y'all gon' do?"

"One question at a time, potna. She doesn't care for the dude and doesn't want anything to do with him. But she said if I thought differently then she'd give it a shot."

"So what's up? Whatcha gon' do?" Genesis took this seriously. They were so close he felt like a problem of Prodigy's was a problem of his. There was no way he would let anything threaten the cohesiveness of his friend's family.

"I don't know."

"Whatcha mean, you don't know?"

"G, I preach responsibility every day to my kids at the center and their parents. I've basically dedicated my life to getting fathers to take a more active role in their kids' lives. I can't just say that when it's convenient. A man has a right to see his child. Unless he did something immoral to the child."

"I know, and you see him every day. That dude ain't no man. Blake never even seen him. Fuck him. How he gon' show up disrupting thangs? And what he did was more immoral than anything I could ever think of. He left his child hanging out to dry, to fend for himself at one got-damn day old and hasn't been around since. Man, fuck him."

"I feel ya. But I told him I'd meet him and talk about it."

"Damn, P, you getting soft. Man, to hell with that dude. Where's he been all this time?"

"Locked up."

"Oh, I guess he's reformed and wanna spend time with his kid? Man, fuck that nigga. This is some straight bullshit and you know it," Genesis said, visibly upset.

"He said he's a Muslim now and wants to right his wrongs. You know how they do when they first get out. They're all motivated. I wanna see if he's real. If he proves himself, then Blake can only benefit from it. If not, I'm always gonna be here."

"Man, everybody's a damn Muslim when they get locked up. His punk ass probably joined up for protection. Blake damn near nine years old. Half of his childhood is over with. What's he trynna prove? Fuck him," Genesis said, wrinkling the space between his eyes—a true sign he was upset. Most of the time when they disagreed it was because Prodigy was trying to be a saint or a peacemaker. This time was no different.

Part of Prodigy knew that Genesis was right, but the other part had to put himself into the other man's shoes. He could not deny a man the right to see his child.

"How are you and the future Mrs. Styles doing?" Prodigy asked. This time he was the one to change the subject.

"Aggravating as hell. This wedding planning is about to drive me up a damn wall. Did Nina put you through all this crap when y'all got married?"

"Yep! Women like weddings. They get a kick out of all that shopping and decorating and whatever else it is that they do. Like I said, just go with the flow, dog. How long do you guys have before the big day?"

"Three months!" Genesis said, sighing deeply. He didn't look so sure and Prodigy picked up on it.

"Why did you ask the girl to marry you if got to be acting all scared?"

"I ain't scared. That's my baby. Just headed into some uncharted territory for a brother, that's all." Genesis perked up a little.

"Well, stop acting like you're about to die or something. Marriage is a good thing, especially for your hoing ass. It's about time you calm down anyway. HIV shutting folks down, permanently."

"Why you gotta put that negative karma out there? And don't act like you wasn't sweatin' bullets before you got married. I can see your ass now when Nina was walking down that aisle. You didn't look so sure ya damn self," Genesis joked, just for the fun of it.

"Nah, what I wasn't sure of was why I asked you to be a grooms-man." Prodigy thought back to that June day two years ago. Every step Nina took down the aisle, Genesis, who stood right beside Prodigy's cousin and best man, Jermaine, would whisper, "It's almost over, dog! Here she comes! P, you better run! Haul ass, nigga!"

"I had to do everything in my power to keep from laughing at y'all silly asses," Prodigy said as he smiled at the memory of how funny his wedding had been because of Genesis and Jermaine. From the rehearsal to the dinner to the actual wedding, they'd been a two-man comedy team.

"Yeah, that was a cool day. You done good for yaself, dog. You know Nina was the best thing that ever happened to you. Before her, you had no class," Genesis said.

"You crazy. If it wasn't for me, you'd still think that Jordache jeans were hot. I'm the only reason you even know that personal tailors exist."

"Stop taking credit for Nina dressing you. Speaking of clothes—you know, ever since Terri moved in I can't find a damn thing. I done lost about five shirts and how in the hell you lose a sock? I mean you come home with two socks on, but somewhere between the hamper and the washer Terri manages to lose at least one a week."

Prodigy laughed. "Boy, you're crazy. But women will try to take over if you let 'em. Especially if they don't like something you wear. They start plotting ways to get rid of it. Nina tried that, but I had to put the foot down. Now she only throws away drawers with the holes in 'em."

"Terri better not even start that. That's when my drawers get comfortable."

"If you can't find your clothes then she already started, dummy."

"I'mma kill her. Did you see all them flowers and plants in every room? I feel like I'm in Wild Kingdom or someplace. Scented candles, potpourri, panty hose, panty liners, and damn tampons! Damn bedroom smells like fingernail polish remover," Genesis said, his expression turning sour. "Got me painting over my pimp colors. Shit, I didn't say nothing about all them damn Delta elephants all over the place."

"Nina the same way with all that red and white. I think they in some kind of cult or something. But you need to paint, brighten up that place. Every time I come to your spot, I feel like I'm in a dungeon. Why you like all those dark colors on the walls anyway?" Prodigy asked.

"Cuz it's stylish like me, get it . . . Styles."

"I can't believe you came out of your mouth with that corny shit."

"What I don't need is for her coming to my house trynna take over. Putting up curtains and thangs."

"Aw, calm down, dog. Plus it's not your house anymore, it's hers. And she's just making the crib feel like home. You were gonna have to take the sheets from over the windows one day, playa. You the only cat I know with sheets up over the window. Yeah, you're stylish all right," Prodigy said, shaking his head.

"Yo, P, wait until you see how many pairs of shoes she has, dog," Genesis said.

"To have spent so much time with women, you sure didn't pay any attention to them. Women like to shop. You might as well get use to that because it doesn't get any better."

"You know she took my closet. Guess where all my clothes at? In the guest bedroom! I got to get up and walk down the hall, around the corner, and into another room just to get dressed."

"That's cuz you a lil bitch," Prodigy said, laughing.

"Oh, I know you ain't talking with yo henpecked ass. 'Nina's my friend,'" Genesis mocked Prodigy with a whine. "Friend my ass, Nina got you in check."

"I ain't the one walking all over my house just to get dressed."

"That's strictly temporary."

"Yeah, right."

"I'm serious, I'm calling a contractor tomorrow to add a closet in that bonus space over by the window. You know that spot that looks out of place?" Genesis said. "I gotta hurry up before Terri puts a damn palm tree or some shit in there."

"If it's larger than the one she just took, she's taking the new one too."

"I'll be damn. I'm about to get me one of them custom joints with an island in it. A whole section for your shoes. Like the rich white folks and bougie-ass blacks have. I don't know how I'mma pay for it, but I'm getting it."

"Oh, if you get that, she's taking it for sure."

"Watch."

"I will and when she does I'mma talk about yo little punk ass. My good friend Poppa Doc use to say, 'You can't get no peace if your woman ain't happy.' And that nice closet will make Terri so happy. She might even give you some."

"That why you so damn henpecked?" Genesis shot back. "Nina be rationing out the sex?"

"I just pick my battles wisely, brah man. Let me put you up on something. Women are catty; they like to nitpick on every damn thing. So let them have what they want and don't say shit. That way when you do say something, they know you really mean whatever it is you spoke up on. Plus, I ain't trynna sit in the house and argue all day about nothing. You can't outargue no woman."

"She ain't getting my closet."

"Who you trynna convince, me or yourself?" Prodigy looked at his friend and immediately knew that they hadn't touched the surface of what was really bothering him. "G, you wanna tell me what's really on your mind?"

Genesis looked at Prodigy and knew it was time to come clean. "Work. Growing up, I only focused on basketball. Now that's not happening, I'm screwed because I didn't have a plan B. Now, I got this wedding coming up, and I don't know how I'm going to pay for all this crap. Man, I'm starting to feel like a failure. Everyone's talking about how good the economy is, but I can't tell. I've been looking for a job for about two months, and nobody's biting. This personal trainer thing ain't paying the bills. I got about two thousand dollars to my damn name. I owe six thousand on the wedding. My truck payment is behind, and so are all the credit cards. The only thing I'm current on is the house. And the only reason I'm current on that is because I paid it up for a year when I got my last check from overseas.

"Man, why didn't you say something before things got so bad?"

"Man, you know I ain't the handout type. I pull my own weight. I'll figure my way out of this just like I do everything else. I'm suppose to be getting a check from my agent, but since I ain't playing no more, he be taking his time with my loot. He still owes me about fifteen grand."

"Yeah, but before, it was just you. Now you got someone else to think about and it's not about taking handouts. Call me first thing Monday morning and we'll get you back in the game," Prodigy assured his friend. He knew Genesis was a proud guy and would never take a loan, so he had to figure out a way to get him some decent money at the youth center.

THEY PULLED INTO the Home Depot's parking lot as Genesis's cell phone rang.

"Hello?"

"You know I'm through with you, don't you?" a female's voice said.

"Hey, baby. I was gonna call you tonight," Genesis replied, smiling.

"I'm glad I didn't want to tell you I was dying. I'd be dead by now and you would've missed your favorite sister's funeral."

"You better stop talking like that, Grace."

"Tell Grace hi for me. I'mma run in and get those covers while you chat," Prodigy said as he got out of the truck.

"Prodigy said hi."

"Tell my baby I said hello. I just spoke with Nina."

"Oh yeah, so how's life treating you in New York?"

"It's hot! But I called to tell you my good news," Grace said.

"You pregnant?"

"No, boy, and what would be so good about bringing a child into this mixed-up world?"

"My bad. What's the good news?"

"Two things. One, I'm moving back home."

"When?" Genesis asked, excited.

"Don't know yet. Still got some things to work out with my finances but I'm coming. Momma doesn't sound too well and I need to be there for her. Have you been checking up on her?"

"I go by the house a few times a week. She looks fine to me."

"Every time I talk to her she seems to be out of it. Something's just not right. Anyway, she's getting up there in age and she needs someone there for her."

"What's the other good news?"

"I'm going to divinity school. I want to become a minister."

"A minister, huh? What brought about that career move?"

"It's not a career move, it's a spiritual move."

"Yeah, well, I know some pastors getting so paid that they're named after money."

"That's true, but my reasons are not money-driven. I've got to get some closure on a lot of things. Our family is in some bad shape. Momma hasn't been the same since Daddy died. Sigmund Freud himself couldn't figure Grover out. Phyllis hates herself so much that it's virtually impossible for her to love anyone other than her son. I'm so afraid to trust anyone that I'm destined to live a lonely life. And you ..."

"Hey, slow down. Nothing is wrong with me other than the fact that I'm damn near broke," Genesis defended himself before Grace could get started.

"No, you have the same issues that I have and a few more that you won't admit to. I'm just searching for answers. I wanna get married one day and have a family, but I can't seem to let anyone get close to me. Anxiety sets in, and I push people away. There's not a better time for me to start the healing process than right now. And I'm going to do my part by trying to put all of the bad blood between Phyllis and me behind me. And that's going to be pretty hard. Is she still the same?"

"I wouldn't know. I don't talk to her that much. I see her every now and then. But if I know Phyllis, she's still the same. I know Momma talks to her."

Grace took a deep breath, "Well, I'm calling Momma to get her number. This will be a big step for me to talk to the woman who killed our father."

"Grace, we can't bring Daddy back," Genesis comforted his sister as he heard her try to hide a sniffle.

"I know, and I'm still coming to grips with that, but let's talk about something happy. So are you getting ready for your big day?" Grace asked.

"Yeah, as ready as I'll ever be."

"Genesis, are you doing right by Terri or are you being like your daddy?"

"Not you! Daddy's little girl got something negative to say about him? What is this world coming to."

"I'm not a daddy's girl, never was," Grace said flatly.

"No, you didn't! Everybody knows that you were a daddy's girl. You'd damn near lose your mind when someone got on his case about all that drinking."

"True, but that wasn't because I was a daddy's girl. It was because I understood that alcoholism is a disease. Y'all wouldn't have been fussing at him like that if he had cancer. I just saw things differently, that's all."

"True, true."

"Daddy wasn't the kind of man that was capable of letting anyone get close enough to be a daddy's girl. I was working on him though. And he was changing, that's why I can't understand why Phyllis did what she—oh, never mind." Grace stopped midsentence. She wanted to put those bad memories in an old lock box and throw them away.

"You okay?"

"I'm fine. But I asked you a question. Are you treating Terri right?" Grace asked.

"Yeah, I'm doing her right," Genesis lied.

"All right, I'm going take you at your word. Well, let me go. I have a long road to travel with your sister. Hey, do you know if Jalen got the box I sent him for his birthday?"

"Don't know, what was it?"

"I sent him a Game Boy video thing."

"I'll check on that for ya. I hope Grover didn't get the package, because if he did, I'll have to pick it up from the pawnshop."

"Oh my God, has he gotten that bad?"

"Baby sis, just be thankful that you don't have to see him every day. He's enough to make *you* start drinking, and he looks terrible.

Won't wash, won't work, and I know he's worrying Momma to death."

"Dag! I really hate to hear that." Grace sounded like someone had deflated her bicycle tires. "Well, gotta run. I love you, big brah."

"I love you too."

four

GIRL TALK

O nce the men were out of the house, Nina and Terri put the wedding planning aside for a minute. It was time for them to play catch-up. They had been the best of friends during undergraduate school at Hampton University in Virginia. Nina was always the serious one, and Terri always kept the party going. Nina could never figure out how Terri kept such a high grade-point average with all the fun she had. Nina was Terri's first friend in the United States after she moved from Canada to attend school.

"So what's been up, girl?" Nina asked.

"Oh, where do I start? This wedding, my bookstore, my man." Terri rolled her eyes and shook her head when she said "my man."

"You wanna talk about it?" Nina asked calmly, noticing the tension written all over her friend's face.

"Yeah, but hold on." Terri ran to answer the ringing doorbell.

"Hey, girl," Terri said to her friend Shanice, a very dark-complexioned girl with naturally curly hair. She got a lot of attention from men due to her extremely curvy bottom and huge breasts.

Shanice walked in, hugged Nina, and took a seat at the table. "What's up with you heifers?" Shanice asked.

"Nothing new. How's everything with you?" Nina said. She couldn't figure out if she was in the mood for Shanice.

"Good. I haven't seen you down at the salon. Where you been?" Shanice asked Nina.

"Oh, if I could only find the time to get my hair done, I'd see you once a week," Nina lied. She thought Shanice's styles were a little on the ghetto side, but she admired her for owning her own business.

"Girl, you gonna have to make time. I can see split ends from here. But anyway, what y'all in here doing?"

Nina glared at Shanice and shook her head.

"We were just about to talk about men. You still wanna stay?" Terri joked. Shanice was the queen of single. Whether she got rid of her men or they got rid of her, she was always single again in less than six months.

"I'm single by choice, thank you," Shanice defended herself.

"What, you decide to leave him alone after he stopped calling?" Nina said.

"I know you ain't trynna jone," Shanice said.

"Stop!" Terri put a halt to the verbal jabs before they could get started. "Just stop it right there, you two. We were talking about my wedding and I'd like to keep it peaceful. Now! I know Genesis is a good guy, and I love him, but I worry if he's ready for marriage. And my momma swears that something isn't right with him. And you know she thinks she's a psychic. 'I got a bad vibe 'bout that boy there, Terri. Every time I was in the same room with him, my foot started itching. Something ain't right.'" Terri mocked her mother's reaction when she first met Genesis. "And Genesis thinks he's so slick. Gonna run in here today and head straight for the shower. I can smell his funky butt a mile from home when he works out," Terri said, slowly shaking her head.

"Okay, am I missing something?" Nina asked.

"I didn't smell him today. But he claimed he was at the gym."

"Did you ask him about it?"

"Nah, he'll just come up with one of his creative lies. But that's another thing I don't want to do. I don't want to stress him out about his antics and force him into cheating. I know plenty of men that said, 'Well, damn, if I'm gonna be accused of screwing around then I might as well screw around.'"

"First of all, Momma don't lie. Second of all, if a man is gonna cheat, he's gonna cheat. And most men do," Shanice said.

"I don't know. Oh, I just have so many negative thoughts running through my head right now. Did you go through this with Prodigy?" Terri ignored Shanice like she always did when it came to matters of men.

"Yeah, it's called prewedding jitters," Nina said.

"What kind of jitters did you have?" Terri asked.

"I had a lot of apprehensions at first. Prodigy was a player in every sense of the word. And after Blake's father pulled his disappearing act—by the way, y'all know he had the nerve to call me?"

"No, he didn't," Shanice said, surprised.

"What did he want?" Terri added.

"He said he wanted to see his child. I asked him who his child was? He didn't even know Blake's name. Didn't even know if he was a boy or a girl. But I guess he wouldn't since he didn't stick around for the first trimester. Anyway, I hung up on that nut. But he called right back. Finally I told him that I didn't want to ever see him. Told him that he donated his sperm to create a beautiful little boy that I named Blake. Told him that Blake was outside playing basketball with his daddy. Told him my life was just fine, and I didn't want him ever calling my house again," Nina said as she counted out her statements on her fingers.

"Where was he all this time?" Shanice asked.

"Jail," Nina said.

"Typical. Men ain't shit. That's why I use they asses for what I want and kick 'em out before the sun comes up," Shanice said.

"Girl, you're crazy. You know what that make you, don't you?"
Terri asked.

"What's that?" Shanice asked.

"A ho," Nina and Terri said together as they shared a laugh.

"Both of y'all can kiss my ass. At least I know what to expect.
Y'all heifers up here playing house with men that y'all know gonna
cheat. If they haven't already."

"Anyway, Nina, what did Prodigy have to say?" Terri asked.

"I told him that he called and Mr. 'I Got to Practice What I
Preach' wanted to meet with him. I finally told him to do whatever he felt as far as that nut was concerned. But I told him that I
never wanted to see him. Didn't want him anywhere near my house,
and that Blake could never go anywhere with him. And I meant
that."

"Dag. Girl, you've been holding out. Why didn't you tell me?"
Terri asked, with a stunned look on her face.

"He just called yesterday. I don't even know how he got the
number. Then he had the nerve to ask me if I still looked good. Jerk!"

"Like I said, men ain't worth a damn. How's he gonna call and act
like nothing ain't happened?" Shanice asked.

"No, he didn't. Did you tell Prodigy that he was tossing hints at
you?" Terri asked.

"Nah, the less I talk about that boy, the better I feel. But anyway,
back to you. When I first started dating Prodigy, I didn't have a lot
of patience for men and their games, and after Blake's sperm donor
pulled his Houdini act, you can see why. So I held him at arm's
length from my heart. The same feelings you're having, I had them
too, but the difference between you and me is that I had to think for
two. Blake was my first priority. But that man loves Blake more
than he loves himself, and he showed me that. So I prayed about it,
and God let me know in so many ways that he was the right one for
me."

"Yeah, it's different when you have kids. I've always liked Prodigy. He's a good guy," Terri said.

"For now! He's a man, so you still gotta watch him," Shanice chimed in.

"Shanice, you know what you remind me of? One of those old behind women that wants everyone to be miserable just because they can't find happiness. You need to stop being disrespectful. That's my husband—not one of them one-night flings that you're used to," Nina snapped.

"Oh, she's just being Shanice, the manless she-devil," Terri said, trying to calm Nina down.

"Y'all know the one thing you can always count on with me is honesty," Shanice said.

"Being honest is one thing. You're just plain old cynical. Nina, what were you saying about Prodigy?" Terri asked after putting Shanice in her place.

"My *husband*"—Nina stressed the word while staring at Shanice—"is a gem, but we still have some major issues."

"Say what? Tell me y'all doing okay," Terri said as she stood and poured three glasses of white wine and sat back down.

"We're fine but the issues we have are major to me. You see, Prodigy didn't grow up with his father around; he passed away before he was born. And when I met him, he was just getting out of that womanizing, hustling thing. But now he's so proud of the person he's become that he overdoes it. He spends half of his time at the youth center and the other half with Blake. Not to mention his monthly trips to New Jersey to see his daughter."

"Oh, how is little Arielle doing with her cute self?" Shanice asked, trying to get back in her friends' good graces.

"She's doing fine, getting big. She calls me Mommy Nina." Nina offered a proud smile. She considered Prodigy's daughter from a previous relationship to be one of her own. "But let me finish my story, girl. Don't get me wrong, I'm proud of the man that my husband has turned out to be, but dag, I need more attention. It's bad when a sister has to schedule a moment to get her groove on."

"Did you tell him how you feel?" Terri asked.

"Well, he getting it from someplace," Shanice said, laughing, as she stood and walked to the bathroom. "Men just ain't gonna go without. Don't be no fool."

"I can't stand her," Nina said, smiling. Actually, both Nina and Terri liked Shanice a lot. She was the kind of friend everyone needed. Anytime she was called on to lend a helping hand, you never had to ask her twice. The strain always came when the conversation turned to men. "Anyway, I told Prodigy, and he tries so hard. He'll cancel everything that was on his plate and spend all of his time with me for about a week, but then I'm smothered. You know, after seeing him all day every day, I'm usually happy when he gets back to his hectic schedule. I know I sound crazy but ... we're just gonna have to work something out."

"Girl, I wish that was the only problem I had with Genesis. I don't have any proof but I have a gut feeling that his player days aren't over."

"So you think Genesis is still out there, huh? He seems so into you. Even Prodigy said that he's seen a change in him since you guys met."

"I'm not saying he hasn't changed, but changing from a rottweiler to a damn poodle isn't saying much. Ya still a dog," Terri said, as she took a sip of her wine.

"Well, soror, you have to trust your heart," Nina said.

Shanice returned from the bathroom and took a long swallow of her wine. She took her seat. "Whose sorry-ass man we on now? I'm just kidding, girls, y'all know I got nothing but love for ya lil men."

Terri and Nina ignored Shanice. They knew she never meant any harm.

"Anyway," Terri said, shaking her head at Shanice, "most of the time Genesis is as sweet as he can be. He makes me feel like I'm the only woman in the world. Then there are times when I just don't know. It's never directly him. It's always other things that incriminate him. Little signs like today, when he came home and made a beeline for the shower. Like the phone calls from the different women. Like the fact that he shuts down his computer whenever I walk in the room. Damn Black Planet."

Shanice frowned and shook her head. "Now you're getting ridiculous. How in the hell can he cheat on you with a damn computer?"

Nina smiled and gave Shanice a high five. "What does surfing the Web have to do with him cheating?"

"I know the difference between surfing the Web and cyber sex." Terri took a big gulp of her wine. "One day I just popped in that office that we have in the guest bedroom and you would've thought I walked in on him having sex with somebody. He jumped up and turned the monitor off and tried to act like he was fixing the computer. I didn't say a thing to him. Let his guilt eat him up."

"Do you think he loves you?" Nina asked.

"Oh, I know he loves me. But love's not the issue here. I'm looking for a total commitment. I'm a busy woman, and the last thing I need is to have to worry about my man being in the streets playing hide the hot dog with some little biddy. I don't have the time nor am I petty enough to be playing detective with him. I believe that whatever's done in the dark will come to light. If he's being sincere, then it'll show, but if he's not, I'm gonna kill him," Terri said as she picked up the corkscrew and held it like a knife.

"Trust, Terri, you have to trust the man," Nina said, laughing.

"No, what you gotta do is find you a old man. One that's tired of running the streets. That's about the only way you gonna get any peace with a man," Shanice said.

"Shanice, why are you always giving advice on men, and you can't keep one for more than a week?" Nina asked.

"I don't want one, and I don't want y'all to get hurt either. That's why."

"Well, I'll take my chances, but thanks for looking out," Nina responded, rolling her eyes. She always ran out of patience with Shanice's raving before Terri did.

"Listen, when we first started dating, back when things between us weren't that serious, I found out Genesis had been spending time with this other young lady. I approached him about the situation and he denied the whole incident. I even had proof but he still denied it. So finally I told him that I didn't have time for his shit and to call me when he was ready to give me what he was asking me to give him. Do you remember when I use to smoke weed?" Terri said.

"Yes, how could I forget? I know you had to ruin at least five of my favorite blouses with your funky little habit."

"For real? Did I pay you for them?"

"No," Nina said as she held out her hand for payment.

"I don't remember that. You know weed makes you forget," Terri said as she playfully slapped Nina's hand.

"Uh-huh, how convenient." Nina rolled her eyes.

"Were you mad, Nina?" Terri asked, smiling at the thought of some of the things that they went through in college.

"As hell. You would always get my good stuff." Nina shook her head.

"Sorry." Terri gave a sad face then went back to her normal perky self. "Anyway," Terri started.

"Yeah, get back to Genesis," Shanice said, adjusting her big butt in her chair.

"You get a kick out of this, don't you?" Terri asked Shanice, but didn't wait on her response. "Anyway, Genesis came over to my apartment one night, and I was getting my buzz on listening to my

Nina Simone. He went off. 'Damn, I didn't know you was a pothead. You gonna have to cut that shit out. Yo lips gonna get black,'" Terri said, mocking Genesis's hand movements. "Realizing that I really liked the brother, I agreed to give up my Mary Jane after he tried to make me feel like a damn addict. Even though I only smoked about once a month. So I made a deal with him: I'd give up my weed, and he'd stop trying to play me for a fool and keep it real with me. Fair enough deal, right? But now I'm beginning to think that he just got slicker."

"Well, Terri, you just said that you didn't have any issues with him cheating, didn't you?" Nina asked.

"I said I didn't have any proof."

"That's cuz you don't want no proof. Read the signs. I done told you read the damn signs," Shanice said.

"Why are you still here?" Nina said to Shanice before turning her attention back to Terri. "Look, girl, you're just going through what every bride-to-be goes through. It's normal. I went through all kinds of doubts with Prodigy. The devil was mighty busy the days leading up to our wedding."

"I'm telling y'all blind asses a man is gonna cheat. It's too many women in this world for a man to commit to just one woman. It's just not in his nature. Look at the way God did things. A man can get a woman pregnant and fifteen minutes later get another one pregnant. The only reason they lil asses are here in the first place is to multiply. So that faithful thing ain't gonna happen. As long as the man is respectful then shut up and move on. But he's gonna cheat," Shanice said.

"Thank you for that long-winded, philosophical piece of crap, Shanice. Like I said, Prodigy was a player, and you know how women can be." Nina shot another look at Shanice, who threw her hands up in surrender.

"Girl, I went through the same things you're going through. I was receiving calls in the middle of the night. Women were dropping by his house acting like they didn't know I moved in. I had all kinds of drama, and if I would've let those women get to me, I would have missed out on one of the best things that has ever happened to me."

"Oh, you're so damn mushy." Terri gave a playful frown.

"Nina, you might've gotten a good one cuz Prodigy is all right," Shanice admitted.

"Well, thank you, Shanice," Nina said, not buying her halfhearted apology. "The thing I had to do was pay attention to Prodigy. He didn't show me any signs that he was doing anything those women would have had me believe. My loyalty is to him, and I'll be damned if I let some miserable little chick force me to move out so that she has a chance to move in. So don't let others dictate what goes on in your relationship. You know how scandalous some women can be." Nina frowned and looked at Shanice. "Especially those lonely ones."

"Yeah, you're right," Terri said as she reopened the bridal magazine. "Maybe it's just the fact that the day is approaching. I just want it to be right. I sure would hate to have to kill him."

"I'm sure everything will be just fine. Other than your prewedding suspicions, how's everything else?"

"Oh, and one more thing. You know that buster won't share his finances with me. I mean, he has to be running short on funds. He don't work. I know that basketball money has to be getting low. Ain't like he played in the NBA for ten years. I try to pay for things, and he gets all upset. I'm like, damn!"

"Well, he must be doing all right. He got you that big pretty ring," Nina said. "What's that, ten carats?"

"No, it's two." Terri looked down at her sparkling engagement ring.

"That is a bad ring, girl. It might be a cubic. Did you get it appraised?" Shanice laughed, playing on her own negativity.

"Shanice, shut up." Terri wiggled her finger just to see her platinum ring sparkle. "It's nice, but anybody can get a credit card."

"Now, how you know he paid for it with a credit card?" Nina twisted her lips because she knew better. Genesis had called her up when it was time to go ring shopping. After they found the perfect ring, Nina witnessed him pay cash for his purchase.

"I don't know how he paid for it but I know what I see. I know how he used to act when money wasn't an issue. Plus he's always complaining about how much the wedding is costing."

"Oh, girl, now you're tripping. Leave that man alone. Y'all will work out who pays what. Sit down and talk about it. How's everything else or should I ask?"

"Uh-oh, I gotta run," Shanice said as she stared at her pager. "I got a date with a baller." Shanice stood up, hugged Terri and Nina, and was out the door.

"That woman gets on my nerves. She's too pretty to be acting like that," Nina said, taking a sip of her wine. "She just came in here and did her best to ruin the mood. You know how she is. Why did you invite her over to help plan a wedding?" Nina asked, confused.

"That's my girl, plus she is one of my bridesmaids," Terri said.

"Shanice got issues. Anyway, what's up with the bookstore?" Nina asked.

"Oh, that's going really well. We're about to add a coffee and bagel shop. But you know how dealing with us can be. Why are black folks so against other black people advancing?"

"What happened?"

"Business has been going pretty good so I treat myself to a much-needed car. But why did I have to go and buy that Lexus truck? A used Lexus at that. Ah, hell, I shouldn't have to explain why I bought a car. But ever since I purchased it, I swear to you that at least ten of my regulars have stopped coming in the store. I mean, these are people that I had some sort of relationship with. People talk, and I heard the word on the street is that they are not going to help me pay for that Lexus. Ain't that nothing?" Terri said as she took another sip of her wine.

"Oh, I hate to hear that. Crabs in the barrel! You'd think they'd wish you well. But don't let that get to you," Nina said.

"I'm not worried, nor am I discouraged. It just pisses me off that the hate is coming from my own people."

"Yeah, but those same folks will be back when you're a big success. People want to be associated with the best, and your bookstore is a hot spot. I haven't missed a Thursday night poetry session with the live jazz yet." Nina gave her soror a high five.

"Yeah," Terri said. "We gotta get our people to start reading more and turn off that damn radio and television."

"And don't forget video games. I had to kick your man out of my house last week. He had my son up till one-thirty in the morning playing that video football or something."

"On a school night?" Terri asked.

"No, it was last Friday, but Blake's bedtime is twelve on the weekends."

"You know what, I meant to call you and ask you if he was lying when he told me that he was over there."

"Trust, Terri. Trust," Nina said, grabbing Terri's hand.

"Oh, I trust him, it's them damn prewedding jitters again. You know, all this could just be my hormones," Terri said.

"Yeah, that time of the month makes the jitters worse."

"No, it's not that. We agreed not to make love again until our wedding night."

"Oh, that's so sweet."

"Sweet, hell, I'm tired of masturbating until my fingers cramp up," Terri said before they got back to some serious wedding planning.

five

DANCING WITH THE DEVIL

Phyllis looked down at her pager and recognized her home telephone number. She let out an exasperated breath and sucked her teeth. She didn't want to talk to Carl, but he might be calling about Zach. Phyllis decided to call the baby-sitter to check with her instead of returning the page. The sitter informed her that Zach was fine and playing video games. Whatever it was that Carl wanted would have to wait. Phyllis was having a good time and was in no hurry to ruin it by dealing with her husband.

"Is everything okay?" Nathan Pryor asked as Phyllis returned to the bar to continue her conversation.

"All is well, but thanks for asking," Phyllis said with a genuine smile. "So when will you be moving to Atlanta?"

"We're still in the preliminary stages but everything should be finalized within the next three to four weeks."

"Wow. I'm impressed. Baker, Covey, and Hawthorne is one of the top law firms in the city. It says a lot about you when they offer a partnership. They go all the way back to preschool with their background checks," Phyllis said, only halfway joking.

"That's what I'm told. So if everything works out, will I be able to count on you for a tour of the city?" Nathan said, inching toward Phyllis in a subtle yet flirtatious way.

"Absolutely. I was born and raised here so you'll be in good hands." Phyllis wasn't flirting, just enjoying the stimulating conversation that she was having with the tall, exotic-looking man with hazel eyes. She gave up very little information about her background, but asked some probing questions about his. She found out Nathan was born and raised in Baltimore, Maryland. He was the first male in his family ever to attend college, but it was the men in his family who footed the bill for his entire tuition at the University of South Carolina. He graduated magna cum laude, majoring in political science. Then he was offered a scholarship to the University of North Carolina Law School. After graduation he was hired by a pharmaceutical company in Texas, but was now leaning heavily toward an offer to move to Atlanta to pursue corporate law.

"So what happened to your friend?"

"Barbara? Oh, she had to rush off." Phyllis chuckled as she thought about the look on Barbara's face when she looked at her watch and realized that she had only paid the escort service for two hours.

"Looks like everyone else is starting to follow suit. Where is the phone you used? I need to call a cab."

"Where are you staying, Nathan?"

"Call me Nate, and I'm at the Swissotel in Buckhead."

"Oh, that's not far from here. I'll give you a lift," Phyllis offered.

"You sure? I mean, I can call a cab."

"It's nothing. Are you ready?" Phyllis asked as she finished off her glass of Chardonnay.

"Careful now. Are you sure you'll be able to drive?"

"I'm a prosecutor. I know all of the cops in the city. Plus that was my only glass. I'm fine."

"Well, in that case, let's ride," Nathan said, sliding Phyllis's barstool back as she stood.

They drove north on Peachtree Street until they saw the tall silver building that was the Swissotel. Phyllis pulled into the circular entranceway and stopped.

"Would you like to join me for a nightcap?" Nathan asked, hoping to spend a little more time with this beautiful sister.

"Maybe some other time. It's getting late, and I have a ton of work to do in the morning, so I better get on home. But thanks for the invite."

"Well, at least call me when you get in to let me know that you made it home safely."

"I'll be okay. How long will you be in town?"

Nathan pulled out one of his business cards and scribbled his room number on the back. As he handed it to Phyllis he held on to her hand just long enough to let her know that this could be more than a business meeting.

"I'll be here until Sunday. That gives me two more days to listen for the phone. I really enjoyed talking with you tonight, Phyllis. You're a very delightful person. I could learn a lot from you."

"Hey, you're the one that's being offered a partnership with one of the big three. It seems like you can teach me a thing or two."

"Well, maybe we can teach each other a few things. Hope to hear from you soon," Nathan said, and disappeared through the mirrored doors of the luxury hotel.

Phyllis stared at his handwriting on the back of the card and smiled. She laid her head back against the headrest and closed her eyes for a moment. She hadn't felt like this in a very long while. She couldn't put her finger on what was making her feel so attracted to Nathan Pryor. He didn't really come on to her; he was just a sweet, intelligent, good-looking man with a sense of purpose. And that to her was a turn-on.

Phyllis put her car in drive and smiled all the way down Georgia 400. She was halfway to the baby-sitter's house when her cell phone rang.

"Why didn't you return my page?" Carl asked.

"What did you expect me to do, drop everything and call you?" Phyllis snapped.

"What if it was an emergency?"

"I called the baby-sitter, and Zach was fine."

"Is Zach the only person that you're concerned with? Never mind, don't answer that. I'm leaving you. I've spent the night packing most of my things. I'll be back sometime this weekend to get the rest. I'll call you to make arrangements about Zach. 'Bye."

"Have you been drinking?" Phyllis asked calmly. She had been down this road before. Carl wasn't an alcoholic but he definitely was a jerk when he drank.

"Doesn't matter, but after dealing with you and your ways for the last ten years I deserve a few. I'll call you to talk about Zach."

"What about Zach?" Phyllis shot back.

"Zach's going to be living with me. You work too much, and you're never home."

"You *must* be drinking!" Phyllis said as she let out a sarcastic chuckle. "If you feel like you need to leave, then leave, but you're not taking my child to live with you in God knows where. Don't be irrational."

"What's irrational about what I said? Who works sixty, seventy hours a week? Who's never home? Who cooks for Zach every morning and night? And you call me irrational? I think you're the one that's been drinking!"

"We need to sit down and talk," Phyllis said, relenting a little as the truth started to hit home.

"Now you want to talk? Too late for conversation. That's your problem; you want to talk after all the damage has been done. I'll call you to make arrangements about Zach." Carl hung up.

Phyllis turned off her radio and let the driver-side window down a few inches. The air was cool for a June night in Atlanta. *Carl had to be drinking and needed a little drama to end his night,* she thought. Was Carl serious or was he just looking for some attention? If he was serious, how would she juggle a custody battle with everything that she had going on? Just yesterday, she agreed to teach a law class twice a week at Georgia State University. She had heard a rumor tonight that she was getting a promotion to deputy district attorney. Life was just starting to get good for her, at least career-wise. And now Carl was throwing a monkey wrench in her plans. Just as her head began to hurt, Phyllis pulled into the upscale neighborhood where her baby-sitter lived. After a few turns down some long, winding roads, she pulled into the driveway and stepped out of her car. Since it was almost two in the morning, Phyllis used the brass door knocker to tap lightly.

"Hi, Mrs. Olsen," Melissa, Zach's baby-sitter, said.

"Hello, Melissa. How was he?"

"He was fine as usual. I feel like I'm ripping you off, you know, him being such a fun kid and all."

"Well, give me my money back then," Phyllis joked with the preppy white teenager.

"You know I would, but I'm saving up for my senior class trip to Cancún. I'm trying to show my dad that I'm responsible so I'm trying to pay for it myself, and every dollar helps, you know?"

"I understand. Where is he?"

"Oh, that's the only thing. When Zachary falls asleep, he's out like a light. I tried to wake him when I saw you pulling up, but as you can see ..." Melissa said, pointing at the comatose Zachary.

Phyllis nodded her head and smiled at her sleeping child. He looked so innocent. Phyllis snapped out of her *Zachary means the world to me* trance and tried to figure out a way to get her son up and out of there. Normally Carl would be with her and he'd just pick Zach up and carry him to the car. But at seven, Zach was almost as big as his mother, and she had no intention of even attempting to pick him up. Phyllis walked over to the couch where her son was sleeping and tried to rouse the youngster, to no avail.

"Man, this boy is going on a diet first thing in the morning," Phyllis said as she struggled trying to lift her overweight son.

"Where's Mr. Olsen?" Melissa asked.

"He's at home. I don't know what I was thinking. Zach is always asleep when we pick him up late."

"I'll go wake my dad—he won't mind," Melissa said, hurrying out of the room and up the stairs before Phyllis could protest.

Melissa's white-haired father came down the stairs in a set of silk pajamas and a pair of leather house shoes.

"Hello, Phyllis. Haven't seen you in some time now. Congratulations on your promotion," he said.

"Well, I didn't get promoted yet, but I heard about it tonight. I thought it might be a rumor," Phyllis said, looking a little confused. "How'd you hear about it?"

"Disclosure of evidence clause. You know the prosecution must turn all evidence over to the defense in a timely manner. Plus I have to keep up with my adversaries," Jack Rudolf said as he reached out and hugged Phyllis. They had gone to law school together. Jack had gone on to defend Georgia's "innocent" men and women who were charged with breaking the law and got rich in the process, while Phyllis had gone on to prosecute the criminals and made a middle-class salary.

"Well, someone's doing their job a little too well. I need to see it in writing before I get excited."

"You need to tell them to take that job and shove it so you can come on over to my firm. We could always use a lawyer of your caliber to fight this oppressive system," Jack said seriously.

"That's a conversation we'll have to have another time. Right now I need those scrawny arms of yours to carry my child to the car."

"You know he beat me in Scrabble tonight? I was so impressed," Jack said as he slid a hand under Zachary's back and the other under his chubby legs. He lifted him and carried him outside to the car, laying him on the backseat.

"I think his favorite book is Webster's dictionary. He beats his dad all the time," Phyllis said.

"How is Carl anyway?"

"Don't get me started. We'll have to do lunch," Phyllis said as she made a frustrated face. Jack got the message and left that one alone.

"Well, Melissa, I thank you kindly," Phyllis said, pressing forty dollars into her hand.

"Thanks, and don't forget to call me if you need me again," Melissa said before running back into the house.

"I will. Jack, call me tomorrow and we'll talk," Phyllis said as she plopped down in the driver's seat.

"Saturday is all-day golf. I'll call you Sunday, and remember what I said about coming to the firm. That invite has been open for years, and it still is. We could use you—but more importantly, your people could use you."

"Thanks, Jack, but I respectfully decline." Phyllis closed her door and waved good-bye to Jack.

Phyllis thought Jack was a good guy with a good heart. His wife left him a few years back, but he hadn't missed a beat raising his daughter alone. However, Phyllis always disagreed with him when he brought race into the issue of law. Her thoughts were that wrong was wrong no matter who was doing it. So as far as she was concerned, race didn't matter. She didn't buy into that redundant dialogue that blacks were treated unfairly, and she didn't have any patience for people who did.

Phyllis made it to her home in Duluth County in forty minutes. When she pulled in the driveway and hit her remote for the garage, Carl was standing in her parking space looking at his watch. It was almost 3:00 A.M.

"Do your banquets last longer when I'm not there?" Carl asked as he looked at his watch. "Or did you go elsewhere?"

Phyllis took a deep breath before opening her car door. She was not in the mood for Carl tonight. All she wanted to do was get out of her high heels, take a quick shower, and cuddle in the softness of her white cotton sheets.

"Carl, it's late, I'm tired, and I'm really not in the mood," Phyllis said, brushing past him. She was right, he had been drinking. He smelled like a liquor still. Now she knew she wasn't about to waste her breath talking with him.

"I don't give a shit what you're in the mood for. I'm tired of dancing to your fiddle," Carl said as he roughly grabbed her arm and turned her around to face him.

"Carl, let my arm go."

"We need to talk."

"Let my arm go. Now, damn it," Phyllis yelled.

"I'll let your arm go when I good and goddamn please. Thought you said we needed to talk? And I'm not letting anything go until you stop acting like everything has to go your fucking way," Carl yelled back.

"Nothing has to go my way. I'm just tired. Can we talk tomorrow?" Phyllis tried to soften her tone.

"No. I'm leaving you and I wanna get some things straight before I go," Carl said, slurring a few of his words.

"And you can't wait until tomorrow? You absolutely have to talk now?"

"Damn right."

"Carl, you're drunk, and you're being obnoxious," Phyllis said in a low growl.

"Obnoxious? You wanna see obnoxious? I'll show your ass obnoxious." Carl lost it. He reached out and ripped the front of Phyllis's dress, exposing her bra.

Shocked, Phyllis stood looking Carl in the eyes. Her instinct was to fight, but for some strange reason she stood frozen in place, trying to collect herself. She looked like all of her mental functions had shut down.

"What took you so long, huh? Who were you with? I've been to plenty of your funky little functions and never made it home past one o'clock. Let me smell your fucking panties," Carl yelled. He roughly turned her around and pushed the back of her head down on the hood of her car. Phyllis didn't resist as he lifted her dress and violently snatched her panties off, ripping the material at her hip. He placed the silk thong under his nose and took a deep whiff.

"Why couldn't you return my damn page? Who were you with?" Carl asked as he took another whiff of her panties.

Phyllis didn't make a sound. She didn't protest or try to fight him. She looked to be under some sort of hypnosis. Her eyes were wide open but life no longer lived there. She couldn't move.

Carl looked at Phyllis's exposed rear end with her dress hoisted up around her waist and became aroused. He ran his hand over her round behind and slid his hand between her legs.

Carl leaned over Phyllis and whispered in her ear, "Who is he? Got to be somebody. You sure ain't giving it to me. So, so maybe I shouldn't be so nice all the time. Maybe I should be obnoxious and take it, huh? I didn't get married to have to jerk off all the damn time."

Then Carl was hit in the back by a small hand.

"Get off of my momma," Zachary cried, swinging his arms and connecting blows to his father's leg. "I hate you. Stop hurting her."

Carl stood frozen. He pushed himself off of Phyllis and looked around the garage as if it were unfamiliar territory.

Zachary went to his mother's side and wrapped his arms around her back.

Carl realized that something wasn't right. Phyllis wasn't moving.

He was drunk but he still expected more of a fight from her. What he was doing was wrong and he didn't know how he'd ever face his son again.

Carl tossed Phyllis's ripped panties at her head and looked down at his lifeless wife. He shook his head, trying to clear it, and placed his hands on Phyllis's neck to see if she still had a pulse. Once he found one, he backed out of the driveway as if he could rewind the night's episode.

Carl turned and almost ran to his car, stumbling along the way. Once he made it inside his car he looked back into the garage and noticed Zachary frowning at him. Carl thought about going back to apologize to his son and his wife and beg them for forgiveness. But why should they forgive him? What could he say? How much did Zachary see? Carl felt ashamed of his actions and lowered his head as he sat in his car gripping the steering wheel tightly. A sick feeling came over him as he made eye contact with his son, who was now standing straight up and pointing a deadly finger at his father. Carl broke his gaze and saw that Phyllis was still bent over on the hood of her car, motionless. Carl felt like a coward as he started his motor and backed out of the driveway.

Once Carl was gone, Zachary felt it was okay to go and check on his mother. He shook her. "Mom. Mom." He shook her harder. "Mom, Mom, wake up," Zachary cried.

Phyllis started breathing hard and shook her head as if to wake herself. She looked around the garage, trying desperately to bring herself back to reality. She looked down at her son and at her panties, now on the hood of her car. She stood and noticed that her dress was up around her waist. She quickly snatched it down and began rubbing her left arm. She bit her bottom lip and tried not to cry. She reached down and hugged her son. She was fighting hysteria but she had to be strong for Zachary.

"Mom, what was Daddy doing?" Zach asked in a tearful voice.

Phyllis grabbed her panties and Zach's hand and hurried into the house without a word. She locked all the doors and rushed to put the alarm on instant alert, so if Carl returned she would know immediately.

"Sweetie, do you mind sleeping with Mommy tonight?" Phyllis asked, finding her voice but still holding back her tears.

"Mommy, where is Daddy going?" Zachary asked. "Is he coming home?"

"Don't worry about that right now, baby. Just go and get in Mommy's bed."

Zachary followed his mother's advice and went upstairs and crawled into her bed.

Phyllis went into the kitchen and got a medium-size knife. She double-checked the doors and hurried upstairs into her bedroom. She looked in on Zachary and found him stirring under the covers. Her heart skipped a beat when she wondered what her child witnessed in the garage. She walked into the bathroom and stood in front of the mirror. As soon as she caught sight of her torn dress, she lost the fight with her tears. She covered her face with her hands and tried to muffle her moans so she wouldn't wake Zachary. Phyllis backed away from her reflection and bumped into the wall. She slid down to the floor and cried. She whispered to herself, "Why, God? Why?"

AFTER SITTING ON the bathroom floor for more than an hour, her arms wrapped around her knees, Phyllis stood and disrobed. She turned on the shower and placed her hand under the water to make sure it was as hot as she could stand it. Once she was satisfied with the temperature, she stepped in and stood directly under the nozzle, letting her tears blend in with the water. She grabbed her pink sponge and squeezed out four times the amount of body wash that she would normally use. She needed to cleanse herself of the crime that was just committed against her, in her own home by her own husband. Phyllis stayed in the shower for almost an hour, washing every inch of her body. She cried and scrubbed—cried until no more tears would flow from her eyes and scrubbed her skin so hard she felt raw.

Phyllis made herself a promise that what happened to her tonight in the garage would never happen to her again. She didn't like the helplessness she felt. She was fully aware of what Carl was doing but she was unable to make a move to stop him.

She went through a range of emotions in that shower. She felt sick that she married a man who would do such a thing. She felt angry with herself for not fighting back. Then she did what most victims do, and blamed herself. But she made herself snap out of that sort of thinking and went back to being angry. After her emotional roller coaster came to a slow halt, Phyllis stepped out of the shower.

After drying herself with a thick white cotton towel, Phyllis walked out of the bathroom. She sat on the side of her bed, picked up the telephone, and dialed 911. She was placed on hold even after she informed the switchboard operator that she had an emergency. In the time she was on hold, she thought about how she would answer the questions when she informed the police that she was sexually assaulted.

"Do you know the perpetrator?" "Yes, my husband!"

"Do you have any visible bruises?" "No!"

"Are you divorced or separated?" "No."

"Do you have a restraining order?" "No."

"Did he sexually assault you?" "He fondled me."

"What did you do to stop the perpetrator?" "Nothing!"

Phyllis hung up the telephone as she realized the same laws that she spent her days enforcing would do nothing to help her. Just the thought of an attorney asking embarrassing questions that would make her seem as if she was on trial was enough to make her hang up the phone. She wished she had someone to call and talk to about this horrible night, but she didn't. *How did I let myself become so alone in this world?* she thought. Phyllis hadn't been close to her mother since she was eleven years old. And although she loved her brothers, she felt no connection with them. And the last time she spoke with her little sister, Grace, she told Phyllis to never contact her again.

Phyllis lay down beside Zachary and pulled the covers up to her neck. She slid closer to him and kissed his forehead. She finally fell off to sleep while clutching her son's hand.

AFTER LEAVING PHYLLIS and his son, Carl drove around Atlanta in a state of disorientation. He felt like a criminal for doing what he had done to his wife, yet he wasn't sure what actually happened. Everything was a blur to him from the time Phyllis pulled into the garage. But the memory of his wife half dressed and his son's pointing made him understand that he'd done something very bad. He hated the way alcohol dulled his senses. When he drank too much, logic and reasoning went out the door. He tortured himself by remembering the look of helplessness on his wife's face and the hate and disappointment coming from his son's eyes. How did things escalate so out of control? Tonight wasn't supposed to happen like that. He was upset with Phyllis for just being an overall ass, but he never meant to hurt her.

When Phyllis left the house earlier that evening for the banquet, Carl had gone to his neighbor Fred's house to shoot some pool and to get his mind off his troubles. To make their game a little more interesting, his neighbor suggested they play for shots. The loser had to drink shots of Cuervo Gold tequila.

Before long, Carl was caught up in the moment. To make matters worse, every once in a while Fred's wife, Karen, would come into the poolroom and check on them to see if they needed anything. He could tell that Fred and Karen shared something special. The look in her eyes told Carl that she was a stand-by-her-man kind of woman. Karen made him think about his own to-hell-with-my-husband wife. He took a swig of liquor before he even leveled his stick to take his first shot.

Eight losses and ten shots of tequila later, Carl stumbled home. He paged Phyllis to see if she was willing to give their marriage a shot at counseling. He waited about twenty minutes, then paged her again, but she still didn't return the call. As he roamed around the house wondering why his wife was such a bitch, he was thankful to Fred for letting him take the remainder of the liquor home with him.

Carl took a quick swig, then his thoughts took a turn for the worse. *Maybe she has someone else and that's why she never wants to talk or do anything with me. Maybe Fred was right,* he thought. For more than an hour, Carl entertained thoughts of Phyllis with another man, and became furious. He thought back to the many playful conversations he'd had with Fred about black women and white men. Fred joked that there were only two reasons his fellow black sisters would ever date white men. The first was because of money, and the other was the fact that white men couldn't control them and would let black women run all over them. Carl understood that Fred was joking, but now he began to think there was some truth to what Fred had tried to mask with laughter. That's when Carl realized that no amount of counseling could ever change the way Phyllis was. The only thing left to do was leave.

Carl picked up the telephone and called Fort McPherson's temporary lodging. After confirming his reservations with post housing he began to pack his belongings. Before the liquor really settled into his system, he called Phyllis again, this time on her cell phone. It was already after one o'clock in the morning when she answered.

Carl loaded his car with his things, then sat on a stool in the garage and waited for Phyllis to return, sipping on what was left of the tequila until his nostrils burned. He stood when he saw her headlights approaching and that was the beginning of the end.

CARL DROVE AROUND Atlanta, drunk, and trying to find the highway that was usually right around the corner from his house. *I wonder who moved the damn street? The asshole could've told somebody,* he thought. Carl was wondering why everyone was blinking their lights and honking their horns at him. Then things really went black.

six

MAN TALK!

Damn, I can't believe I'm really giving up my playa card, Genesis admitted to himself as he headed out the door of Terri's old apartment. He had agreed to do the final walk-through with the leasing manager for her. Genesis stood in the doorway looking back at the empty place with a sinking feeling in his stomach. He felt as if he was making the biggest mistake of his life. He almost wished he could pull a genie out of a bottle and make all of Terri's things reappear in her apartment.

Genesis leaned against the door frame as his life as a player flashed through his mind. Lisa, Crystal, Michelle, Delana, Kim, Jackie, Ebony, Amber, Tammy, Yvette, Kameka, Vickie, Sheila, Dee Dee, and at least another hundred ladies had spent time beneath, on top of, or in front of Genesis the lover man. Now all of that bumping and grinding was about to come to a screeching halt. And why? To spend the rest of his life with one woman. *Damn, that just don't seem fair to a brother,* he thought.

Genesis took a deep breath and closed the door on his freedom. He walked to his truck as if he were walking to his execution. He climbed behind the wheel of his Blazer, looked into the rearview mirror, and ran his fingers through his twisted hair.

"Hell no, I don't wanna ride with you to see the reception site. Spending all this money on one day's worth of hoopla! That's crazy," Genesis said to himself, frowning at the thought of all of the madness that had been going on around him lately.

The wedding was only two months away. Sixty-one more days and he'd be a married man. As he pulled out of the parking lot, the doubts started creeping back in, so he quickly adjusted the mirror and turned up the volume on the radio.

Genesis pulled into the parking lot of the Atlanta Youth Center and parked next to Prodigy's truck. He hopped out and walked into the single-floor building, smiling at the progress that Prodigy had made with the old place. The youth center was once a grocery store, and then it closed down due to the locals stealing more than they paid for. The place stayed closed and gutted for a few years until Prodigy came along searching for a site to house his vision.

The walls were painted with murals of small kids wearing professional apparel. There was a little African-American boy wearing a white doctor's jacket with a stethoscope around his neck, checking the heart of a Caucasian boy wearing an Atlanta Hawks uniform that was about ten sizes too big. Farther down was a pretty young girl sitting behind a desk in what appeared to be a law office.

Just as Genesis turned the corner, he noticed Prodigy leaning down talking to a light-skinned little boy who looked to be on a comb or pick boycott.

"Why you crying, little man?" Genesis asked the boy as he walked up and slapped Prodigy on the back.

"They won't let me play basketball no more," the little boy said.

"Prodigy, what kind of ship you running around here?"

"Well, I'll tell you what," Prodigy said, reaching into his pocket and handing Genesis the keys to the gym. "It's your ship now. Kevin, you stop crying and go back in the gym. Find something else to do. When you lose a game you have to wait your turn to play again. Okay? And find you a comb. I already told y'all about coming up in here looking like you just rolled out of bed."

"Okay."

"Man, it's a lot of kids in here for a Saturday morning," Genesis said as he looked through the window of the gym and saw about fifty kids running every which way.

"Yeah, it's like this all the time, and you really haven't seen anything yet. Wait until the afternoon. It's bananas up in here," Prodigy said.

"This place isn't as big as I thought it was. It's nice though."

"Yeah, I know. I'm working on a grant right now that will allow us to add on to the gym and buy a few pieces of gymnastics equipment."

"Black folks don't do gymnastics," Genesis said, looking at Prodigy with a wrinkled lip.

"Yeah, we don't play golf either. Shut up. You don't see a lot of us doing it because we don't have the access to the equipment, but we're trying to change that. Whatchu doing here so early all dressed up? I didn't expect you until one."

"I gotta meet with Dr. Ben. He told me you got him over here doing some volunteer counseling a few days a week."

"Yeah, Dr. Ben's the man. The kids set up appointments with him just so they can laugh at his tight-ass suits. I wonder if your sister Phyllis would come over and talk to the kids sometimes. I got about twenty or thirty kids in here that say they wanna be lawyers. It would be good for them to actually see one outside of an arraignment at the courthouse."

"Good luck. You'd probably have a better chance of getting Johnnie Cochran."

"She's that busy, huh?"

"Nope, she's just a bitch!" Genesis called his sister out of her name with the greatest of ease.

"Ahh, don't talk about your sister like that. Come holla at me when you finish with Dr. Ben. I gotta take care of this grant stuff or I'll be here all day."

"Oh yeah, Terri told me that your wife said that you spend too much time up here. Said she's always lonely," Genesis said.

Prodigy thought about what he just heard and nodded. *Damn, I let it happen again,* he thought.

"Handle your business now. You can't preach to me about fucking up if you fucking up too, even if yours is justified. Feel me?" Genesis said, happy to play the adviser for a change.

"Yeah, let me get outta here. You got the keys to the gym and front door. I'll call you later to give you the code for the alarm and get all your info so Candy can put you on the payroll," Prodigy said as he looked around the gym for Blake.

"How's Candy doing with her fine ass? Damn, I'd like to hit that. She won't give me no play," Genesis said, shaking his head.

"Get some scruples about yourself," Prodigy said with a sigh. "Blake! Blake, it's time to go!" Prodigy called out to his son.

"P, you work up here with that fine-ass woman every day and ain't try and hit it?"

"You ignorant, you know that? Blake," Prodigy called out to his son. "I know that boy can hear me calling him."

"I'll take him home. You take your whipped behind on and spend some quality time with your wife. Jalen will be here in a minute, and he'll be a little upset if Blake's not here."

"Okay, call me if y'all need anything," Prodigy said just as Blake ran up. "Never mind, dude. I'm about to leave but Genesis is gonna bring you home."

"Where's Jalen?"

"You wanna speak first?" Prodigy reprimanded his son.

"Hey, Uncle G. Where's Jalen?" Blake said, in a rush to get back to his basketball game.

"What's up, scrub?" Genesis grabbed Blake and put him in a headlock. "Jalen will be here in a few. I'm making his daddy walk him around here."

"Oh. Tell him to come in the gym, okay?" Blake said, after wiggling himself free and running back to his game.

"Let me show you where your office is," Prodigy said as he walked into his modestly furnished office space and reached into his desk drawer to retrieve a key.

"Uh-oh, I got a office," Genesis said, smiling.

"Yeah, all of the staff have offices. Yours is in the gym." Prodigy unlocked a door to a small office with a glass front that allowed its occupant full view of the gym.

"Oh, this is straight. I might not be here long, though. I spoke with my bucktooth-ass agent this morning and he's working on a coaching spot with the WNBA."

"Oh, congratulations, dog," Prodigy said. "You think you'll be safe around all those fine women?"

"I'll be married by then and I told you I'm going to be a faithful man, damn it."

"Yeah, you did say that," Prodigy said. He seemed to be preoccupied ever since Genesis told him that his wife had a need that he wasn't meeting.

Genesis shook Prodigy's hand and shook his own head. He couldn't believe the drastic change in his friend. *Done went from a super lover to a damn wimp,* he thought. Genesis walked down the hall and tapped lightly on the office door of Dr. Ben Rogers.

"Man, you look like a million bucks. I wish I was five or six sizes smaller, I'd make you give me that suit," Dr. Ben said, as he rubbed his chubby hand over his large belly, admiring the gray custom-made blazer and slacks that Genesis wore with a simple white silk T-shirt and black Mezlan shoes.

"Congratulations on your recent engagement. I'm proud of you."

"Thanks," Genesis said, letting out a deep sigh and plopping his lanky body down on the leather love seat. His worry showed on his face.

"Well, let's talk. What's on your mind?" Dr. Ben asked, walking behind his desk and taking a seat.

"It's hard to make a woman your wife, when you've been humping married women for most of your life." Genesis cringed. "I heard that years ago on a Big Daddy Kane song."

"A who?" Dr. Ben asked with a confused frown.

"Ah, don't worry about it. I can't get that phrase outta my head, man. It's just ... you know, what comes around, goes around. That's the thing that's on my mind daily. Dr. Ben, I ain't crazy. I know you can't keep doing wrong and expect everyone to do you right. But I still don't want my girl out there cheating. That's the ultimate slap in the face."

"Do you feel that it's okay for you to cheat?"

"Nah, I'm just saying. I look at it different if a woman cheats. I sort of lose respect for her."

"Why?"

"Because somebody has to have some morals. It might as well be my wife."

"What about your morals?"

"You know what I mean."

"You said that you would lose respect for your lady if she was unfaithful, but would you be able to forgive her and move on if something like that was to happen?" Dr. Ben asked.

"I might be able to forgive her but I could never move on and be with her again."

"What if you were to cheat and she found out, would you want her to forgive you and move on with your lives?"

"Yeah, but like I said, women are different."

"How?"

"Well, we put them up on a pedestal." Genesis sat up in his seat with his elbows on his thighs. "You know, that's my queen and she should never violate that position. It's hard to explain, but I'd be too hurt, and the trust could never be the same."

"Trust. What does that mean to you?"

"It means believing in a person. Knowing that she won't do you wrong."

"Now, do you trust Terri?"

"To a certain extent."

"Why not fully?"

"I don't trust anybody fully."

"You can't believe in something a little bit. Belief is one of the few things in this world that is absolute. All or nothing! So you're saying that you don't trust anybody," Dr. Ben said with a straight face.

"If you put it that way then I guess not," Genesis said, leaning back in his seat.

"Your father was the same way. He ran from commitment like it was a bad storm. But, I'll tell you another thing, your father was a very unhappy man. He never fully gave of himself; therefore he never experienced true love. You have to give in order to get, young man."

"I understand."

"I think you do. But you'll have to develop a different frame of mind if you are to ever have a fulfilling relationship. Otherwise it'll always be touch and go. Now, what's up with you and married women?"

"It's not like I go looking for them, they come to me. But I'm not going there anymore. I'm starting to look at that a little different now. I'm starting to put myself in the other man's shoes," Genesis said, thinking about the venomous monogrammed bath towel.

"What brought about that change?"

"I'm just getting older, and I need something different now. Something more fulfilling than sleeping with just any ol' body. I want what Prodigy and Nina have."

"How old are you now, Genesis?"

"Twenty-nine. Damn near thirty years old," Genesis said, staring up at the ceiling as if he were trying to find some answers there.

"Plus, I've contributed to my share of broken homes. I had an affair with a woman one time, and her husband found out. He beat her up so bad that you couldn't recognize her. He went to jail, and she went into hiding. One woman lost everything she had: her house, cars, bank accounts, and to top it all off, lil buddy took the kids—all because of a fling with me. That's why I know some shit is coming back at me. I mean, how can I cause all that drama and have a happy-go-lucky life with my wife?"

"Genesis, you do understand that you can't go into this marriage with feelings of infidelity, don't you? You'll drive yourself insane. Trust is one of the most important attributes of any relationship."

"Dr. Ben, I done slept with *a lot* of married women, and I know every one of them started out all in love," Genesis said. "You know, now that I'm about to get married, I think about all the reasons why the women came on to me in the first place."

"And why was that?" Dr. Ben asked, twirling a Mont Blanc pen skillfully between his fingers.

"The need for attention! 'He doesn't hold me anymore, he works too much, he's this, he's that.' Most of the time I agreed with the dude. I just played that compassionate role to get the panties," Genesis said with a straight face.

"And how did that make you feel?"

"Whatcha mean, how did it make me feel?"

"How did it make you feel that you slept with another man's wife?"

"I didn't feel anything. Not for him, I mean. If he was taking care of home, then she wouldn't be with me in the first place, now would she?"

"Well, if you truly feel that way, then you have nothing to worry about with Terri. Just take care of home."

"Women are high-maintenance, man, and nobody can keep up a pace like that."

"You're contradicting yourself, but go on," Dr. Ben said as he pulled the hairs on his long gray goatee with one hand and twirled the pen with the other.

"To keep a woman totally happy is a twenty-four-hour-a-day job, and nobody has that kind of time," Genesis argued.

"Why do you feel that way?"

"When my father was alive…" Genesis closed his eyes and quickly crossed his heart. "We used to talk about women all the time, and we could never figure them out. He spoke of a time when a woman wasn't that hard to please. All you had to do was treat her right and provide for her. Now you got to jump through all kinds of hoops to please they asses. They ain't that easily impressed anymore either. You pull up in your 500 Benz, and I'll be damn if that trick don't have a 600."

Dr. Ben laughed. "Those are just material things, Genesis. At the end of the day a woman still needs a man to be a man, and you need for her to be a woman. Is Terri materialistic?"

"No, she's cool."

"Then why are you making things complicated? Why worry about any other woman, whether she's impressed with you or not? If Terri's happy, then no one else should matter. The Bible says to married people, 'Let no man or woman put them asunder.' "

"I hear you, but a woman is a complicated creature."

"Have you ever given any thought as to how women got the way that you say they are?"

"All the time."

"And what did you come up with?"

"They're just greedy and money-hungry. Plus, they think because they make their own money they don't need a man."

"What about you? Have you ever thought that you made them that way?"

"Me! How did I make 'em that way?"

"As men, sometime we can be trifling. I'm sixty-nine years old, and I can remember when my own father was living. He'd step out on my mother all the time. I knew what was going on, and my mother did too. But I never once heard her complain. Now, my father was what you would consider a 'good man.' He would take care of all the bills and fix whatever was broken. But when I look back at him as a man, I'm not proud. My mother was the real hero. She didn't have time to run the streets because she had a job to do with all of us kids. She stressed education to all of us, but especially to my sisters." Dr. Ben turned around and opened a small refrigerator and removed two bottles of water. He handed one to Genesis and opened the other one before continuing.

"Now, just think of the women who don't have a man around at all. They're not gonna prepare their daughters to be wives and take care of the household duties. They're gonna teach their daughters to take care of themselves and their children, if they have any. How could they teach their daughters how to be wives if they haven't been one themselves? They're going to teach their daughters to be self-sufficient, and when those daughters grow up, all they're going to know how to do is take care of number one. Guess what, Genesis? You're dealing with those grown-up daughters now and they weren't taught the meaning of compromise. It's damn near impossible for her to forget everything that she was ever taught and let you call all the shots. Especially if they're dealing with a man that can't keep his eyes off of other women long enough to lead the family. You're dealing with an educated woman now, Genesis. She's not the same woman your father was talking about." Dr. Ben paused to catch his breath and take another sip of water. He knew that he talked too much for a psychologist, but this younger generation didn't have anyone to talk to them at home, so he felt obligated.

"Now, if this young lady does meet up with a good brother who wants to take care of home and be the head of his house, it's still hard for her to go back to being second in command and now you got chaos. And you're right, she *is* very hard to please. And what about the little boy that grows up in a home with a single mom? Who's going to teach him how to be a man—his momma? She's not a man, therefore she can't provide him with the necessary tools that are essential to his survival in this world. It's hit-and-miss. Some of us make it out of single-parent homes and do really well, but the majority of us are falling like flies. Every Wednesday when I teach at the juvenile detention center, I see the ones that have fallen victim to what I call the 'trifling daddy syndrome.' What I see are mostly young black faces, and you know the one thing that ninety percent of them have in common? No daddy at home!"

"So where does that leave us?" Genesis asked, soaking up all the information he had just heard.

"Genesis, all we have to do is start being men again. Stop running away from our responsibilities as husbands and fathers. You make a child—be man enough to take care of that child until he can take care of himself.

"We have to start thinking before we go jumping in the bed with just any ol' lady that makes your pecker rise. Being a father is a lifetime job. You young guys are running around here committing genocide. Kids are having kids.

"I met a thirty-year-old grandmother the other day at the detention center. Her fifteen-year-old son is doing time for murdering someone else's black child. And she was bringing his son to visit him. The mother had to be fourteen years old herself when she had him and her son only emulated what he saw at home. So the cycle of destruction continues. Sooner or later we won't have much of a black race."

"Man, I never thought about it like that," Genesis said. "I got my work cut out for me. When I have kids, I don't want them to look at me like my nephew looks at my brother." Genesis pictured his little nephew, Jalen, sitting on the front porch waiting in vain for his dad to do daddy things. He wondered if Grover had gotten Jalen up to the center yet. Genesis and Grover had, on several occasions, come to blows over the way Grover treated his son.

Genesis wasn't perfect, especially when it came to being faithful to Terri, but he was an exceptional role model when it came to Jalen or any other kid. He made a conscious effort to keep his sneaky dealings with women out of his nephew's sight.

"One day Grover will come around. We just have to pray for him."

"He needs more than a prayer. It's bad when you don't like your own brother."

"Back to you. Is Terri hard to please?" Dr. Ben asked, making a mental note to come back to the conversation about Grover on another day.

"Nah, she's straight for now. But she's still a woman, and I understand what you just said, but the fact remains that they asses are crazy. Like all this here," Genesis said, sweeping his arms around the doctor's office. "My momma and Terri got me up in here. I mean, I enjoy talking to you, but this some ol' corny woman shit. Premarital counseling! If a marriage is gonna work, then it will; if not, then it won't."

"Boy, watch your mouth. There's nothing wrong with getting some advice from people who have been there," Dr. Ben said, stepping out of his counselor's role and into that of family friend. He'd been friends with Genesis's father ever since the two of them were small, so he looked at Genesis and his siblings as his own.

"Sorry," Genesis said. He dropped his head, realizing he had overstepped his bounds.

"If you feel that way, then why are you here?"

"You know how my momma is. Plus, this is suppose to be some kind of family tradition or something, ain't it?"

"It's customary for young couples to seek counseling before they embark on their lives together as husband and wife. This session will only help if you allow it to. It's intended to give you a better understanding of married life."

"Didn't you counsel Carl and my sister?"

"Yes, I did. How are they doing?"

"My momma said that Carl left Phyllis last night. You know how Phyllis is. That's another woman that nobody can understand. I mean, she's my sister, and I love her, but . . ." Genesis shook his head.

"Are you still upset about the decision she made with your dad?"

"Nah . . . never mind her," Genesis said, wanting to change the subject. It had been ten years since his father had passed, but the wounds were still fresh. Especially since there were still questions about whether he had to go when he did.

Taking his cue to change the subject, Dr. Ben said, "You know, I think you're worried about nothing at all. Terri seems to be a wonderful young lady, and I think she'll make you an awesome wife."

"Awesome wife? Ain't that an oxymoron?" Genesis said, as they shared a quick laugh.

"Do you love her?"

"Yeah."

"Well then, act like it and give her your all."

"I hear you. But what about four or five years down the line? When she starts all that nagging. What about when I put her on mute because I don't wanna hear all of that drama and she starts getting attention from somebody else? See, that's when I'm going to snap," Genesis said, clapping his hands together and startling Dr. Ben, who just gave him a look that said, "Don't do that again."

"It seems you're preparing for the worst. That's a good trait to have if you're expecting a flood or a tornado, but a very bad one when it comes to human beings—and an even worse one with relationships. Remember, you can plan the picnic but you can't predict the weather. Hit your knees and hope for the best."

"I'm just being realistic." Genesis leaned back in his chair and ran his fingers through his hair. "Ya know, I never wanted to get married in the first place. She forced me into this."

"Oh, and how did she do that?"

"She threatened to leave. She said that she was going to hire someone to run her store and she was gonna go to NYU to earn her master's," Genesis said, shaking his head at the thought of Terri leaving. It wasn't until after he was faced with the reality that she wouldn't be around that he realized how much he loved and needed her. That's when he proposed.

"But you said you loved her."

"I do. I just wasn't trying to get married."

"But why not? What are you afraid of?"

"I don't know, it just seems so final."

"It should be. You've finally found the right one, and now it's time to settle down. You can't play forever, Genesis."

"I know, she's a good girl, and I'm really not trying to be with anyone else, anyway."

"Then what's the problem? Genesis, I don't think you give yourself enough credit sometimes. You focus on the negative way too much. You can't keep doing that and keep people around. Negativity drives positive people away."

"I'm not negative," Genesis responded, feeling a little put out.

"Yes, you are. Listen to yourself sometime. You haven't said one positive thing today without finishing it with something negative. I swear you're like your father. God bless his soul."

"You know, my mother and my father spent the last fifteen years of his life sleeping in separate bedrooms and basically ignoring each other. Now, I wonder how you go from being all lovey-dovey to that kind of life."

"Have you ever sat down and asked your mother how they got to that point in their relationship?"

"Nah, cuz Momma's gonna be one-sided, and I need to hear Daddy's point of view too."

"You'd be surprised at the kind of information you'd get if you just gave it a shot. I think speaking with your mother will give you a ton of insight on your own relationship. And maybe help you conquer your fears."

"I don't know, Doc. This marriage thing ain't no joke. I don't mean to be negative, but I don't know anybody that's been married for more than three years and still happy."

"Nonsense, sure you do."

"Who?"

"Give it some thought, and I'm sure you'll come up with someone. I'm happily married, and you've been knowing me all your life."

Genesis thought about every time he visited Dr. Ben's house and found him in the basement and his wife, Clara, upstairs. *Now, if that's what I have to look forward to, then I'm in some trouble.*

"You know what's strange about this relationship, Doc? I don't wanna cheat."

"Well, then don't. It seems to me that you're fighting your maturation process."

"I'm starting to see the light. I realize I have a diamond and I don't wanna mess it up. Sometimes I feel like there's a war going on inside me. Terri treats me like a king, even after some of the dumb things I done pulled. I got to reward her for that."

"What makes you think you're rewarding her? When you say things like that, it gives the impression that you're doing her a favor. From the way you describe your past behavior, she's the one that's doing you a favor. You just have to open up your eyes and see it."

"Well, I didn't mean it like that, it's just that she's been the one wanting to get married. I never wanted to get married. But I wanna give her something for all that she's done for me."

"Well, marriage is the supreme commitment. You need to be sure, Genesis."

"I'm sure I wanna marry her, I'm just not sure I can keep my jimmy in my pants."

"Why do you feel that way?"

"Cuz like my man said on that movie, *The Best Man,* ain't nothing better than some coochie, except some new coochie."

"Well, I saw a movie once myself that said, 'What's old to you is new to the next man.' If you plan on keeping your woman at home, keep that in mind. Look, I gotta get out of here. Tell your mother I asked about her."

"But what about karma? I know something is going to happen for all the cheatin' that I did."

"Pray and repent. You'll be just fine," Dr. Ben said as he stood and shook Genesis's hand. "What did your mother say when you told her about your engagement?"

"She asked me did I love Terri and I said yes, then she asked how do I know that it's love and I said that I can feel it and she said, 'Ah, boy, that ain't nuttin' but gas.'"

They laughed and walked out of the office together. Genesis noticed a pretty young lady waiting in the lobby. He looked at her long, shapely legs and round rear end. He hesitated a moment but kept walking toward the gym. He smiled at himself. That was a big move for him.

seven

MISERY LOVES COMPANY

Phyllis was startled awake by the sound of a ringing telephone. Her heart was pounding, so she lay still for a moment, trying to collect her thoughts. She was dreaming that she was drowning in a swimming pool, surrounded by men, and none of them would jump in to save her.

Phyllis gathered herself long enough to look at the caller ID. It read "line error." She decided to let the machine pick it up. She glanced over at the clock on her nightstand and saw that it was only five-thirty in the morning. That really put her in a foul mood. Just as she closed her eyes, the phone rang again. This time she picked it up and placed the receiver to her ear without a greeting.

"Hello? Hello? May I speak with Phyllis Olsen, please," the caller stated.

Realizing that it was not Carl, Phyllis finally spoke. "Who's calling?"

"This is Officer Joe Jackson with the Atlanta Police Department. Is this Mrs. Phyllis Olsen?"

"What can I do for you, Officer?"

"Is this Mrs. Olsen?"

"Yes, it is," Phyllis snapped. "What can I do for you?"

"Mrs. Olsen, we have your husband down here. My supervisor asked me to call you before we processed him for DUI. Looks like he had one too many to be behind the wheel. He ran into a ditch, but he seems to be okay. But as a professional courtesy, we'll release him to you."

Phyllis didn't respond. The thought of Carl had taken her back to last night. She held the phone to her ear without speaking.

"Ma'am! Mrs. Olsen, are you there?"

"Yes, I'm here."

"Well, will you be coming to pick up your husband?"

"Officer Jackson, I would like for you to treat Mr. Olsen just as you would any other person that breaks the law. I appreciate the call," Phyllis said before hanging up.

She lay back down and tried to catch the sleep that had left her when the phone rang. Just as she was on the edge of unconsciousness, the phone rang again.

"Damn it," Phyllis said before picking up the telephone. "Hello," she snapped.

"Phyllis Olsen, this is Major Parham with the Atlanta Police Department. We have your husband down here."

"I know that. I already told the first person who called here to do what you would normally do. I didn't ask for any favors. Mr. Olsen is an adult. If he wants to drive after he's been drinking and place other people's lives in danger, then he needs to be in jail. Please don't call me anymore. I have a child here, and we're trying to get some rest."

"Phyllis, he's down here tossing your name around. I know that you're up for a promotion, and I just thought that was the kind of attention that you don't need. Won't you come on down here and pick him up?"

Phyllis had known Major Parham since she first became a prosecutor, and she knew he meant that some people would blame her for Carl's actions. But she would not help Carl, even if it meant that her career would have to suffer.

"Major, I'm sorry, but I won't be able to do that. He's on his own."

"Okay, Phyllis. I'm sorry to bother you."

Phyllis hung up the phone and picked it back up to see if she had a dial tone. Once she heard the buzz she placed the receiver on the floor instead of in its cradle. She placed a pillow over the phone to muffle that irritating sound the phone made when it was off the hook too long.

Once again, she tried to go back to sleep, but after a few minutes of tossing and turning, she realized sleep wasn't going to happen. Phyllis gave up and sat on the side of her bed. She looked at her son as he slept peacefully and rubbed her hand over his forehead. She thanked God he didn't look like Carl. As far as she was concerned, Carl was the Antichrist.

Phyllis stood and walked around the house, tossing anything that reminded her of Carl into a trash can. She went into their bathroom and emptied the contents of his drawers and cabinets into a plastic trash bag. She noticed his wedding band was sitting on the counter. She picked it up and stared at it, thinking back to the day she had purchased it and the emptiness she felt inside. She didn't feel anything like a lady in love would feel searching for the ring for the man she was about to marry. All she remembered feeling was numbness. She sucked her teeth and tossed the ring in the toilet and hit the flush lever.

After her *Waiting to Exhale* moment, she went into the kitchen and made herself a pot of coffee. Realizing that if she were to get over last night's episode, she would have to do something to take her mind off it, she picked up her briefcase and sat at the kitchen table to go over her caseload. As she flipped through folder after folder, she noticed mug shots of one black face after another, but she felt nothing for the accused.

Phyllis frowned as she stared at the mug shot of a young boy who looked to be only a few years older than Zachary. His lips were curled into an evil snarl, but his eyes said that he was afraid, lonely, and helpless. When she looked farther down the sheet to find his age, she closed her eyes and took a deep breath. He was only twelve years old.

Oh, my goodness, she thought. *Where are his parents?*

Nothing was unusual about her prosecuting young black men. As a matter of fact, blacks made up more than three-fourths of her caseload, but they seemed to be getting younger as the years passed.

Phyllis walked over to her computer in the den and tried to log on to the Internet, but kept getting a "no dial tone" message. Then she remembered that her phone was off the hook in her bedroom. She ran up the stairs and walked into the room just as Zachary was coming out of her bathroom.

"Momma, why was Daddy's ring in the toilet?"

"What are you talking about?" Phyllis said, remembering that she flushed the ring.

"His ring was in the toilet. Did he drop it?" Zachary handed his mom the ring. "Is Daddy home?"

"No, he's not," Phyllis said calmly as she sat on the bed and patted a spot next to her for Zachary to sit. He followed her lead.

"Your father won't be staying with us anymore." Phyllis waited to see her son's reaction, but there was none.

"Did he hurt you?" Zachary asked, staring at the floor.

"Yes and no. Your father and I hadn't been getting along for a very long time, and now it's time for us to go our separate ways. You'll still see him, and you'll still get to spend time with him. He just won't live with us anymore."

"I hate Daddy. I don't wanna see him again. I saw what he did last night, and I don't like him no more."

Phyllis sat with her eyes closed for a second, contemplating what to say to her son. She had to will herself not to cry. "Zach, your father was drinking last night, and when a person drinks too much alcohol, he doesn't do a whole lot of thinking. And your father just wasn't thinking last night. He's still the same daddy you've always known. So you'll have to forgive him, and you guys can still have a relationship. Okay?"

"No. I hate him. He was being mean to you. I don't wanna see him again," Zachary cried, as he got up and ran to his bedroom and slammed the door. Phyllis decided to give him some time. She rolled Carl's ring between her thumb and forefinger, then threw it in the trash can that sat by her nightstand. She reached over and put the phone back in its cradle. Less than a minute after she hung up, the phone rang. She picked it up without looking at the caller ID.

"Hello," Phyllis snapped.

There was a pause, then she heard a faint "Hi."

"Hello," Phyllis said, a little nicer after she realized it wasn't about Carl.

"Hi. This is Grace."

"Grace, how are you doing?" Phyllis said in a dry tone. It had been at least four years since she heard her little sister's voice.

"I'm good, how are you?" Grace spoke in measured tones.

"Oh, I'm doing. How's New York?"

Grace sat on the other end of the line, shaking her head. She couldn't believe how nonchalant and uncaring Phyllis seemed.

"New York is fine. How are Carl and Zach?"

"Everything is great. What made you call me?"

"I'm moving back home and I—"

"You need a place to stay!" Phyllis finished.

"No, I don't need a place to stay. I don't need anything from you. I just wanted to talk. Is that too much to ask?" Grace was seething on the other end of the line. She wanted to hang up but she made herself stay on the line.

"What do you want to talk about? I recall you telling me that you never wanted to hear from me again. Do you remember that con-versation?" Phyllis was hurt, as the memories of that day came crashing down on her, but the only defense mechanism she knew was attack.

"Yeah, I do. But I'm really trying here, Phyllis, and if you like things the way they are between us, then I can't force you to change, and I won't try. I'm just extending an invitation to bury the hatchet."

"I never had a problem with speaking with you. It was your decision to run off to New York. You're the reason we've been estranged for I don't know how long."

"I understand that *you* think I'm the cause." Grace felt herself losing control. "Wait, I think I better go."

"Suit yourself, you're the one that called."

"Phyllis, why are you such a bitch? You act as if you don't have any faults. Everyone has a problem except you. You're always so condescending. I haven't spoken with you in years, and all you can do is place the blame. So what I left—you killed my father. I'm trying to move on."

"First of all, I didn't kill anyone. Second of all, I realize that I'm not perfect and sometimes fall short of the grace of God, but you could never handle criticism. Never have, and I see you haven't changed."

"And I see *you* haven't changed either, Phyllis. You're still the same self-centered, egotistical winch with a superiority complex. Forget I ever called." Grace cursed herself for using profanity. She ended the conversation by slamming the phone down in its cradle.

PHYLLIS SAT ON the edge of the bed, cradling the phone to her chest as if it were Grace herself. In her own way Phyllis missed her little sister. Even though Grace had said some of the meanest things to her that night in the hospital when their father died, Phyllis forgave her and still wanted a relationship with her. She placed the phone back down in its cradle and looked up to the ceiling as if to ask God for some answers.

The phone rang again. Phyllis snatched it up. "Grace?"

"This is Carl. Phyllis, we need to talk."

Phyllis wanted to kick herself for not letting the phone ring long enough for the caller ID to work. "I'm not prepared to talk to you right now. I don't want anything to do with you right now."

"Phyllis, I'm sorry for what happened last night but we need to talk," Carl pleaded.

"Carl, I don't want to talk to you right now. All we'll need to discuss from this point on is Zach, and right now he doesn't want anything to do with you either. So do yourself a favor and go away."

"Why does everything always have to be your way? Why can't you compromise?"

"My way? You sick son of a bitch! I can't believe you even have the audacity to call here. First you tear my clothes off, and then you attempt to rape me in the garage. What could you have to say, Carl?"

"I didn't try to rape you. I just wasn't thinking."

"What do you call it? Huh? I call it attempted rape. And you're lucky I don't file charges against you. You're a vile individual, and I never want to see you again."

"First of all, how in the hell can you call what I did rape? I didn't have sex with you," Carl yelled. He knew what he did was wrong but it wasn't rape, and he resented Phyllis saying that.

"Carl, leave it alone. You can call here to speak with Zach after I speak with him. But he needs some time."

"How much time? I really need to talk with him." Zachary had been on Carl's mind all night. When the police pulled him out of the ditch, all he wanted to know was if his son was all right. They finally convinced him that his son wasn't in the car, and he felt better. Once the liquor wore off and he sobered up, all he could think about was Zachary. They were so close, nothing like him and his father, but he knew that Zach was a momma's boy. How he was going to straighten out the mess that he made last night with his son was beyond him. Carl kept seeing the hate in Zach's eyes when he was pulling out of the garage. *Damn,* he thought.

"Okay, Phyllis. I'm sorry, and I realize that we are done. Hell, we never really began. We've just coexisted for the last ten years. But let Zach know that I love him, and I'm sorry for what he saw."

"That's your job." Phyllis hung up the telephone.

MIC CHECK

rodigy and Genesis pulled up to Genesis's mother's house in the rough area of southwest Atlanta. Jalen was sitting on the wooden steps that led up to what used to be a screened-in porch, playing with a Game Boy. He smiled a little and stood when he saw the flashy truck pull into the dirt path used as a driveway. Before the truck came to a complete stop he was standing at Prodigy's door.

"Hey, Prodigy. Where's Blake?" Jalen asked in his low, raspy voice.

"What's up, dude? Blake's at home." Prodigy reached out the truck's window and bumped knuckles with Jalen.

"Hey, Uncle G."

"How you doing, man?"

"Fine."

"How was school today?" Genesis asked.

"Fine."

"What's wrong?" Genesis asked, noticing sadness in his nephew's eyes.

"I'm hungry," Jalen said as he looked down at the ground.

"Why didn't you eat?"

Jalen didn't respond, and that sent Genesis's antenna up.

"Jalen, why didn't you eat? Didn't Momma cook?" Genesis asked with a little more firmness in his voice.

"Yeah," Jalen answered softly.

"Then why didn't you eat?"

"My daddy ate all the food," Jalen said.

"Got-damn it," Genesis growled. "Get in the backseat, Jalen. I'll be right back, P," Genesis said as he stormed out of the truck and into the house.

Genesis walked into his hot and stuffy childhood home and shouted out his brother's name. "Grover. Grover."

"Why you doing all that yelling, baby?" Virginia Styles said calmly. She felt something was about to happen between her two sons, but life had taught her to let her children deal with their own battles.

"Hey, Momma. Where's Grover?" Genesis softened his tone as he walked over and kissed his mother on her cheek.

"What's the matter? Why you all frowned up? You look ugly like that," Momma Styles said, trying to inject a little humor. She was well aware of her youngest son's distaste for her oldest. It hadn't always been that way, but the last few years their relationship had been strained to say the least. She said a prayer every night for her children to come together and act like a family was supposed to, but her prayers had yet to be answered. So whenever she could, she would put a halt to her children's run-ins.

"Why didn't Jalen eat?"

"I don't know, I thought he did. I cooked," Momma Styles said as she put a hand on her waist and limped to the chair and took a seat.

"Momma, what's wrong with you? Why are you limping?"

"Old, that's all."

"Well, we're gonna have to get your old good-looking self to see a doctor. I'll call and make an appointment in the morning. Phyllis still got you on her insurance?"

"I guess so," Momma Styles said as she wiped the sweat off her face with a wrinkled handkerchief.

"Uh-huh. I knew something was wrong with you," Genesis said, looking at his mother, nodding his head.

"What you talkin' 'bout, boy? How you figure something wrong with me?"

"Cuz you didn't protest like you do all the other times."

"I don't always protest. I just don't like them doctors poking me every which-a-way."

"Well, they need to check you out, Momma. Have you been taking your insulin shots for your diabetes?"

"Every day!"

"That's good. Where's Trifling?"

"I didn't name any of my children that so I don't know where whoever you just said is. You ain't too big that I won't put a strap to your butt," Momma Styles said, and she meant it.

"Okay, Momma," Genesis relented. "Where's Grover?"

"I think he's in the back. Now look here. I don't feel like hearing all that fussing today. My blood pressure already too high so if you can't talk like somebody decent then don't go back there messing with him."

"Momma, where's the VCR?" Genesis asked as he looked on top of the floor-model television set he and Grace purchased for her this past Christmas.

"A tape got stuck in it, and Grover took it to the shop."

Genesis took a deep breath and strode slowly and methodically to the back of the house. Grover was in the last room on the left, sitting in an old beat-up chair with a forty-ounce bottle of Old English malt liquor resting between his thighs. He was watching a baseball game on the thirteen-inch television Genesis had bought for Jalen.

"Why did you eat all the food, man? Jalen didn't eat." Genesis struggled to be calm at the sight of his worthless brother sitting in dingy clothes and run-over sneakers.

"Shit," Grover said, an immediate frown coming over his face when he saw his younger brother standing in the doorway of his bedroom. "What the hell you want?"

Grover was about an inch or two shorter than Genesis, but they shared the same medium-brown complexion. Grover was once a top prospect for basketball recruiters, playing three seasons in college at South Carolina State University. He returned to play his senior year but found out that the school had hired a new basketball coach. Since he and the new coach didn't see eye to eye, he left school and returned to Georgia. He worked odd jobs here and there but nothing seemed to hold his interest very long. Then one day he disappeared and stayed gone for almost two years. When he finally returned home, he had the look only a mother could love. He knocked on the door dirty, unshaven, and carrying a crying baby.

No one knew why Grover made the decision to do drugs, but everyone was in agreement that he'd never been the same since. That was more than ten years ago. Now his days were spent trying to find the next high.

"Listen, man. I know you don't give a fuck about nobody but your sorry-ass self, but let me come over here again and my nephew is hungry because his bitch-ass daddy ate all the food, I'mma whip yo ass. You hear me?" Genesis was talking low but his words were strong as steel.

"You always talkin' that shit wit' yo righteous ass. I was hungry, hell, how was I spose to know the lil nigga ain't eat? I just got home. He need to open his damn mouth sometime," Grover said as he ran his hand through his uncombed beard and took a long gulp of his beer.

Genesis walked over to his brother and snatched the bottle out of his hand and tossed it out the open window. Grover jumped to his feet, only to be pushed back down. He knew that his days of being the bigger and tougher brother were long gone, but he still tried from time to time to buck his new omega status in the family hierarchy.

"You open *your* damn mouth. You ask him if he ate. He's a kid, you free-loading punk. I buy the groceries in this house. What do you do? Not a got-damn thing but sit around with your hand out." Genesis stood over his brother, getting more pissed off with each passing second. "Grover, I'mma fuck you up for real. And where's the VCR?"

Grover didn't answer. He just looked out of the window.

"Tomorrow. You got until tomorrow to find Momma's VCR or you getting the hell out. I don't care what Momma says." Genesis stormed out of the room and back to the front of the house.

"Momma, I'll be back, I'mma run and get Jalen something to eat. You need anything?"

"I need to know who died and made you chief. And where you get off talking like that in my house? I don't wanna hear that kind of talk round here no mo', ya hear me?" Momma Styles said.

"Yes, ma'am," Genesis said as he walked out of the house.

Genesis got back into the passenger seat and released a deep breath. He had a headache from the tension that was taking over his life. Terri and his infidelity! Grover and his child! The big wedding that was expected and paying all of his bills on next to nothing! It was only a matter of time before all his savings were gone. His daddy used to say, "A man wit' no money ain't much of a man." He now knew what he meant.

"Is everything cool?" Prodigy asked as he read the frustrated expression on his friend's face.

"Naw, it's Grover, man," Genesis said as he turned around in his seat to face Jalen. "Jalen, I don't want you walking around here hungry. You've got my cell phone number. If you don't eat, call me, and if Grover puts a hand on you, let me know," Genesis said sternly.

"Okay," Jalen replied.

"Grover still acting up?" Prodigy asked.

"Ah, I can't understand that dude. It seems like you'd get tired of that life after a while."

"Yeah, I feel ya. But check this out. I got something that should cheer you up," Prodigy said, smiling from ear to ear.

"What's that?"

"You know I got that hip-hop producer JP coming out to the youth center for Talent Night next week, right?"

"Right, but what does that have to do with me?"

"Slow down, potna. Guess who gave me a tape? And it's banging?"

"Who?"

"Jalen."

Genesis looked back at Jalen, who returned his look with a blank one of his own.

"Check this out." Prodigy pushed the cassette in and pumped up the volume as the funky bass line kicked in. Then Genesis looked at Prodigy in amazement as Jalen's thirteen-year-old voice came across the top-notch sound system loud, clear, and angry.

I'm from a family full of alcoholics, thugs, and drug dealers.
Inebriated, schizophrenic, psychopathic niggas.
My pops is a drunk and my momma was a fiend, I was born in the
*   midst of the crack scene.*
Holla if ya hear me, I'm screaming in pain.
A damn shame what cocaine has done to this young man.
I wake up to a zombie figure of my dead momma.
Screaming: Lord . . . please . . . stop . . . the . . . drama!
I'm pleading, I'm begging, I'm calling your name.

I'm needing your blessing, so come break these chains.
What do you call a crack baby when he gets older?
I'll tell ya . . . a pistol-packing soldier.

Genesis pushed Stop and stared at the tape deck as if he'd heard a ghost. He didn't mumble a word. A single tear made its way down his cheek. Then more tears rushed to catch the first one. He didn't bother to wipe them away. He looked at Prodigy, then turned and stared out the window. In the thirteen years that his nephew had been on God's green earth, he had never heard him utter that many words at one time. Never mind the fact that he was doing it to music. He couldn't help but feel the hurt his nephew had so elo-quently stated in hip-hop eulogy. Genesis thought of Jalen as if he were his own son. He hated Grover for bringing a child into this world addicted to crack. He couldn't help but hate Jalen's dead mother, Sara, for putting a pipe in her mouth while she was carrying his nephew. He hated every drug dealer for being selfish enough to push poison to his own people. He hated the school system for labeling Jalen emotionally handicapped. He hated himself for not digging further into his nephew's mind to find out what his true feelings were.

"He wants to perform, dog," Prodigy said.

"Jalen, you wanna do this?"

"Yeah, you mind?" Jalen asked, his head down.

"Nah, I don't mind. You got skills, boy. I want you do anything you wanna do and I'm proud of you," Genesis said, filled with emo-tion.

Jalen's eyes lit up but he kept his smile to himself. He was a shy kid but the look on his uncle's face let him know that he really was loved.

After grabbing a bite at Applebee's, Prodigy and Genesis dropped Jalen off with a promise to pick him up the following Friday a few hours before the talent show was to start.

"Can you believe that little dude?" Genesis said, still astonished at Jalen's lyrical ability.

"Yeah, he's tight. I'm not even into hip-hop anymore but you can't front on Jalen's skills," Prodigy said.

"What you mean you're not into hip-hop?" Genesis said, holding up a DMX CD.

"Oh, that's the dog. I can't just go cold turkey. But this new generation of rappers is full of shit. Bling-bling-pow-pow and any other ignorant thing they can find to say. I hate that shit with a passion."

"Not you. You were Mr. Hip-hop."

"Ol', but now I recognize the game. The record companies put these kids out there, give them a few dollars, and let them come up with some of the ignorantest shit they can—is that a word?" Prodigy laughed at his Don King moment before continuing. "These kids don't know how to separate fantasy from reality. So they wanna have everything they see in these fake gangstas' videos, not knowing that all that shit is rented. But they see this, and they go out and try to get it and end up getting locked up. Trying to be like a fool they saw in a video with a mouth full of platinum. Most of them rappers don't have a pot to piss in, but they got a Bentley in the video. Get the hell out of here. You got grown-ass men been rapping since I was in high school talking about kidnapping babies and spittin' at ladies, all in the name of getting paid. They don't give a damn that these kids take what they say as the gospel and are steadily feeding the prison system the fresh black souls," Prodigy said.

"I agree with you, dog, but it's the parents' fault. You gotta watch what your kids listen to, and if you don't agree, shut that shit off. Let 'em be mad. Better them be mad than letting Lil Wayne tell him to go and get a Glock if he gotta problem with someone," Genesis said.

"Bullshit. You can't watch your kids twenty-four hours a day.

These assholes gotta take some of the responsibility too. Getting paid has its place."

"But how can you tell a child that's hungry not to bust a few raps? If you hungry, you wanna eat," Genesis said.

"I'm not talking about the hungry ones. I'm talking about the ass-holes we see in the *Forbes* magazines. The ones with multimillion-dollar clothing lines," Prodigy said.

"Yeah, I feel ya," Genesis agreed. "Yo ass is like Malcolm X or some shit. Why you take this stuff so personally?"

"Cuz I messed around and started giving a damn. Plus I have kids. I don't want one of these fake-ass gangstas to stick a gun in my son's face because he's trying to be like some ignorant-ass rapper."

"Arnold and Sly kill fifty people every movie. It ain't just the rap-pers," Genesis said.

But Prodigy wasn't having it. "You sound just like one of them dumb-ass rappers when they get locked up trying to live out their corny-ass studio image. Ol', it's entertainment now. These kids can't relate to Sly or Arnold, but they can with the Cash Money Mil-lionaires and Snoop Dogg."

"True, true. Enough of that shit! I'mma have to take you and my momma to the hospital for high blood pressure if you keep on. What's up with my bachelor party?" Genesis said, changing the subject. He knew that Prodigy was really passionate about what affected kids and he didn't want to hear it all night.

"Oh, we got you. Trust me it's gon' be sick," Prodigy said, nodding his head.

"I guess that's my last shot at some sin-free coochie, huh?" Genesis said, trying to read Prodigy's thoughts.

"Boy, you got issues," Prodigy said, laughing. He knew he couldn't change Genesis. And at that point, he decided not to try anymore.

They pulled up to Genesis's place and made plans to see each other at work on Monday.

nine

IT TAKES A VILLAGE

The voice of a person who was a little too happy for six in the morning interrupted the peacefulness of Genesis's sleep. Genesis reached over Terri and hit the snooze button to silence the loudmouth radio personality. He looked at his still-sleeping fiancée and shook his head. *Girl,* you'll *sleep through a shoot-out,* he thought. He lay back down for a few seconds to prepare himself for his first day as athletic director of the youth center.

Just as Genesis's head touched the pillow, he glanced over at Terri and noticed her left breast hanging out of her nightgown. He rolled over on his side and ran his tongue across her chocolate nipple. Terri moved a little but remained asleep. Genesis closed his eyes and began to lightly suck on the soft nipple. First gently, then a little harder. He slid his hands over her firm but soft satin-covered body. The more he felt her softness, the more he became aroused. It had been nine months since they had made love and as far as he was concerned that was long enough. Sex was one of the main reasons that he agreed for them to move in together. He just let her believe that saving money for the wedding was the reason.

Genesis reached down and pulled her gown up just enough to give him access to her panties. As he slid his hands over her closely shaved pubic area, Genesis felt like he was about to explode. He slid down on the bed to start his oral journey but that was a little too much movement. Terri woke up and grabbed his head.

"Stop."

"Come on, Terri. I don't wanna do this no more," Genesis pleaded as he looked up at her from between her legs.

"Do what no more?" Terri asked as she tried to maneuver her legs closed.

"I don't wanna wait until we're married. I need you now," Genesis said, holding on to her legs for dear life.

"Genesis, we agreed. Now move your hand."

"That's foul, Terri, and you know it. How you gon' expect me to keep sleeping in the same bed with you every night and not have sex?" Genesis asked as she pushed her legs together and sat up on the side of the bed.

"Just like you been doing. Come on, Genesis, this is important to me. I wanna halfway do something right." Terri slid up behind him and put her arms around his shoulders. She knew he was getting frustrated and tried to ignore his unsuccessful sneak attack.

"But we already did it before. So what difference does it make?"

"I know, but we shouldn't have. So I'd like to wait until we're married before we make love again."

Genesis stood and walked into the bathroom and closed the door hard enough to let Terri know that he was upset.

Terri lay back down on the bed and took a deep breath. She wanted to make love, too, but she reminded herself that she got down on her knees and repented for the first and only time that they made love and had no intention of asking God to forgive her again for the same sin. Masturbation would have to tide the both of them over for the next two months.

Genesis walked out of the shower as naked as the day he was born. Terri looked at his perfectly chiseled chest and had to close her eyes and ask God for a little more strength.

"Are you upset?" Terri asked.

"Nah, I'm straight. Horny as hell, but what's new," Genesis said, trying to act normal but it was clear that he was mad as hell.

"Genesis, do you understand that I have to do this?"

"Yeah, if you say so," Genesis said as he walked out of the room.

Terri heard him fumbling around in the guest bedroom for a few minutes, then she heard the front door open then close. She heard the deadbolt lock and the screen door shut.

Damn, I guess he's upset. He never leaves without giving me a kiss, she thought. Terri hated it when they didn't talk. History told her that his silent treatment would normally last a few days before he came around and wanted to be friendly again. Before when things like this happened he would just go home and not call for a little while, but now they lived together. Terri thought it would be interesting to see how they handled their differences under the same roof. She wanted to please her man, but not at the cost of committing another sin.

There were only two men in her life with whom she had shared herself, and she wished that she could take both of those experiences back. The first was her slick-talking high school boyfriend, who told her that if he didn't have sex, his penis would swell up and he would die. She kicked herself for falling for that stupid lie, but she was only sixteen and had very limited experiences with the opposite sex. The second was Genesis, and even he caught her at a moment when she wasn't feeling good about herself. Nothing was going right in her life and she was doing a lot of self-evaluation. She had cut off her shoulder-length hair to sport a close-cropped natural and wasn't feeling very good about the results of her new hairdo. Genesis came along and made her feel pretty and wanted again. Lonely and vulnerable, she gave in to him. But right after it was over, she told him that sex between them would not happen again. Terri expected Genesis to stop calling since he knew that he wouldn't be getting any more but he surprised her by being supportive and respectful of her wishes. Before Genesis, Terri thought she'd spend the majority of her life alone. All because she wanted to wait until she was married before making love.

Terri cleared her mind of thoughts of Genesis and his libido and tried to go back to sleep. Her bookstore didn't open until noon on Mondays.

GENESIS DROVE TO the youth center in silence. "How in the hell does she expect me to be faithful to her if she's holding out on the sex?" he kept repeating to himself. He tried to stop himself from being upset with Terri but kept remembering how fine she looked as visions of her thick chocolate thighs kept popping into his mind. He turned on *The Tom Joyner Morning Show* and prayed that J. Anthony Brown made it to work on time today. He could use a good laugh.

Genesis kept looking at his cell phone. He was tempted to call Shaneka, his ghettofied backup. Shaneka was always down for something freaky, but thoughts of her quickly disappeared after Genesis remembered their last episode, when one of her bad-ass sons stood on the bed and urinated on him while he was still asleep, yelling, "You ain't my daddy."

As Genesis pulled into the parking lot of the youth center, he noticed Prodigy sitting in his truck talking on his cell phone. Genesis got out of his vehicle and tapped on Prodigy's window, snapping him out of what seemed to be an intense conversation. Prodigy hit the unlock button, and Genesis hopped in.

"Yo, man, I need a favor," Prodigy said as he closed his cell phone.

"What's up?"

"One of my kids got locked up last week, and I need to talk to your sister Phyllis."

"I'll give you her number, but don't expect anything from her. I told you she's an asshole," Genesis said as he reached in his pocket and pulled out his PalmPilot to retrieve the number. He tapped a few times with the stylus and beamed the number into Prodigy's PalmPilot.

"I got to give it a shot, dog. This is a real good kid. One of the best ones around here," Prodigy said, looking worried.

"What they got him for?"

"Grand larceny. He robbed this lil drug dealer around his way. He's only thirteen years old but he gotta play daddy to a little sister and a little brother. His momma's out there doing something that has all of her attention. Little man's the only one around there trynna maintain for the family."

Genesis could tell by the look in Prodigy's eyes that he was really affected by this.

"Damn, that's messed up," Genesis said, his thoughts going immediately to Jalen.

"Yeah, tell me about it."

"What jail is he in?" Genesis asked.

"Atlanta City. I hope your sister can find an ounce of compassion. Somebody has to look out for these kids. Everybody wanna lock 'em up. Joey don't deserve jail."

"I can tell you care for this kid, but damn, P, he did rob somebody."

"Ah, man, Joey's been telling me about this cat for a while now. Said he sells right in front of his house and is always tossing money at his little seven-year-old sister. I guess he just got fed up and went and got a gun."

"Do you know how old the drug dealer is?"

"Not exactly, but I don't think he's too much older than Joey. The way Joey talked about him made me think that he was a young boy."

"Yo, P, even if Phyllis gets a wild hair up her butt and decides to help, how do you know she can? I mean, sometimes things are out of her hands. I know there were a few times when Grover got locked up, and she couldn't do nothing."

"She's the one who's prosecuting his case. I just got off the phone with this cop that does some volunteering up here, and he told me it's her case."

"Well, dog, I'll see what I can do, but I wouldn't put too much hope in Phyllis. Start thinking of a plan B."

"At this point I don't have much of a choice. He has a prior for receiving stolen property."

"I know Phyllis used to get into her office at eight but I haven't spoken with her in a while. Just keep in mind what I told you about her."

"Yeah, I got you. Did you work on any plans over the weekend for the after-school kids?"

"Yeah, I think I'mma set up some teams. And get some kind of conditioning program implemented. I see too many fat kids walking around here."

"What you gonna do, put 'em on a diet?"

"Nah, man, make 'em work out. It's them damn video games. All these kids do nowadays is sit around and play videos. I never see kids out in the streets no more playing football like we did."

"True," Prodigy said, preoccupied with his thoughts. "I'm sure you can make it happen."

"So when are you meeting with Blake's fake-ass father?"

"Damn, I almost forgot about that dude. I'm supposed to see him on Saturday."

"Has he called since the first time?"

"Nah. I haven't heard anything else from him. I assume he's still down."

"Maybe you'll get lucky, and his ass will disappear for another nine or ten years."

"That would be fine with me. I really don't need any more drama."

"Well, I'm going with you. Just in case he wanna act a fool."

"So you my bodyguard now? You're welcome to roll, but I think I can handle it. Let's get inside. I need to call your sister."

"Let me call her first. Then I'll let you know the deal." Genesis really didn't want to call Phyllis, but under the circumstances he would make this exception.

"All right. But let me know something either way as soon as possible," Prodigy said as he scribbled all of Joey's information down on a piece of paper and handed it to Genesis.

"You got it, dog."

Genesis made it to his office and dialed Phyllis's office number.

"Phyllis Olsen's office. How may I help you?"

"May I speak to Phyllis Olsen?"

"May I ask who is calling?" the female's voice said.

"Genesis Styles. I'm her brother."

"Oh, hi, Genesis. This is Barbara! Congratulations on your engagement."

"Thanks, and how are you doing?"

"I'm hanging on in there. What about yourself?"

"I'm okay. Hey, Barbara, maybe I don't need to talk to Phyllis. I have a problem. There's this kid that's a member of the youth center where I work, and it seems like he done went and got into a little trouble. He's a real good kid, and I'd hate to see him get caught up in the system over some bad judgment."

"What's his name?"

"Joey Martin. He's thirteen, and he got arrested last Tuesday for grand larceny. He robbed a drug dealer."

"Yeah, seems like they're getting younger and younger. I don't know if it's the parents or the low tolerance of the system. But let me see what I can find out for you. Give me a call-back number."

Genesis gave her his number and thanked her before hanging up. Ten minutes later his phone rang and he heard the dreaded voice of his older sister, Phyllis.

HARD TO LOVE

"What can I do for you, Genesis?" Phyllis asked, sounding rushed.

"How you doing, Phyllis?"

"I'm fine. Now what's going on that has you and Grace calling me?"

"I didn't know that Grace called you," Genesis lied. He didn't want to get into a long conversation with Phyllis about anything other than what he had called for.

"Well, she did, and I haven't spoken with either of you in ages. So what can I do for you?"

"The calls are not related. How's the family?" Genesis asked, using what his father taught him. A little small talk always helped to ease into business.

"Everyone is fine, Genesis, now cut the crap. I have to prepare for court, and I don't have time for idle chatter," Phyllis said, obviously having missed that lesson from their father.

"Okay, well. I work at this youth center, and one of our young members was arrested this past week. We found out you're prosecuting his case."

"And?" Phyllis said.

"Well, Phyllis, I'm asking you for a little consideration with this kid. He's had it rough all of his life and I'm—"

Phyllis cut Genesis off. "I know, either his mother's gone or she's on drugs, and either he's never met his father or he's in prison. He's had it so bad you wanna give him another chance. Well, I'm not going to help you, Genesis. He'll have to stand trial just like everyone else. What do I look like, a get-out-of-jail-free card? How do you think he'll learn what he did was wrong if he's not punished? I have to go—please don't call me anymore wanting favors." Phyllis hung up without so much as a good-bye.

"Ol' heartless bitch. Didn't even consider the boy's situation. Got-damn sellout," Genesis said to himself, staring at the telephone before placing it back on its cradle.

Genesis stood and started on his way to give Prodigy the bad news, but realized he needed to calm down. He decided to call Grace and vent a little.

"Hello," Grace said, picking up the phone on the first ring.

"Well, damn," Genesis said. "Who you expecting to call you at this time of morning?"

"Oh, hi, sweetie. I thought you were my job. I'm working from home for a few days. I just got my transfer, so I'll be back home a little sooner than I thought," Grace said.

"Oh, that's straight. Where are you staying? You know you can stay with us."

"I think I'm going to stay with Momma for a few weeks until I can get reacquainted with Georgia."

"Well, you know it's not the same over there. Hell, I want Momma and Jalen to move, but you know how she is."

"Yeah, the old girl is a bit stubborn. Has it gotten that bad over there?"

"Put it like this, you can sit on the front porch and watch a live episode of *Cops* any night of the week. Plus with your stealing-ass brother in the house, you won't be able to put anything down without watching it like a hawk."

"Dag, Genesis, you don't make coming home sound all that appealing."

"I'm just keeping it real. You've been gone for a long time, and things haven't gotten any better."

"Well, we can't keep running away from our own people. I'm going to give it a shot. As long as I don't fear for my safety, I'll be fine."

"Okay, but my offer still stands. Oh, and Jalen did get his game. He was playing with it the other day when I picked him up. Did you know he can rap?"

"Rap?" Grace sounded surprised. Even though she moved away, Grace felt a special connection to Jalen. She always made sure he had all the things he needed for school. But after all she had done for him, he still never said more than a few words to her at a time.

"Yeah, and this Friday he's rapping at the talent show we're having here."

"You've got to be kidding me. I'm there. Okay, I'm going to figure out how I can close all of my business out so I don't have to see Manhattan for a while. I'm not missing my baby do his thing. Oh, my God. I'm so proud of him. He won't say two words to me when I call the house."

"I know. He's slowly but surely starting to open up, though. I was super shocked when I heard him. He's a little rough with his lyrics, but considering what he's been through, he deserves to tell his story how he sees fit."

"Well, glory be to God. Tell him I'm proud of him."

"I will, but anyway I almost forgot why I called, you talk so much," Genesis said, joking with his sister.

"Shut it up."

"Did you know that your sister is a complete asshole?"

"Stop cursing, and yes, I did."

"She told me you called."

"Yeah, I called that woman, but you tell me your war story first. She had *me* cursing."

"Not you?"

"Yeah, me. You know it took a lot for me to call her after what she did, but I tried. After I heard her sounding like everyone has a problem but her, I just lost it."

Genesis relayed the details of his early-morning phone call with their big sister.

"Well, I'm going to continue to try and reach out to her. I don't think she wants to be the way she is," Grace said. "I think she's hurting inside about something and I still love her in a funny ol' kind of way."

"You know what I realized? That you don't have to love your family! You can't choose who you're related to, so why should you be obligated to be all in love with 'em?"

"Genesis, you need to stop thinking like that. Nobody said you had to be all in love with anyone, but you should love your family."

"Why?"

"Because that's the way God wants it."

"Well, you know I can't argue with you when it comes to the good book, but it just don't make no sense that we have to love folks like Grover, the drug addict, deadbeat dad, and thief, and Phyllis with her mean ass."

"Like I said, there's more to it than what appears. That's one of the reasons I'm coming home. It doesn't make any sense that we're the way we are with one another. Daddy's not coming back, and Momma's getting up there in age, so it doesn't make any sense for us to walk around and act like strangers."

"I feel you, but don't be naive. You can't do everything by yourself. They have to want to change too."

"I know, but somebody has to open up the lines of communication. It might as well be me. And you!"

"Me? I didn't volunteer for no makeup mission. I'm cool with the way things are now. They stay away from me, and I'll do the same," Genesis said. He wasn't too excited about seeing Phyllis or Grover any more than he already did.

"Come on, Genesis. You don't mean that. You can't tell me you don't miss the closeness of the family when Daddy was alive," Grace said, trying to refresh her brother's memories. "We had some really good times together."

"Yeah, we did have some good times, but things have changed. And people grow apart."

"I don't think we grew apart. I think we all have some unresolved issues that we need to get out. Only then can we work on repairing our family."

"I hear you, Dr. Grace the psychologist."

"I'm for real, but hold on a minute." Grace clicked over to answer her other line. She was back a minute later.

"Hey, sweetie, I have to run, but I'll call you with my flight information. Will you be able to pick me up?"

"Oh yeah. I'll be there."

"Okay, gotta run. Duty calls. I love you."

"Love you too."

PHYLLIS SAT AT her desk, staring at the mug shot of Joseph Marion Martin. He was a good-looking little kid who seemed to be well kept. He didn't have those ugly cornrows or a mouth full of gold teeth, which were the ugliest things she'd ever seen. His lips were twisted into a menacing snarl but his eyes said he was a lost child. But Phyllis had seen the rap sheets of boys twice as cute as Joey with records that would make some career criminals look harmless, so she wouldn't be swayed by the innocent look in Joey's eyes.

Phyllis was trying to decide if she was going to seek the maximum sentence of fifteen years. She decided against the maximum and wrote eight years on his file jacket. Phyllis figured that Joey would be out of jail in four years if he acted right, less if the prison he was sent to had overcrowding issues. She closed the file jacket and moved on to the next case.

Just as she opened up another folder of yet another young black boy, her telephone rang.

"Yes, Barbara," Phyllis said as she set the folder down on her desk.

"Hi, there's a Nathan Pryor on line three for you," Barbara said.

"Nathan Pryor?" Phyllis smiled. They had been talking a lot in the last few days. Every time she hung up with him she felt better. Especially when he called just to tell her he was thinking about her.

"Hold on, Mr. Pryor, Mrs. Olsen is on the line."

"Hi there, Phyllis. Did I catch you at a bad time?"

"There's never a bad time for you," Phyllis said, smiling at the memory of the extremely handsome man on the other end of the line. "How are you?"

"I'm good. I was just sitting here and, as usual, you crossed my mind."

"You're too sweet." Phyllis's heart skipped a beat. *Why am I so attracted to this man that I've only seen one time?* she thought.

"I'm not trying to be. You must bring out the best in me."

"Well, don't start something that you can't finish."

"I'll remember that. Did you get your roses yet?"

"I sure did. They're beautiful; I'm looking at them right now. I knew who they were from even though you didn't send a card with them," Phyllis lied. She had tossed the roses in the trash the minute they were delivered, thinking they were from Carl in one of his shallow attempts to make up.

"Well, why didn't you mention it?"

"You didn't give me a chance to say anything. You just called," Phyllis said as she pulled the flowers out of the trash basket.

"Okay, I'll go with that."

"So how are you doing? Any news on the partnership yet?"

"Yeah, I just got off the phone with those guys, and it looks like I'm headed your way."

"That's great. Congratulations."

"Thank you. I'm really looking forward to seeing you and my tour of the city."

"Me too. We'll have fun."

"Phyllis, I have a favor to ask of you."

"Shoot! This seems to be the morning for favors, so go right ahead."

"Are you being bombarded? I mean, this can wait. I know how it is to be overwhelmed."

"No, go ahead. It was only my brother wanting me to drop the case against this child that robbed somebody."

"Child? How old?"

"Thirteen."

"Any priors?"

"One, for receiving."

"Are you going to help him out?"

"Why should I? I see case after case of these little hardheads come through here, and I'm not about to get soft on them. The last thing I need is to let this young man off, and he ends up murdering someone."

"I understand your concern and that's the favor that I wanted to ask you. I want to locate a few at-risk, underprivileged youths so I can try and make a difference in their lives."

"That's very noble of you, but we're dealing with an almost hopeless situation here. More than sixty percent of my caseload is young black males, and the majority of them are rotten to the core," Phyllis said, sounding unconcerned.

"Well, that's where we come in. It's our obligation to help these young men. You know as well as I do that the system doesn't rehabilitate. It only punishes, and the way some of these jails are run, it's more like a vacation to a lot of them. More than just the lives of a few young black men are at stake—our whole race is in trouble if we don't do something."

"Our?" What the hell did he just say? Phyllis thought.

"Did you just say *our* race?" Phyllis asked.

"Yes, I did. Are you surprised?"

"Well . . . I didn't know." Phyllis didn't know how to respond to that.

"Well, I'm black. My mother is Irish-American and my father African-American. Is that a problem?"

"Oh no. Why would it be a problem?"

"Just asked a question, that's all. The way you responded made me wonder. It's always better to ask."

"No, it's not a problem." Phyllis took a deep breath and exhaled. The reality of how she lived her life came crashing down on her. The disappointment she felt when Nathan informed her of his race made her realize that she had some issues. It was a hard pill to swallow.

"Well, I'll tell you what is a problem and that's the state of black America," Nathan continued, unaware of Phyllis's internal battle. "Like I was saying, these jails are just warehouses for blacks. Prisons are big business and unfortunately, young blacks are the commodity."

"Well said, Mr. Pryor, but you don't have to work here every day and see the destruction these young men cause. I do realize that a lot of them don't have any accountability at home, but some of these crimes are just mind-boggling. Listen." Phyllis grabbed a stack of folders and began going through them. "Twelve-year-old male; charge: pimping a ten-year-old female. Nine-year-old male charged with attempted murder of a police officer. Fifteen-year-old male charged with rape, kidnap, and assault with a deadly weapon. Need I go on?"

"I hear you loud and clear. All I'm saying is it's only going to get worse if we don't do anything about it."

"I am doing something about it. I'm putting them right where they need to be, behind bars. I don't care what anyone says, some people don't need to be walking around free."

"I agree, but the majority of 'us' are in prison, and these kids are coming out of prison worse off than they were when they went in. All you're doing is prolonging their criminal life. Once they're released from prison after ten or fifteen years, what do they have to look forward to? We have to reach them while they're young."

"I hear you, Nathan," Phyllis relented. She didn't want to have this conversation right now and wanted to kick herself for letting it get as far as it had.

"I didn't mean to be so abrasive, but I grew up in a neighborhood where a lot of us have given up hope of ever being anything other than dope dealers. I just want to do my part, that's all. I apologize if I came on too strong. I'm really passionate about our children," Nathan said.

"I see. Well, I agree with you that something different needs to be done, but enough of that. When will I see you again?" Phyllis surprised herself by flirting. Nathan had proved that he was a good man no matter what color he was and as far as she was concerned, Carl was out of the picture. If she never saw him again, that would be too soon.

"Soon, real soon. I'm looking forward to it. I haven't stopped thinking about you since I last saw you."

"That's good to hear," Phyllis said.

"Oh, and I'll need some help finding a suitable neighborhood to live. I hear you can get a mansion in Atlanta for around three hundred grand."

"In some areas you can."

"Sounds like the place for me. I'll call you soon. Do you still have my number?"

"Yes, I do."

"Use it, it's good for another week. Talk to you later."

" 'Bye, Nathan."

"You can call me Nate."

"I'd rather use Nathan, if you don't mind?"

"Suit yourself. See you soon."

Phyllis hung up the phone feeling like a high schooler with a crush on a boy she knew was no good for her. She swiveled in her chair, smiling uneasily. Like it or not, for the first time in her life a black man had her attention. Even if he had to pass for a little while in order to get it.

eleven

I CAN'T HELP IT

Genesis lay on his back, looking at the ceiling with a disgusted look on his face. He was disappointed in himself for what he had just allowed to happen. He looked at the clock on the nightstand and rolled out of bed.

Just last night he had a man-to-man talk with himself about his sex situation with Terri, and he felt better. After all was said and done, he realized that he had a woman with principles, and that's exactly what he always wanted. If Terri wouldn't sleep with him, then he could almost guarantee she wasn't going to be out there messing around with someone else.

For the life of him, Genesis couldn't figure out how he had let what just happened happen. Especially when the day started out on such a good note. Genesis woke up extra early in order to prepare Terri her favorite breakfast: French toast and a vegetable omelet. He served his fiancée her food in bed and gave her a dozen long-stemmed roses that he had purchased the night before. He had made a personalized card further expressing the joy he felt from having her in his life. They kissed and admitted how much they meant to each other. Then Genesis was off to the youth center, feeling like a million bucks.

At twelve o'clock sharp, Genesis left the center to pick up Grace from the airport, but en route got a call from her on his cell phone informing him that her flight was delayed. Genesis had just turned around and headed back in the direction of the center when Amy called.

Genesis had helped Amy out a few times with a workout plan when he was trying to be a personal trainer. She was a very attractive white lady in her early thirties and, judging from the different high-priced luxury cars she drove to the gym on a regular basis, she and her husband were doing well in the finance department.

"Hi, gorgeous, are you alone?" Amy asked.

"It depends! Who is this?"

"Amy!"

"Amy? Oh, Amy! How you doing, sexy?" Genesis smiled as he thought about how fine the body was that belonged to the voice on the other end of the phone.

"Where are you?"

"I'm in my truck leaving Hartsfield Airport. What's up?"

"Is this a bad time?"

"Nah, what's up?"

"Well, I've been thinking about you, and if you're available I'd like to see you."

"You know I'm not training anymore."

"Okay, but I still want to see you," Amy said.

"Where are you?" Genesis asked, feeling his heart beat a little faster.

"I'm in my car, but why don't you go to the Airport Westin, and I'll meet you in the bar area."

"How far away are you?"

"Fifteen, twenty minutes tops."

Ten minutes after Genesis ordered his first cranberry juice, Amy walked in and kissed him on the cheek. She sat down and ordered a golden margarita.

"So, I finally get to spend a minute with you alone, huh?" Amy said.

"I didn't know you were trying to spend any time with me," Genesis said, playing dumb. He knew the white chick with the Florida suntan and sister booty had a thing for him.

"I thought I made that clear. Maybe I didn't," Amy said as she reached over and placed her hand where it didn't belong.

"I have to pick up my sister at four-thirty," Genesis said, smiling at her aggressiveness but not bothering to move her hand.

"Well, that gives us a good two hours. Let's not waste it talking." Amy stood and walked over to the front desk and paid for a room. A few minutes later, she waved Genesis over with the room key card.

"I AIN'T WORTH a damn!" Genesis's conscience ate at him as he dried off after his two-hour sexual rendezvous. "This my last time doing this shit."

Genesis walked out of the bathroom into the sleeping area of the hotel room. "Amy, I gotta run. I'mma be late picking my sister up," Genesis said, looking at his watch. He had about twenty minutes to make it to the airport, park, and catch a train to the gate.

"Don't leave without your gift," Amy said. "I have a little surprise for you." She was still lying in the bed naked with the sheet up to her chest. She pointed to a white envelope that sat on the nightstand.

"What?" Genesis asked as he walked over and picked it up. He opened the envelope and saw five one-hundred-dollar bills.

Damn, I didn't know I was a gigolo. But I'm keeping the money, Genesis thought to himself as he blew Amy a dry kiss.

"That's a wedding gift. I might be a little more generous the next time around," Amy said with a naughty smile.

Ho, please. Ain't gon' be no next time. Can't you see I'm trynna be faithful, Genesis thought.

"I'll holla," Genesis said as he ran out the door and raced toward the elevator.

Genesis made it to his truck and drove like a madman to pick up his sister. When he arrived fifteen minutes late, Grace was standing by the baggage claim waiting on her bags.

"Hey, boy! Look at your hair. I like those little twisty things," Grace said as she reached up and hugged her brother. "I missed you."

"I missed you too. Sorry I'm late. Traffic this time of day is murder. How you doin'?"

"I'm okay. I'm just happy I finally made it. I've had about as much as I can take of airports for a while. LaGuardia wasn't made for naps. My neck, my back, and my arms hurt, and I have a headache. Other than that, I'm doing just fine."

"You hungry?"

"Starving. Have you eaten?"

"Nah, I was waiting on you. You wanna go to Red Lobster?"

"Sounds like a plan," Grace said as she pointed out her bags to Genesis.

GENESIS AND GRACE made it to his truck and pulled out of the airport parking lot. Grace looked over at her big brother and reached up to play with his twisted braids, but stopped when she noticed a long strand of blond hair on the shoulder of his navy blue Polo shirt.

"Is this why you're running late? You done got a case of jungle fever?" Grace asked, waving the long strand in Genesis's face.

"Oh, that ain't nothing. It's not what you think." Genesis tried to play it off.

"Now, the one thing I could always count on was you being real with me. Has that changed, too, since I left?"

Genesis looked straight ahead. He was busted. He and Grace were the tightest of siblings. As long as he could remember, they always had a special kind of kinship.

"Ahh, go ahead now. Why you trippin'?"

"Genesis, why? Why do you feel the need to run around on Terri? I mean, you said it yourself, she's the best thing that ever happened to you."

"She is, and this little thing kind of just happened. It wasn't like I was planning on messing around on her," Genesis said.

"Oh, that's so lame. I bet if Terri just kind of slept with some dude, you'd lose your mind. I'm so disappointed with you, Genesis."

"Why you mad? It ain't like Terri your home girl. Hell, y'all barely know each other, and you going off."

"She's a sista, and you're my brother. Why can't you exercise a little self-discipline sometime? You're just like your father."

"Now why you gotta go there," Genesis said, getting upset. "Daddy is dead. Let him rest. What, you hate men all of a sudden?"

Grace frowned and wondered where that had come from, but decided to answer anyway. "I love men! I love you, but I'm tired of men doing women wrong just for the fun of it. People's hearts are nothing to play with. Just be a man. A real man."

"Grace, how you gon' tell me about being a man? The last time I checked, you were of the female species."

"And that's supposed to mean I don't know what a real man is? As a woman, I'd like to think I'm an authority on men, and I don't think running around trying to sleep with everything that looks good qualifies you as one."

"Let's talk about something else."

"It's not your fault, but you're paying for it."

"What's not my fault?" Genesis asked.

"The fact that you're a ho. You got that from your daddy."

"Why all of a sudden you going off on Daddy?"

"Because I'm searching for answers. I loved my father, but he was dead wrong for the way he ran around on Momma. He was dead wrong for the way he gave Grover beer at seven years old. He was dead wrong for taking us to his girlfriends' houses and making us wait in the living room while he committed adultery."

"Grace, let's talk about something else. You just got here, and we have plenty of time for you to do your soul searching."

"That's fine, but we're going to have to deal with the sins of our father if we're ever going to move on as a family."

"I hear ya, but let's focus on Momma for now."

The mere mention of their mother put Grace in a foul mood. Her conversations with the doctors didn't leave much hope of having things like they used to be.

"Have you been praying for Momma?"

"I'll leave all that praying up to you. I just hope for the best."

"Genesis, have you turned into a nonbeliever?" Grace asked, eyeing her brother carefully.

"I grew up in the same church that you did. I'm just not a fanatic. I don't think about church and God and all that stuff on a regular basis."

"What do you mean 'all that stuff'?"

"Man, most of these preachers around Atlanta ain't about nothing but the dollar bills. They'll tell you anything you wanna hear for the right amount of tithes. Hell, in some churches they have reserved seats for the one with the biggest tithe."

"Genesis, don't ever put your faith in man. God is the final answer. Now, all these so-called pastors with money on the brain will pay for their sins. You should only focus on the word of God. Oh, we have to talk."

"I hear ya, lil sis, but it's time to eat," Genesis said as he whipped his truck into the Red Lobster parking lot.

twelve

A FAMILY AFFAIR

P hyllis was steaming at what she just heard on the telephone. She slammed the phone down and leaned back in her chair, closing her eyes to help relieve the tension.

Carl had left a message in a manner that left no doubt in Phyllis's mind that he was a certifiable nut case. "Phyllis, since you're not accepting my calls, I'll tell you what I have to say on your little machine. If you want a divorce, I'll give you one. But I want a blood test to make sure that Zachary is mine."

"Oh, obviously you don't know who you're dealing with," Phyllis said to the phone as if it were Carl himself.

Just as Phyllis picked up the phone to call her lawyer, she was surprised by the presence of a familiar face in her doorway.

"Hi."

"Well, hello," Phyllis said as she stood and walked around her desk to embrace her younger sister, Grace.

"I had the hardest time finding this place. Why do they have you guys all the way back here?" Grace asked, hugging her sister.

"We're prosecutors. After you sentence a person to twenty years, you need not be too accessible," Phyllis said as she walked back around to her desk and sat down. "Have a seat."

"Congratulations on your promotion," Grace said, taking a seat across from Phyllis.

"News gets around fast," Phyllis said dryly. "Thanks."

"When I called to get directions, your secretary told me that you're now the assistant district attorney."

"Yeah, and I'm not looking forward to all the work that comes along with this job, but what can you say? So when did you get in?"

"Today. Are you going to see Jalen tonight?"

"See Jalen? Where is he?"

"He's performing in a talent show tonight. He's a rapper."

"A rapper? I didn't know he could even talk," Phyllis said, as if she could care less.

Grace tried to control herself. "Yes, he can talk, he just chooses not to. You should come on out and see your nephew."

"Where is this talent show?"

"At the youth center where Genesis works."

"Where is that?"

"Over by Momma's house. Are you going to come and support your nephew?" Grace asked, almost begging with her eyes.

"I'm not going in that neighborhood unless it's absolutely necessary."

"Phyllis, did you not grow up in that house? Don't your mother, brother, and nephew live there?" Grace was trying her best to control her temper.

Phyllis sighed and stood, opened her desk drawer, and removed something. She walked over to the door, opened it, and said, "Let's go."

"Are you putting me out?" Grace asked, shocked, as she turned around in her chair.

"No, I thought you wanted to go to the talent show," Phyllis said, smiling for the first time in a long time at her baby sister. She remembered a couple of nights ago when she wished she had Grace's ear. Maybe this would be a start on repairing their relationship.

"That's what I'm talking about," Grace said as she stood with renewed hope.

"But before we leave we have to go and pick up your other nephew. How did you get here?" Phyllis asked as she held the door for Grace.

"Genesis dropped me off."

"Oh, he couldn't come in to say hi? I guess he's upset with me," Phyllis said with a smirk.

Grace rode with Phyllis to the after-school center to pick up Zachary. Because she and Phyllis didn't get along, Grace had only seen Zachary twice his entire life. But that didn't stop her from leaping from Phyllis's car when her chubby little nephew ran up.

"Hey, Zach. I'm your aunt Grace."

Zachary smiled and said a sheepish "Hi."

"How are you doing?"

"I'm fine. Are you going to live with us?" Zachary asked, smiling.

"No, I'm going to stay with your grandmother for a little while. Then I'm going to get my own place. Are you going to come and hang out with me?"

"Yeah, if my mother says I can. Mom, can I?"

"You sure can," Phyllis said. *But not in that neighborhood,* she thought. "Now get in the car."

Grace got caught up with the lives of Phyllis and Zachary. Grace was surprised at how open Phyllis was about her problems with Carl in front of her son. Grace was also surprised at the dispassionate attitude that Phyllis displayed about her marriage and how cool she was handling their mother's illness. She didn't seem all that concerned with much of anything. But then again, that was Phyllis's way from way back in the day. They pulled up to the youth center and noticed a few hundred kids standing around the parking lot.

Grace noticed Genesis standing with Prodigy by the front entrance of the youth center. She led the way as they all walked over.

"Hey, boy. Where is Jalen?" Grace asked Genesis as she reached up and hugged Prodigy.

"Backstage, like the star he is," Genesis said proudly. He also made a mental note that Grover was a no-show, even though he said that he'd be there for his son's first performance. Genesis looked at Phyllis and turned up his lip. Phyllis ignored him too.

"Prodigy, have you ever met my sister Phyllis and my handsome nephew Zachary?" Grace asked.

"A long time ago. I think it was one of those summers in Philly, but it's nice seeing you again. What's up, little man?" Prodigy said, extending his hand to Phyllis and then Zachary.

"Nice seeing you again too, Prodigy."

"I guess I should take this opportunity to ask you if you would come and speak with the kids here sometime," Prodigy said.

"I'll have to check my schedule," Phyllis said, noncommittally. "But that doesn't seem like it would be a problem."

"Well, the kids would be happy to see one of their own in your position."

Phyllis just nodded. Then there was a loud scream and a few more hundred screams followed as a long black limousine pulled up. The driver stepped out and held open the back door for the multiplatinum producer, JP, who was wearing his customary jogging suit and a ton of platinum jewelry. The bodyguard ushered the braided wonder kid through the crowd of screaming teenagers until he was slapping hands with Prodigy and Genesis.

"Let's get you in here before you get mauled," Prodigy said.

"I'm cool. I love my people. They usually get used to me after a minute or two. How y'all feelin'?" JP asked as they all rushed into the building and locked the doors on the overzealous fans.

"I'm glad you made it. I know you're a busy man collecting Grammys, doing movies, producing hits," Prodigy said.

"Man, I always got time to show love to my folks. You never too big for that. And the minute you get too busy for your own is just about the time when you lose touch with who the hell you are."

"I hear ya, and I like that. Some people get their piece of the pie and don't look back," Genesis said, as he stole a peek at Phyllis.

"So, Zach, do you have any of JP's albums?" Genesis asked his nephew.

"No, my mom won't let me listen to rap. But I like his stuff that they play on the radio."

"Phyllis, why you won't let Zach listen to rap? That's black folks' music," Genesis said, finally acknowledging his older sister.

"Don't question me on how I raise my child," Phyllis snapped back.

Grace gave Genesis a look that said, "Don't say another word." He turned away again with his lip turned up.

"Most of the rap that's getting played today I wouldn't let my own kids listen to," JP said. "But I'm trying to change that."

Phyllis looked at her young ally with surprise and a newfound respect. She had seen JP on television several times and could never make it past his attire and broken English long enough to realize he was a decent young man.

Prodigy led everyone to the gymnasium. Grace, Phyllis, and Zachary took their seats beside Terri and Nina. Prodigy gave the go-ahead for security to let the crowd in. JP followed Prodigy and Genesis backstage.

Jalen and Blake were sitting on a bench looking like two seasoned entertainers preparing for a big show. In their matching white Sean John overall sets and navy blue FUBU boots, they were looking too cool. All the other performers were moving about the room doing their last-minute tune-ups. Some looked nervous and some didn't, but they all lost their minds when they saw JP. Everyone jumped up and ran to meet their idol, who shook their hands and gave them all autographs.

"Blake, you rapping too?" Genesis asked.

"Nah, I'm the hype man. I might bust one, though," Blake said, smiling at his dad.

"What you gon' do with him, P?" Genesis asked Prodigy.

"I have no idea," Prodigy said, rubbing Blake's head and knocking his hat off in the process.

"Oh, Dad. You messing up my waves," Blake said, moving out of his father's way.

A few minutes later Prodigy was onstage with the microphone in hand.

"I'd like to thank all you for coming out this evening. We have a lot of future stars showcasing their talent here tonight and you guys can say you knew them when.

"I'd like for everyone to be respectful. Remember we are one community, therefore we're all family here, and you don't mistreat your own people. First I'd like to introduce the judges. Me." Prodigy stopped talking long enough to take in the loud applause from the audience. That alone let him know that he was not only appreciated but loved. "We have Mr. Genesis Styles, who is the new athletic director for the center." Prodigy stopped again to hear respectable applause for Genesis as he walked out and took his seat at the judges' table. "We have Mrs. Monica Kofmier from Channel Two News." Once again Prodigy stopped for the applause. "And yes, we have Atlanta's own hip-hop extraordinaire, movie star, Grammy Award winner, American Music Award winner, Essence Award winner, Soul Train Award winner, and overall good guy, Jaaaay to the Peeeee." Prodigy had the place so hyped that by the time JP walked out, there was near pandemonium. JP walked over, and Prodigy handed him the microphone.

"You know, I grew up hanging out in a place just like this. I want y'all to recognize the true work my man Prodigy is doing over here and know that everything that he does for you comes from the heart. Now let's get ready to see who's gonna be the next star on my label, y'all ready?" The crowd went wild. JP handed the mic back to Prodigy and took his seat at the judges' table.

The first guy came out and tried his best to imitate Carl Thomas, but the crowd wasn't feeling him, and they let him know by a shower of boos that would make amateur night at the Apollo Theater look tame. The second guy didn't fare much better. Then a little girl who looked to be about eight years old came out and ripped up a Kelly Price song. The crowd went crazy. A young man came out trying to do comedy and immediately got booed off the stage. Then it was Jalen and Blake's turn. Prodigy called for them twice but no one came out. After looking backstage, Prodigy asked Genesis to go and check on the dynamic duo. He called the next act in the meantime, a group of girls. One was reciting poetry while the others did an African dance.

Genesis walked backstage and called out to Jalen. A little boy pointed toward the bathroom. Blake was pleading with Jalen, who was sitting on the floor shaking his head, to come on. Genesis walked over to Jalen, who was nervously rubbing his hands down the front of his overalls. He looked at Genesis and pleaded with his eyes. Genesis tried to comfort his nephew. He lifted him up and took him into one of the stalls to try and calm him down.

"What's up, man? You all right?" Genesis asked, as he leaned down face-to-face with Jalen.

"Um, I . . . Um, I don't wanna rap no more. They gon' laugh at me and boo me."

"No, man, you're real good. They gonna clap for you."

"No." Jalen shook his head. "I don't wanna do it."

"Okay, man, you don't have to if you don't want to."

"I can't think of my words. I forgot my rap," Jalen said nervously. He looked like he was about to cry.

"It's cool, man. You don't have to rap if you don't want to."

Genesis gave his nephew a hug and assured him that he wasn't upset with him and that everything was going to be okay.

Genesis made his way back out to the stage and informed Prodigy of what happened. Prodigy leaned over and told JP something.

After all of the votes were in the Kelly Price girl and the dance team ended up in a two-way tie. JP offered to donate the extra two hundred dollars so that they both could get first-place prizes. He also gave the crowd a surprise performance of two of his best songs. After JP gave the crowd more than they'd bargained for when they bought their five-dollar tickets, he met Prodigy back in his office.

"I have something I think you should check out," Prodigy said as he popped Jalen's tape in his stereo.

JP wore a look that said he had heard a million demo tapes and really wasn't too thrilled to hear another one.

"I know you get this all the time, but you gotta hear this kid," Prodigy said, reading the look on JP's face.

"Go ahead."

Prodigy pressed the Play button on the boom box sitting on his credenza, and Jalen's voice blasted from the speakers.

"Whoa," JP said as he sat down in the chair. "Who is that?"

"That's Jalen, the little kid that wouldn't come out tonight. The one with the white overalls on."

"Oh, lil man got skills and a nasty delivery. Why wouldn't he perform?"

"He got a little stage fright."

"You his manager?"

"No, he doesn't have a manager. This is all new to him."

"Well, he's going to need one because I want him. Prodigy, promise me that I can have lil man," JP said.

"He's not mine to give but I'll let you holla at his uncle," Prodigy said as he stood and called out in the hall for Genesis to join them in his office.

Genesis walked in and told JP all about Jalen's history and why he wasn't able to perform. JP said he understood and still wanted to sign him as a writer to his label.

"Just like that?" Genesis asked.

"Yeah, that's how this business is. You gotta be on the move or you'll get left behind."

"Well, how much does something like this pay?" Genesis asked.

"Let's see, I normally start my writers off with an advance of about one hundred fifty thousand. But we can talk about this a little further on Monday if you're interested."

JP wrote a phone number down on a piece of paper and stood and walked out of the office.

"Genesis, looks like you have a future star on your hands," Prodigy said, smiling from ear to ear.

"Damn, dog, thanks for the hook-up. I can't believe this. Jalen 'bout to be in there. I gotta tell Grace," Genesis said, just as Grace, Phyllis, Terri, and Nina walked in.

"Y'all ain't gonna believe what just happened. JP just offered Jalen a contract as a writer," Genesis said excitedly. "One hundred and fifty thousand dollars to start."

"Look at my baby!" "Well, all right then!" "Go Jalen," Grace, Nina, and Terri said, respectively.

"He was offered what?" Phyllis asked.

"A songwriting contract with JP's record label," Genesis repeated.

"He's gonna need a manager, Genesis, so you might wanna get the ball rolling on that," Prodigy said.

"Phyllis, do you know anyone that can help in that area?" Grace asked.

"I could take a look at the contract, but let's get it first," Phyllis said. "And even so, one hundred fifty thousand isn't that much money, so why are you guys getting so excited?" Phyllis said, shaking her head.

"It's a lot of money for Jalen. I bet *you* don't make that much money a year. Why you always gotta put a damper on shit? I'm going to find Jalen and tell him his good news," Genesis said, storming out the office. He was even more upset when he thought about Grover. Here his son was being offered something that a million kids dream about, and he was probably somewhere getting high.

"That boy is so sensitive. Do you guys understand what I'm saying? I mean, with taxes and other expenses that these record companies charge?" Phyllis asked, looking around the office for some sort of support. When she found none, she asked, "Where is Zachary? I hope he's not hanging around those thuggish little boys." Phyllis looked around the hallway, then left the office without saying a word to anyone.

"Y'all please excuse my sister, she has a case of the uppity-butt syndrome," Grace said, shaking her head. They all laughed. "So, Terri, how's the bookstore?"

"It's doing well. I can't keep any good help but I'm surviving," Terri said.

"What about Yolanda? I thought she was a sure thing for you," Grace said, referring to a young lady who was with Terri when she first opened her bookstore.

"Oh, she just up and disappeared. I had high hopes for that girl, but you never know with some people," Terri said, shaking her head.

"Well, dag, I really liked her. I talked to her on the phone more than I spoke with you," Grace said, frowning with disappointment. "How's the teaching going, Nina?"

"It's great. I love what I do. Don't make enough money, but I still love it."

"Well, y'all, I gotta get this place locked up," Prodigy said as he ushered the ladies to the door. "I hope y'all had a good time tonight."

"I had a wonderful time. I wish I could've gotten to see Jalen perform, but—" Grace said.

"Oh, let me give you his tape. That'll give you a taste of his skills." Prodigy popped the tape out and handed it to Grace.

"Well, all right then. Terri, I think I might need a ride. Phyllis has probably left me," Grace said, looking around.

"No problem," Terri said as they strolled outside.

thirteen

CHANGING PLANS

Terri sat in her bookstore office, looking at different honey-moon spots. Planning the honeymoon was supposed to be Genesis's responsibility, but once again he'd found a way to make it her job. Terri smiled because she wanted to plan it anyway. She really didn't trust Genesis with the logistics of almost anything. She only gave him that task so he'd feel involved.

Genesis had walked in the house a few days ago and given her five one-hundred-dollar bills and told her to add it to the wedding budget. That gesture of kindness brought a smile to her face and the extra padding she needed to plan a honeymoon to remember. Terri smiled to herself as she thought about them cruising along the Caribbean Sea in a luxury liner. Now that Genesis was being generous, they would have a few extra dollars' spending cash.

The wedding was only two weeks away and everything was in order. The invitations had been mailed weeks ago. Her eight brides-maids had been fitted for their dresses and shoes. All the grooms-men were lined up and had confirmed that everything was a thumbs-up with them as well. The only thing left to do now was jump the broom.

"Terri, someone is out here to see you," Linda Harris said.

Linda was the mother of one of Terri's sorority sisters. She was retired and since she loved to read, she volunteered to help out at the store full-time for minimum wage.

Terri stood and walked out to the front of her store. She stopped, smiled, and put her hand on her hip as if to say, "Let's hear some sort of explanation."

"Hi," Yolanda said shyly, holding a baby carrier, which she shifted from one hand to the next.

"Girl, where have you been? I know this isn't your baby," Terri said, as she reached over and gave Yolanda a hug. She looked into the baby carrier that Yolanda had placed onto the counter. "Well, I can see it's a girl, with all of this pretty hair and bows. She's beautiful."

"You think so? Thanks," Yolanda said.

Terri lifted the little girl out of her seat and held her to her chest. She rocked the little princess slowly and closed her eyes. Terri couldn't count the number of times she imagined a baby as a part of her family equation but was happy she'd decided to wait until marriage, when she was well on her way in life, before she took on such a great responsibility. "What's her name?" Terri asked.

"Gabrielle! It means 'God is my strength.'"

"That's a pretty name. I guess I don't have to ask you why you left the store then, huh?" Terri asked, still holding Gabrielle.

"Sorry. I just needed to get away and get my head straight. I didn't mean to leave you like that, but you know ... It's just I ... I don't know," Yolanda stuttered before dropping her head.

"Well, you look good," Terri said, complimenting Yolanda on her slim figure and smooth reddish-brown skin tone.

"Thank you."

"How old is this little lady?"

"She's eight weeks."

"Are you one of those mothers that's going to count by weeks until she's ten years old?" Terri said, laughing.

"No, I don't think so."

"Do I know the father?" Terri said with raised eyebrows.

"No!" Yolanda frowned, not looking at Terri.

"Tell me he's helping you."

"No."

"And why not?"

"He doesn't know about the baby."

"Wait a minute. He doesn't know?" Terri asked, shocked.

"I didn't want to ruin his life because of a mistake I made," Yolanda said, showing Terri an immature side of her that had rarely surfaced.

Terri put Gabrielle back into her carrier and strapped her in. "Now wait a minute. You are not going to try and handle this on your own, are you? It took two people to make that precious baby, and there should be two people to raise her. Yolanda, you have to at least let this guy know that he has a child. I mean, think about little Gabrielle. Don't you think she deserves a chance to know her father? Now, I don't care what's going on in this man's life. He should take full responsibility for his child, and if he doesn't want to, then I'll help you find someone that will put him where all dead-beat dads belong." Terri rubbed her hand over Gabrielle's forehead. "You have to give her the best possible chance in this world. You're so young, and I'm sure the father is, too, but it's time to become an adult. You don't come first anymore, it's all about little Gabby now," Terri said.

"Terri, I don't know what to do." Yolanda burst into tears. "I'm so confused. I feel like I've let everybody down. My mom has basically disowned me. She kicked me out when I was seven weeks pregnant. I've been staying in a shelter, but then I moved in with my aunt, and she has this rat-infested place and a roach crawled in my baby's mouth this morning. I can't take it no more." Yolanda cried even harder.

"Come here." Terri pulled Yolanda close to her and held her tightly. "Everything is going to be fine. You can stay with Genesis and me until you get on your feet. And you'll always have a job here. See, things aren't so bad, huh?" Terri tried to make things sound a little more encouraging for her young friend.

Yolanda slowly pulled away. "Terri, I have to do what I feel is best for my baby."

"I agree with you wholeheartedly, sweetie, but things aren't as bad as they seem. You're not alone. I'll do everything I can, and I'm sure the father is a nice young man. We can put our heads together and work this out," Terri said. She reached for Gabrielle as the baby began to cry.

"She's hungry," Yolanda said, still crying, as she reached into Gabrielle's baby bag and pulled out a bottle of milk. "Will you feed her for me? I have to run outside and grab a diaper."

"Sure, I'd be glad to feed the little angel," Terri said. Gabrielle stopped crying as soon as the nipple touched her lips.

While Yolanda was outside, Terri picked up the baby bag and headed to her office in the back of the store. "Mrs. Linda, will you send Yolanda to my office when she comes back?"

"I will," Mrs. Linda said as she stole a peek at Gabrielle. "That sure is a pretty baby."

"Oh, she's an angel. She has the prettiest brown skin and look at her eyes—they are gorgeous," Terri commented.

"Let me hold that baby," Mrs. Linda said, reaching over the counter and taking Gabrielle from Terri.

Terri cringed when she thought about the hard times that faced little Gabrielle. But she knew she would do everything she could to make the road a little smoother for her. As Mrs. Linda cooed with the baby, Terri looked on and said a silent prayer, asking, "God, please bless this baby, watch over her, and never let any harm come her way. Provide the miracle needed to let little Gabrielle have a safe and joyous upbringing. Amen." Terri opened her eyes and reached for the baby. In the short amount of time that Mrs. Linda had been holding the baby, she started to miss her.

Terri walked to the back of her store and into her office. Terri and Gabrielle eased into the love seat and got comfortable. She looked down into Gabrielle's eyes with concern. She could only imagine the trouble that was waiting in the wings for this baby and her young mother. All of a sudden, Terri felt a certain responsibility to this child. She didn't know to what extent and couldn't really understand her feelings, but she knew that whatever it was, it was placed on her heart by God.

Terri's mind automatically went into survival mode. The honeymoon would have to wait or at least be scaled down. There was a larger mission to deal with. Terri frowned. "Oh, Gabby, you stinky winky."

Terri searched the bag for a diaper but she didn't find any. *I guess that's where your mommy went,* she thought.

"Well, little lady, you'll have to stay stinky until your mommy comes back, and I hope she hurries up." Terri placed the baby back on her shoulder and stood. She walked out to the main part of the bookstore.

"Yolanda hasn't come back yet?" Terri asked the obvious.

"No, but she's had plenty of time to run to the store and back by now," Mrs. Linda said as she looked out the window.

Terri walked over to the door and peeked out.

"Give me that baby," Mrs. Linda scolded as she took the baby once again. "You don't have no small child that close to the outside weather without a blanket or something to cover her up."

"I'll be right back," Terri said.

Terri walked out of the store and looked around. It was broad daylight, but Yolanda was nowhere to be found. A bad feeling started to come over her. She walked down to the convenience store on the corner and walked in to have a look around. Still no sign of Yolanda! She asked the clerk if he'd seen a girl that fit Yolanda's description, and the Korean man said, "No can help you." Terri looked at her watch. Yolanda had been missing for about forty-five minutes and from what she knew about Yolanda, that was way too long. She had always been a responsible person. Terri walked back toward her store baffled and confused.

"Muddy, did you see Yolanda?" Terri asked the homeless man who often stayed out in front of her store. "You remember the girl that used to work for me?"

"Can't say that I have, ma'am," Muddy said, quickly looking away.

"Well, okay, have you eaten anything today?" Terri asked just like she always did.

"Just finished eating. Can't believe the amount of food people throw away."

Terri nodded. "Well, you take care."

"Did you see her?" Mrs. Linda asked, the second Terri walked in the door.

"No, no sign of her anywhere," Terri said, as she reached for the baby like she was her own.

"Well my, my, my. Do you know where her parents live?"

"Well, I still have her file in my office." Terri ran back to her office and called the number that was on Yolanda's application, but got the message saying the number was disconnected.

She walked back to the front of her store and told Mrs. Linda the news.

"Well, she said her mother put her out because she was pregnant, so even if I could reach her she probably wouldn't be willing to help."

"Well, you know what this means, don't you?" Mrs. Linda asked.

"No, I don't," Terri responded. "What does this mean?"

"It means you have a choice to make. Either you call the police and report this baby as abandoned and take the chance of her ending up in some horrible foster home or you get to thinking about being a guardian."

"I think we might be jumping the gun here. I mean, she hasn't even been gone for an hour yet. Let's give her a little more time before we start all this abandonment and adoption talk."

"Suit yourself. But now that I think about it, I saw the look in that chile's eyes, and she ain't coming back. She's scared to death. You can delay the truth as long as you want, but it's gonna come back to the same thing I said, adoption or the police," Mrs. Linda said as she wiped down a glass bookcase.

"Oh, my God. You really think she left her child?" Terri asked. All of a sudden she was scared.

"Unfortunately, I do. Just as sure of it as I am standing here!"

"Oh, my God. What will I do? I'm definitely not having her go to one of those awful foster homes. Not with all the horror stories I've heard about what happens in those places. No way," Terri said, as she held Gabrielle tighter.

"Looks like you made your choice." Mrs. Linda smiled. "God uses all of us at different times for different things. We are a family, a black family, and God will bless you abundantly for doing what you're doing," Mrs. Linda said as she walked over and picked up the ringing phone.

"Is it Yolanda?" Terri asked, and was met by a slow shaking of Mrs. Linda's head. She pulled Gabrielle away from her shoulder and looked her in the eyes. "I won't abandon you. I'm going to be there for you just like you were my very own. You can depend on me."

Gabrielle looked at Terri as if she understood what she heard. She even gave a pretty baby toothless smile.

"Looks like the blessings are starting already. Eric Jerome Dickey's publicist called to schedule a book signing in three weeks."

Normally Terri would be ecstatic at the news of another *New*

York Times best-selling author coming to her store. E. Lynn Harris was just in her store last week, but she just nodded and said, "That's great. Will you watch Gabby while I run down to the store and buy some Pampers?"

"Absolutely! Terri, I know I was a little pushy and that's because I put my own values on this situation. I think you should really think about this. Being a parent is a full-time job, but the blessings are so satisfying. I raised three kids on a secretary's salary, and I would do it all over again. My husband got hurt on his job and wasn't able to work much after our youngest girl was born. But I'll tell you this: nothing compares to the joy I feel when my children say, 'Momma, I love you'—and they don't miss an opportunity to tell me either."

"Thank you for telling me that, Mrs. Linda. I'll be back in a minute." Terri gave an uneasy smile and walked out the door.

Mrs. Linda looked at Gabrielle and smiled. "God has truly blessed you with a phenomenal lady in your corner. You're gonna be just fine, chile. But she sure needs to hurry back with your Pampers, cuz you stank."

Terri was stopped by Muddy just outside the door.

"Miss Terri, I . . . I got something to tell you. I can't lie to you after how good you done been to me. I mean, you let me sleep in your store when we had that last winter storm, you feed me when I'm hungry, you let me work on just about anything to let me make some eating change and I can't thank you—"

"Muddy, what do you wanna tell me?" Terri said, cutting to the chase. Her experience with Muddy told her that he could go on forever without getting to his point.

"That girl, Yolanda, got on the Greyhound. She asked me not to say nothin', but you've been too good to me and I just couldn't keep it from you."

"When? What bus?"

"Don't know. For real I don't."

Terri sprinted toward the bus station. She ran through the glass doors and looked around for Yolanda, to no avail. She went to the counter and asked every ticket agent if they had seen her and all of them told her that they couldn't remember with the amount of people that came through their doors.

Now Terri was really terrified as her fears were confirmed. What would she do? What could she do? She walked out of the bus station and began to cry. As she walked back to her store, she looked up to the sky and asked God for some direction.

fourteen

FAMILY

G race looked down at the piece of paper she was holding and stared at the big brass numbers over the door. She had a match. She took a deep breath and rang Phyllis's doorbell. As she waited for someone to answer, she hoped for the best.

Zachary opened the door and Grace reached out and hugged him. "Hey there, handsome."

"Hi. My mom said she's on the way down," Zachary said. "You wanna see my room?"

"Sure, you lead the way."

Grace followed Zachary up the stairs and into his room. The room was very nice, equipped with a twenty-seven-inch television, a Sony PlayStation 2, a computer, and all the other little amenities that would put most children in kiddy heaven.

"You know how to play PlayStation?" Zachary asked, as he walked over to his play area.

"No, can't say that I do. But I bet you're good."

"Want me to teach you?"

"Yeah, man, but not today. I gotta get some shopping done. You have a nice room, Zach."

"Thank you," Zachary said, smiling as if he'd built the room and paid for all of its contents himself.

Zachary and Grace headed back downstairs to wait for Phyllis. Zachary pointed toward the den and told Grace to have a seat.

"Are you guys going to any toy stores?"

"Maybe. Why, do you need anything?" Grace asked, already knowing the answer.

"Well, I want a new game for my PlayStation 2, but my mom probably won't get it," Zachary said as he dropped his head.

"Have you been listening to your mom and dad?"

Zachary lifted his head when he heard mention of his father. "I listen to my mom. My dad doesn't live here anymore. I made the honor roll."

"Well, you run and write down the name of the game you want on a piece of paper, and Auntie Grace will get it for you," Grace said, smiling with her nephew. Grace wondered what Phyllis had done to drive Carl away, but shook the thought clear from her head. Nothing Phyllis did would surprise her.

"Thank you, Aunt Grace." Zachary broke out into a bigger smile before running up to his room.

Grace looked around her older sister's immaculate place. Phyllis didn't have the biggest house in the neighborhood, but it was probably the cleanest. She thought her sister was on the verge of having some kind of obsessive-compulsive disorder. There were crystal figurines here and there, a white carpet throughout the living room, and the kitchen's cherrywood cabinets and granite countertops looked like they had never been touched. *How can a kid live in here? Poor Zach, he's probably afraid to touch anything,* she thought as she took a seat on a soft leather sofa.

Grace had called Phyllis last night and convinced her to have a sister-girl Saturday-at-the-mall bonding session. She made Phyllis promise to wear sneakers and to let her hair down. Phyllis walked down the stairs in a nice-fitting jogging suit and a pair of running shoes.

"Look at you," Grace said, standing. "Girl, you're wearing that. You look good."

"Thank you. You look nice yourself. After we drop Zachary off at the sitter's we'll head on out to the Mall of Georgia. I heard that place is so big that it takes three days to see the entire place."

"Why don't we take Zach over to the youth center and let him spend some time with his uncle Genesis?" Grace suggested.

Phyllis gave her a look and said, "Don't push it. You better be happy I've decided to cancel my Saturday plans for you."

"Okay, I'll shut up." Grace put her hands up in surrender.

"Let's go. Zachary, let's go," Phyllis called out.

Zachary ran down the stairs and stood in the foyer with his book bag on his shoulders.

"Zachary, you have homework on a Saturday?" Grace asked.

"Yeah, my mom makes me do it before I can play video games."

Phyllis gave Grace another look that said, "Mind your business." Grace hunched her shoulders. "Hey, I think that's great."

"All right, I have to watch you childless people that like to make the rules for parenting," Phyllis said as she set the alarm on her home.

"Oh, I think you're doing a wonderful job. He has really good manners."

"Well, thank you," Phyllis said.

They piled into Phyllis's Mercedes and set out for some sister time. They dropped Zachary off and hit the mall. For the first time in a very long time they felt like sisters. They shopped so much that they had to make two separate trips back to the car to store their bags.

After spending six full hours in the mall they decided to stop at the Cheesecake Factory to have dinner together before they called it a day.

"Girl, I had a good time today. We'll have to do this more often," Grace said.

"Hush your mouth. I can't take too much of this. I'll be in the poorhouse."

"I know that's right. I need to watch my dollars. Momma needs all kinds of repairs over there."

"Yeah, we'll have to come up with a plan to take better care of that old place, since she refuses to move. And since I'm trying to be positive, I won't mention how trifling your free-loading brother Grover is."

"I'm so disappointed with Grover. He didn't even know who I was. He almost put me out." Grace laughed as she thought about how high her oldest brother was when she first walked into the house.

Just when the waiter took their drink orders, Phyllis's cell phone rang.

"Hello."

"Momma had a stroke, you need to come to the emergency room at Grady," Grover said.

"What happened?" Phyllis asked, leaning forward in her seat.

"I'll tell you when you get here. You seen Grace?"

"She's with me. We're on our way." Phyllis ended the call and stood so fast she almost knocked the table over.

"What's going on?" Grace asked, looking at her sister, who seemed to be falling apart.

"Grover said Momma had a stroke," Phyllis said as she placed five dollars on the table and motioned for Grace to come on.

"A stroke! What kind of stroke? How . . . ?" Grace stammered as she stood and followed Phyllis out of the restaurant.

Phyllis and Grace went back to being strangers on the ride to the hospital. They had spent so much crucial time away from each other that they didn't know how to handle a crisis together as a family.

Grace bit her fingernails and cried as she looked out the passenger window, regretting her decision to move to New York. Phyllis wished she had spent more quality time with her mother. She was the oldest, and they had always been close.

Grace borrowed Phyllis's cell phone and called Genesis at the center to inform him of their mother's condition.

Phyllis parked in the emergency room parking lot and they hit the ground running. They walked up behind Grover as he talked with the paramedic that responded to his 911 call.

"I'm not a doctor but I can tell you she's not breathing on her own."

"Is she gonna make it?" Genesis asked frantically as he ran up.

"I can't say at this time," the paramedic said. "But we're doing our very best. She's receiving optimum treatment."

"Where is Jalen?" Genesis asked Grover.

"I sent him next door to Mrs. Jackson's house right when the ambulance got there," Grover said.

A nurse walked out and asked for the family of Mrs. Virginia Styles.

"Where is our mother?" Phyllis asked.

"She's being worked on and we can only allow one of you to go back there at this time," the nurse said.

"Let me go," Grover said as he rushed up to the nurse.

"No, you the reason her blood pressure so high now," Genesis said. "I'm going."

"Man, kiss my ass." Grover turned to Genesis. "My momma laying up in there, and you sitting up here playing God. How in the hell you figure it's my fault?"

"Please, you guys, cut it out!" Phyllis said just below a yell. "Now, I'm the oldest, so I'll go. God knows I'm the only one that's capable of taking care of her." Phyllis took a step toward the area where the nurse pointed to when she asked of her mother's whereabouts.

"No. The last time you made a decision because you were the oldest, we lost our father. I'm going," Grace said with such conviction and authority that no one challenged her.

Phyllis took a deep breath and stepped aside. She wanted to respond to her younger sister's accusations, but now was not the time. Turning and walking away, she pulled out her cell phone and called Zachary's baby-sitter, telling her she would be late.

WHILE GRACE WAS gone, Genesis, Grover, and Phyllis sat in three separate corners of the waiting room. Phyllis was on her cell phone with their mother's private doctor's office and Genesis was on the phone with Terri. Grover sat in his corner staring at the wall.

Fifteen minutes after she left, Grace came back into the waiting room with a scared look on her face.

"What's up? How's Mom? Come on, Grace, spit it out," Genesis said.

"I can't tell. She has tubes everywhere, and she had two seizures while I was back there."

"Seizures? What the hell they doing to her?" Genesis asked as he started to walk toward the area that Grace just left. Grover reached over and grabbed his brother's arm. "Look, she's in capable hands. We just gonna have to be patient," Grover said as he stared Genesis in the face.

"Grover, you better get your fucking hands off me or I'm . . ." Genesis said, trying to pull away from his older brother's tight grip.

"Or what? What you gonna do, you hotheaded little boy?" Grover said. And just like that his big brother status was back in effect. "I know you're upset and want the best for Momma, but you haven't stepped one foot in a medical school, so let these people do their jobs and stop fooling with 'em."

Grace and Phyllis looked on in complete surprise at Grover's outburst. Genesis just dropped his head. He knew Grover was right.

Genesis slid to the floor and cried as he thought about life without his mother. Grover walked over to his younger brother and took a seat on the floor beside him. He debated whether to put his arm around him. They had been on such bad terms over the last couple of years that he didn't know what to do. He took a chance and hugged his little brother. Genesis leaned into Grover and his sobs increased.

"She's gonna make it, baby bro. She's gonna pull through. We gotta stay positive," Grover said as he closed his eyes and rocked back and forth, his little brother in his arms, the same as he did when they were younger on the nights their father would come home drunk and fight their mother.

Grace walked over and sat down on the other side of Genesis and tried to console him. Phyllis felt awkward. She wanted to be with her family, but she didn't feel any real connection at this point. This was how things had been for the longest time, those three together and her alone. She took a seat in a chair at the far end of the room and prayed for their mother's recovery.

"Phyllis, you can join us," Grace said.

Phyllis hesitated, then walked over to her family. She slid down on the floor beside Grace.

Grace asked everyone to join hands and began a prayer for their mother. "God, have Your way with Momma. Let Your healing hand touch her in the places where she needs it most. Bless the hands of the medical staff as they administer to our mother. Bless us as a family, heal us as a family, and keep us as a family. In Jesus' name we pray."

They all sat silent for a few minutes before Grover spoke.

"Hey, Phyllis," Grover said. "How's Zachary and Carl?" Grover was the next oldest and he remembered a time, before Genesis and Grace were born, when Phyllis would take care of him. He smiled to himself as a childhood memory flashed through his mind.

"Everyone is fine. How are you doing, Grover?" Phyllis said.

"Not too good, but it's going to get better," Grover said. "Phyllis, do you remember when I was about seven or eight years old and this girl beat me up and took my Halloween candy?"

"Yeah, I remember that." Phyllis smiled and shook her head at the memory of her baby brother running in the house crying like his world had ended.

"You remember kicking her ass and making her give it back? Right in front of her older sister."

"Yeah, I remember that too." Phyllis smiled again and closed her eyes. "You were my baby. I couldn't have anyone messing with you."

"Yeah, I didn't even know you could fight until then."

"Me either." Phyllis laughed with her brother for the first time in more than ten years.

"You remember when Genesis had the chicken pox and you stayed home from school for a whole week because he didn't want anyone to hold him but you?" Grover asked.

"That wasn't the only time I missed school because of Mr. Genesis," Phyllis said, enjoying this trip back down memory lane. "But what about you and Grace? I thought she was going to have to be surgically removed from your arms in order to go to preschool."

"Yeah, she was my baby. Still is," Grover said, looking over at his little sister. "Do you know that you ran out on the basketball court in the middle of a championship game because I twisted my ankle?"

"I did?" Grace asked, covering her mouth. "How old was I?"

"Old enough to know better, but right and wrong went out the window when it came to your big brother," Phyllis added.

"Oh, Phyllis, don't you talk about knowing better. I remember that time when Momma caught you sneaking in the house, and I got a beating," Genesis said.

"Why did you get a beating for Phyllis sneaking out?" Grace asked.

"Cuz I lied for her. Momma came in the room and asked me, 'What time did Phyllis go to sleep?' and I said, 'A few hours ago.' I'm laying on the bed hugging a bunch of pillows that were supposed to be Phyllis." Genesis laughed.

"How did you get caught?" Grace asked Phyllis.

"Your father pulled up in the yard as soon as I climbed my butt up on the ladder to get back in the window."

"Did you get a beating too?" Grover asked.

"Oh no. Momma was too tired after chasing this one here," Phyllis said as they all laughed at the memory of Genesis's customary act of running around the house begging.

"That boy was something else. I don't think you ever had a complete spanking. Momma and Daddy would usually start laughing themselves and give up," Grover said.

After all the laughter subsided Grace turned serious. "Guys, why don't we make an effort to be close like that again? That's one of the reasons I moved back home."

"That's cool with me. I would hate to have my wedding with all of the ill feelings that I have been having lately," Genesis said. "And that's just being real with y'all."

"Yeah, things have been really strained with our family over the last few years," Phyllis added.

"Well, I'm all for it," Grover said. "I have somebody to get drunk with."

"Ain't nobody trynna get drunk, man," Genesis said with a frown.

"I'm just kidding. Get your panties out your crotch. But on the real, guess what?" Grover said, reaching into his pocket and pulling out a white envelope. "I wasn't going to say anything to nobody, partly because I don't ever talk to y'all anyway but mainly because

I done failed at this thing three times. I'm checking in to a rehab on Monday."

"That's great, Grover," Grace said as she reached over Genesis and gave Grover a hug.

"Let me see that." Phyllis reached over and took the envelope. She scanned the first page and said, "Is this the same place you've gone to before?"

"Yeah, but I'mma try it again. Maybe with y'all's support I can make it this time. Plus I'm tired of getting high."

Genesis frowned as he listened to Grover's rehabilitation speech. He had heard it all before, and even though he longed for the days when he had a functional relationship with his brother, he didn't have any faith that Grover would ever kick the habit. Genesis twisted his lips and shook his head. He thought the only reason Grover was even thinking about rehabilitation was because of Jalen's newfound money. Little did Grover know that Jalen would be the only one to benefit from his talent. Phyllis had set up a trust fund for eighty percent of the royalties to be released to Jalen at age eighteen. The other twenty percent was to be used for living expenses until then.

"Grover, I don't mean to delay your process but let me find a place for you," Phyllis said. "This place is not going to help you. I'm prosecuting the director of this place right now for defrauding the taxpayers. So first thing Monday morning you call me, and I'll get you into a quality treatment center."

"Thanks, Phyllis. I'll do just that," Grover said, reaching over Grace and Genesis to grab Phyllis's hand.

"That's cool, man. Jalen needs you. Did you know that he can rap?" Genesis asked.

"Yeah, I hear him around the house all the time. I came to that talent show the other night too," Grover said.

"I didn't see you there," Genesis said, thinking Grover was lying.

"I saw him," Grace said, turning her attention to Grover. "You were all the way in the back of the gym, weren't you?"

"Yeah. I saw y'all too."

"Why didn't you come over and speak?" Phyllis asked.

"I don't know. Y'all know how thangs is with me," Grover said.

"Y'all know what? I bet Momma would be proud to see all of us talking like this," Grace said as thoughts of their mother returned.

"God works in mysterious ways. Sometimes it takes a tragedy to open your eyes," Grover said.

"Amen to that," Phyllis added as she thought about her own situation with Carl. She thought about what Carl did and the reason she hated black men in the first place. "Grace, will you spend the night with me tonight?" Phyllis asked. "I have some things I need to clear up."

Grace knew she wanted to talk about their father. She nodded her head.

The doctor walked out and gave everyone an update on their mother. They had her stabilized, but she was still in critical condition. He stated that it was too early to tell if she would make a full recovery and that he was still waiting on the results from the MRI and CAT scan. He suggested that everyone go home and come back the next day because there was nothing else they could do that night.

"Well, you guys can go on home, I'mma hang around here. Genesis, will you go and pick up Jalen for me?" Grover asked.

"Oh yeah. I got him," Genesis said, happy to hear that his brother was thinking about his son.

"Well, Grover, you have all my numbers. Call me as soon as you hear something, and we'll come back in the morning," Phyllis said as she reached over and hugged her brother.

"Do you have any money for snacks or something?" Grace asked.

"No, but I'm cool," Grover said.

"Here." Grace reached in her pocket and gave Grover a ten-dollar bill.

Grover looked at it and vowed that he would not leave the hospital in search of drugs.

"Okay y'all, I'm out. I gotta run and pick up my little nephew." Genesis hugged everyone as they all walked out.

fifteen

LET'S WORK!

After leaving the hospital, Genesis went by his mother's next-door neighbor's house to pick up Jalen. Genesis gave him a subtle update on his grandmother and told him everything would be just fine.

They made it to Genesis's house and as soon as they walked in they heard a baby's cry.

"Who is that?" Jalen asked.

"Oh, that must be our new houseguest. One of Terri's friends had a baby and she's watching her."

"Oh. She's loud." Jalen smiled. "Can I see her?"

"I don't see why not," Genesis said as he pulled out the sofa bed for Jalen and walked into his bedroom. He looked over at Terri, who was still asleep, and shook his head.

"Hey, pretty lady. What's all the fuss about?" Genesis reached down into the bassinet and picked up the baby. This was his first time meeting Gabrielle. He had to chaperone a sleepover at the center the night before when Terri brought her home and from there he went straight to the hospital.

"Ain't this something, Jalen? Terri's knocked out."

"Terri needs to get her tonsils taken out. She snores too loud."

"Tell me about it. Wanna hold her?"

"Nah. She's too little. I'm going to bed," Jalen said as he lightly punched Genesis on his arm.

"Good night, dude," Genesis said as he placed Gabrielle on his shoulder. "You're the one that's suppose to be sleeping like a baby, not her," Genesis said to Gabrielle. "Ain't that something? You crying, and she's asleep. Well, let's go in the kitchen and see if we can't find you something for that belly of yours."

Genesis looked in the refrigerator and retrieved a full baby bottle of milk. He boiled a pot of water and set the bottle in the water for a few minutes, just like he did when Jalen was a baby. As Genesis waited on the bottle to heat up, he walked back into the bedroom with the baby on his shoulder to get a Pamper. He smiled as he removed Gabrielle's soggy diaper. "Ooo wee, little girl, I see why you crying." Genesis wiped the baby clean and sprinkled a touch of baby powder on her before putting on a new Pamper. He lifted Gabrielle and walked back into the kitchen. He removed the bottle from the water and squirted a small amount of milk on the back of his hand before placing the nipple in Gabrielle's hungry mouth.

"Now you're back in business. I'm hungry, too, so I'm going to sit you in your seat and prop this bottle up. Now I gotta find me something to grub on." Genesis created some kind of pillow contraption that would hold Gabrielle's bottle while he searched the fridge for leftovers.

"Hey, baby. How's your mother doing?" Terri asked, walking in the kitchen rubbing her eyes. She walked over and picked up Gabrielle.

"I don't know. Doctor says it's too early to tell so we're just gonna have to wait and see," Genesis said as he removed a half-eaten sub sandwich.

"What happened?" Terri asked as she rocked with the baby.

"Grover said she was walking down the hall and fell into the wall.

She said her right leg wouldn't move. Then she had a seizure and couldn't breathe. So he called 911 and the ambulance came. That's about all I know." Genesis sat at the kitchen table and took a bite of his sandwich.

"I'm sorry to hear that. Is there anything you need for me to do?"

"Nah, I guess she's in good hands."

Terri lifted Gabrielle up to her shoulder and began to pat her back. Terri chuckled when Gabrielle burped.

"I guess she's ready for bed now." Terri took Gabrielle into the bedroom, came back out to the kitchen, and sat down.

"Well, are you okay?" Terri asked, concerned for Genesis. She knew how he felt about his mother.

"Yeah, I'm straight. Tell me about your interesting last two days. You left home not wanting to give me none and came home with a baby. That don't add up." Genesis cracked a smile.

"Well, you know I had a little thing on the side, and it just kind of happened like that," Terri joked back. "Nah, but do you remember Yolanda? The girl that used to work for me at the bookstore?"

"No, you done had so many come and go it's hard to keep track, but what's up?"

"Well, she's young and scared. She came in the store and basically dropped the baby off and left. I rode by her old house and a Mexican lady answered the door. She said that the black people that lived there moved six months ago. I rode around asking any and everybody who looked like they might know something, but no one was talking."

"That's messed up that someone would just drop a baby off like that. But that's how it is these days. At least she didn't do something dumb like put the baby in a Dumpster or something. She's a pretty little girl."

"Yeah, so what do you think we should do? I don't wanna send her to a foster home. I've heard too many horror stories about what goes on in those places," Terri said as she pleaded with her eyes for Genesis to agree.

"Well, I know it's a big responsibility, but if you wanna keep her, I'm all for it."

Terri smiled and said, "Good. I called one of my sorors that's a lawyer, and she's gonna get started on the adoption paperwork."

"Whoa. Don't you think you're moving too fast? What if ol' girl comes back and wants her baby? You thought about that?"

"Yeah, the paperwork is only for temporary custody. If she reappears, then fine; if not, fine too. Everything will be in place."

"Okay, if you say so. I'm all for it." Genesis smiled and Terri stood and walked over to him and sat on his lap.

"You're such a good woman. What did I do to deserve you?" Genesis asked as he pulled her lips down to his.

"I don't know but you have the rest of your life to figure it out. Two more weeks, and we're official. No more shacking."

"Your breath stinks. Why you ain't brush your teeth before you came out here breathing all in my face? That's why the baby went back to sleep, you probably knocked her out. Let me go check on my little princess." Genesis acted like he was trying to get up. Terri just sat on his lap and smirked.

"You know how to ruin a mood, don't you? You're lucky I'm trying to stop cursing, so don't make me start back," Terri said and stood to leave.

"Hey, you gonna have to do something about that damn sleeping problem you have. You didn't even hear the baby crying. She could've starved to death messing around with you."

"That's why I have you," Terri said, and walked back into their bedroom.

Genesis shook his head and smiled. He liked the fact that Terri had a sense of humor. He picked the soiled diaper up off the

table and tossed it in the trash can before retiring to their bedroom
himself.

GENESIS COULDN'T SLEEP. Between the baby crying every
hour on the hour and his mother's illness, he realized that no more
sleep was coming. He looked at the clock and saw it was eight-
thirty. He did a quick calculation and realized that he got about four
hours and that was enough for him on most days. He jumped up and
threw on his warm-ups and a pair of Jordan's. He woke Terri and
told her that he was going to the youth center to work out and then
to the hospital. Terri nodded, sat up and took a peek at the baby, and
lay back down.

Genesis was running laps when he heard the door to the gym
open.

"What's up, man?" Prodigy said as he took a seat on the floor and
began stretching.

"Hey, I tried to call you last night. Momma had a stroke," Genesis
said.

"A stroke! Damn, man, is she all right?" Prodigy stopped what he
was doing and stared intently at Genesis.

"Don't know yet. I just called up there and spoke with Grover.
He said he hasn't heard nothing yet."

"Dog, if you need me to do anything, let me know. Did you try me
on my cell phone?" Prodigy asked, still a bit shocked at the news.

"Man, I couldn't think of that number to save my life. But I'm
going up there after I leave here. I had to get some of this stress out
before I passed the hell out."

"Yeah, I hear ya. What hospital is she in?"

"Grady."

"A'right. Well, I'm going to follow you up there if you don't mind.
I know this is family time but . . ." Prodigy said as he joined Genesis
running around the perimeter of the gym.

"Go ahead, man. You know you family. So did you ever talk to Blake's biological thing?" Genesis asked, having trouble giving Blake's biological father a title.

"Oh yeah, he called the house again after missing two appointments with me. I told him not to ever call my house again."

"Good! What did he say then?"

"Ya know that thuggish rubbish. 'I'll kill yo ass. That's my mutha-fuckin' son.' I just hung up on him."

"Yeah, that's what you shoulda did the first time he called after all them years. Niggas get on my damn nerves. He should be kissin' yo ass after what you've done for his seed. Anyway, what's up with the bachelor party?"

"I got you. We're going to have a good time." Prodigy smiled, downplaying the whole thing.

"Well, looks like I won't be getting my groove on. Terri's brother is coming and about three or four of her cousins. I was looking forward to getting my last piece of ass as a single man but them fools gonna jack it up," Genesis said.

"I ain't responding to that," Prodigy said. He couldn't believe that Genesis was still thinking about having sex with someone two weeks before his wedding.

"Good, cuz I don't feel like one of your sermons. You getting some ass at home. I gotta wait until I'm married, so damn that."

"You know you need help."

"I've been faithful for over a week. I done turned down every woman that called me, so give me some credit."

"A week!" Prodigy said, shaking his head. "Man, go get a basketball."

"Oh, I know you don't wanna go there."

"There you go talkin' trash already. I'm trying to get a workout in. I ain't about to kill myself up in here trying to beat you in a funky little basketball game."

"That's cuz you can't beat me. And your ass is getting a little fat," Genesis said as he pinched Prodigy's side.

"For real? Damn, Nina gonna tell me I need to work out. Talking about she needs to be the only one in the house with titties. Ain't that something to tell your husband?"

Genesis looked at Prodigy and cracked up laughing.

sixteen

THE BOOGIE MAN

Phyllis got Zachary tucked into his bed and kissed him on his forehead. She turned his light out and headed back downstairs where Grace was sitting.

"Is everything okay?" Grace asked.

"Yeah, he wants to play with that game you bought him. If Zach had his way, that's all that he'd ever do."

"Kids will be kids."

"Can I get you anything? I'm still hungry," Phyllis said.

"You're gonna eat this late at night?"

"Yeah. Do you want to join me?" Phyllis asked as she pressed the button on her answering machine.

Beep. "Hi, Phyllis. It's Nathan. I tried your cell but couldn't get through. I hope all is well. Call me and let me know something."

Beep. "Phyllis, why in the hell did you change the locks when you know I still have things in there? Okay, you win, but let me say this: I love you. I don't have any excuses for what I did, so I won't give you any. I guess I had a lot of pent-up emotions that got the best of me. Maybe we can move forward as friends. That would be good for Zach's sake. Well, I'll call you later with my contact information. Oh, and Phyllis, I came into this relationship with love; you came into it with hate. I know we'll never be together again. I'm not sure we can, but I want to be there for Zach. Don't let hate influence your decision with him and me. He's my son and I love him. Goodbye, and take care."

I'll deal with you later, Carl, Phyllis thought as she looked at her now bare ring finger. A number of emotions washed over her—anger first and foremost, but also sadness and guilt. I can't think about this now. Another beep shook her out of her reverie.

"Phyllis, this is Prodigy. I really need to speak with you about the young man that Genesis spoke with you about, Joey Martin. Please give me a call, no matter the time."

"Prodigy loves those kids, doesn't he?" Phyllis said as if Grace didn't hear the other two messages.

"Yeah, he's really special. What kid does he want to talk to you about?" Grace already knew the story but she didn't want to let Phyllis know that.

"Some little boy that got arrested for robbery. What do you want to eat?" Phyllis asked as she turned on the big-screen television and flipped the channels until she found her BET jazz station.

"What do you have? Nothing too heavy. I'm not trying to get fat."

"What about some juicy hamburgers and greasy French fries? Just like we used to do when I was in high school on those hot summer nights."

"Sounds good," Grace said as she laughed with her sister. "But I know I'm going to pay for this blast from the past. Back then we had a high metabolism working for us."

"Speak for yourself, my metabolism is just fine," Phyllis said as she pulled out a bottle of Mylanta.

Grace laughed at her sister, then picked up the current issue of *Essence* and waited for her late-night meal.

"So how's your love life?" Phyllis asked, removing a frying pan from the bottom cabinet.

"Nonexistent. I don't know what the problem is."

"Quality of men too low for you?"

"I wouldn't say that. I met some real cool brothers over the years. But I have this issue with trust. I don't care how much a man shows me he's being for real, I don't believe him. I know I've lost a few good ones being that way. I can't say for sure but I think it's the way that Daddy was. You know, running around with all those women behind Momma's back. I guess it's been embedded in my brain that all men are liars. Even though in my heart I know that's not true."

"Well, I'm starting to learn that all men are different." Phyllis surprised herself with her comment. But it was true. Ever since the garage incident with Carl and meeting Nathan, her perspective on men was changing.

Phyllis finished up in the kitchen and headed for the den.

"Enjoy," Phyllis said as she handed Grace a plate with a big hamburger on light bread, a slice of pickle, a slice of tomato, and more than enough French fries.

"You really are trying to kill me, huh?" Grace said.

"You're the one that told me to live a little and lighten up. Now hush your mouth and eat."

"Right, lighten up, not fatten up."

"Hush, girl, and eat."

Grace smiled and took a bite of her burger. "Ohh, what did you put in this? This is good."

Phyllis just smiled and took a bite of her own sandwich.

"I guess I should explain to you what's behind those messages that you heard."

"Only if you want to."

"I want to. You're my sister, and I can't remember the last time I had someone to talk to about my problems. And God knows I have problems."

"That's what I'm here for."

"Well, I'll start with Carl." Phyllis took a deep breath and pushed the rest of her food away. "Carl and I hadn't been getting along for a very long time. I mean, we were like two ships passing in the night. Well, to make a long story short, things came to a head a few months ago. I went to this awards ceremony that my job was giving and thankfully he didn't want to go. Well, when I came home he was really drunk and attacked me in the garage. He ripped my dress and tore my underwear off. He tried to rape me. The only reason that I think he didn't do it was because Zachary woke up and stopped him. Then I got a call."

"Wait, wait. He did what?" Grace asked, stunned.

"He tried to rape me, but let me finish. I got a call letting me know that he was arrested and that I should come down there and get him out. Can you believe that? First he tries to rape me, then he wants to trade on my good name to get him out. You know I work with all of the people at the jail. So now he's trying to jeopardize my livelihood."

"Tell me you didn't get him out."

"Oh, no. After what he did I wanted him to rot in jail. But he got out somehow and called the next day with the same foolishness."

Grace thought about her older sister being attacked by her own husband and felt bad for her.

"Are you okay?" Grace asked.

"Yeah, I'm fine. Whatever it is that I had with Carl is over, and I have to refocus to make sure that Zachary is taken care of. Good thing we didn't have any joint bank accounts. The way he's been acting he probably would've wiped me out by now."

"I guess that explains the other call, huh?" Grace asked seriously.

"Yes and no. I met Nathan the same night that Carl acted up, but he was living out of town. He recently moved here, and we haven't missed an opportunity to talk or see each other. He really has helped me through this whole situation." Phyllis took a sip of her water.

"Phyllis, have you ever thought that what happened to you with Carl is payback for Daddy?"

Phyllis looked at Grace and turned away. "Are you done with your food?" She stood and grabbed her plate.

Grace nodded, and Phyllis took her plate into the kitchen. She dumped the leftovers in the trash and placed the plates in the dishwasher. She walked back into the den and took a seat beside her sister.

"Grace, I have so much to say. I can't tell you how much it hurts me that you think that I killed your father."

"Why do you always say *my* father?" Grace said, frustrated. "He was your father too."

"No, he wasn't! He met Momma when I was five years old."

"He what? Wait a minute. You and I don't have the same father?" Grace said, trying to digest this news.

"No, we don't. I never met my father. So your father is the only dad I've ever known, and he was a good man in his own way. But the father that you knew is a different man than the one I came to know."

"Wait a minute. Why didn't Momma tell us?" Grace asked.

"I don't know. I guess she thought it was best if we keep that information a little secret. Have you ever wondered why all of you guys' names start with a G like your father's and my name is Phyllis?"

"Yeah, but I thought that was something that Daddy and Momma decided to do after you were born. That doesn't mean a thing," Grace said, still looking confused.

"Well, I didn't kill your father. I didn't mourn his death but I didn't kill him."

"Why didn't you mourn his death?" Grace asked.

"Because he killed a part of me a long time ago." Phyllis sat stone-faced.

"What are you talking about?" Grace asked.

"Wait. When the doctors gave me all of the information on his rare liver disease, I realized he would spend the rest of his life as a vegetable, and I wouldn't wish sitting in a chair all day unaware of anything around me on my worst enemy. So I told the doctors not to go on with the treatment. After Momma had her nervous break-down, I was left to make all the decisions. I just did what I thought was best."

"Hmm." Grace sat stoic. She wasn't sure how she felt about Phyllis's explanation but realized holding a grudge would not move their relationship forward. "Why didn't you ever tell me about your situation?"

"Oh, everyone was so set against me by then that I just dealt with it myself. You guys were so young, I doubt if you would've under-stood. I barely understood what I had to do myself."

"Why did you hate him so much? You were always so mean to him," Grace said.

"When Momma and Grover Senior got together he was so sweet to me. I used to be so happy all the time. He was my best friend; he treated me like I was the princess of a large African vil-lage. Everything was perfect. Grover was born, then came Genesis and then you. We were the perfect family. I was about eleven years old when you were born. I remember it like it was yesterday. Your father's brother, Jack, moved in with us so we were living in some pretty tight quarters, but as kids we didn't care. Everyone slept where they could find a spot. Well, I fell asleep in the back room one night and Jack came in. Do you remember him?"

"No," Grace said.

"I don't know where everyone was but . . ." Phyllis started crying and stood to go get some tissue. She returned and sat back down beside Grace. "He came in the room where I was sleeping, and he started feeling all over me. I could smell the alcohol on his breath.

He tried to kiss me. I still remember that scratchy beard rubbing over my face. When I tried to scream, he placed his hand over my mouth really hard. I thought he would break my jawbone if I tried to move again. He lifted my dress and molested me right there in my own house." Phyllis cried uncontrollably now.

"Did you tell Momma or Daddy?"

"He told me if I told them he would kill all of my little brothers and you. I believed him because I knew he had just got out of prison. That's why he was staying with us, so he could save some money and find his own place."

"But Phyllis, if you didn't tell Daddy then why—"

"He knew. When he found out, I wanted him to kill that mean man for hurting me so bad. But all he did was make him leave the house. He said that family sticks together and I was to never mention what happened to no one. I never saw Jack again after he left, but the damage was done. I've hated black men ever since."

Grace reached over and hugged Phyllis tighter than she ever hugged anyone before. At that moment she regretted all the evil things she ever said about her sister. They held each other and cried some more.

"But you know what?" Phyllis said. "I don't hate black men anymore. After what Carl did to me, I realize that ignorance doesn't have a color. When Grover Senior didn't come to my rescue, I told Momma. But all she said was to let it go and to never tell no one. So I hated her, too, for a while, and I felt so alone for the longest time. Then I had Zachary, and he changed all of that. That little boy is the only reason I'm sane."

"You have me, too, and you have two brothers that love you. Phyllis, I'm so sorry you had to go through that. I'm so sorry." Grace couldn't stop crying.

"It wasn't your fault. Do you know, I've never told anyone that story? Over the years I've sort of repressed it. I've dealt with it by running away, joining the army, marrying a white man, and doing everything in my power to disassociate myself from anything that would remind me of that house where all this happened. But now I realize I have to deal with it if I'm ever going to move past it." Phyllis disengaged herself from Grace's embrace and wiped her eyes.

"Phyllis, I love you," Grace said.

"I love you too."

"Phyllis, if you ever need to talk about anything, and I mean anything, you let me know. I'm your sister, and that means more to me right now than anything."

"I know. You're all grown up now, huh?" Phyllis said, looking at her baby sister proudly. "Now, let's go to bed. We have to get up early and check on Momma."

"Where am I sleeping?"

"Where do you want to sleep? There's the guest room or the sofa, whatever you prefer."

"I want to sleep with you if you don't mind."

"Now, why would I mind my baby sister sleeping with me? Just don't wet the bed like you did the last time I let you sleep with me."

"That was a hundred years ago. You need to let that go."

"Some things never change," Phyllis said before walking up the stairs with Grace on her heels.

seventeen

BOOGIE NIGHT

G enesis and his siblings decided to take turns spending the night with their mother while she recovered. Genesis had agreed to drop Grace off for her tour of duty and was anxious to get her out of his truck. Tonight was the night of his bachelor party.

"Why are you rushing me?" Grace asked, knowing full well the reason for the hurry.

"Ahh, girl, come on. You know I got people waiting on me."

"Yeah, I know who you got waiting on you. You *need* to be careful and please remember that you're almost a married man," Grace said as she pulled on the door handle and stepped out of the truck.

"Take care, love. Tell Momma I'll see her in the morning," Genesis said before pulling off.

Just as he exited the hospital premises, Genesis grabbed his cell phone and called Prodigy.

"Yo, man, is everything in straight?"

"Yes, sir. It's ten o'clock. Where in the hell are you?"

"The dancers get there yet?"

"Is that all you're worried about? All of your homies are here. Ain't that enough? As a matter of fact, we've decided that we're not going to do that stripper shit. That's so played. We're going to ride around in this super stretch limo that I rented, drink some Cristal, and talk about the good ol' days. We can go to a strip club any night of the week. Are you gonna pick up Grover?"

"Grover's in rehab and stop playin' so much."

"Rehab! Grover trynna get it together, huh?"

"I guess, but damn that. I want some strippers. I ain't trynna sit around and talk to y'all fools all night unless we talking about which one of them hos was the freakiest. And you know I don't drink. So you better get me some long-legged chicken heads over there cuz I can talk to y'all bastards anytime."

"Well, you might as well stay your little horny ass at the hospital, cuz I canceled the girls. Why can't you just hang with us?"

"P, man, I hope you playing cuz if you not, you getting on my damn nerves."

"I ain't playing, man. I'm gonna help you help yourself. You got a good girl, and it's time you start acting like it."

"It's my bachelor party, and you ain't gonna fuck it up with all your righteousness. Ever since you got your little degree, you always trynna psychoanalyze some got-damn body. You had strippers at yours," Genesis yelled. He was pissed.

"Why you raising your voice?" Prodigy asked, laughing.

"Cuz, man, you get on my nerves with all your sanctified high-and-mighty bullshit. You had strippers at your little party but you sitting up here judging me. I knew I should've let somebody else set up my party."

"Well, you sure should've let somebody else do it. Plus, I'm not like you. I don't have a problem keeping my zipper up. You coming or not?" Prodigy said, trying to hold in his laughter. He was looking at about ten of Atlanta's finest strippers. Prodigy picked out a variety of beautiful ladies. Short with big breasts, tall with small breasts, African-American, Asian, Puerto Rican, Spanish, etc. Each lady had on a different color thong and bra set.

"Go to hell, P."

"You always getting mad. Calm your punk ass down. Are you coming?"

"Oh, I'm coming, and I'mma beat that ass when I get there."

"I'm shaking in my shoes."

"And after I beat that ass, I'm going to the Gentlemen's Club and have my own damn party. You can go to church," Genesis said before he hung up the phone. He was livid at Prodigy for taking this opportunity to preach. *Damn, this is f'ed up,* he thought.

Genesis had his mind set on sneaking one of those curvaceous strippers away for a private show. To hell with Terri's brothers and her cousins. Genesis had only met them a few times but they seemed to be pretty cool guys. All he needed was about fifteen minutes any-way, they would never know he was gone, especially with all of the people that he knew would be there.

Genesis cruised down Metropolitan Boulevard and did a double take. He smiled as he thought about what his next twenty minutes would be like. He turned around and pulled over to the side of the road.

"What's up, shorty? You working?" Genesis said to the tall, sexy lady in fishnet stockings, high heels, and a halter.

"What's up with you?" the lady said.

"It depends. I know what I want to be up."

"What's that?"

"Them long-ass legs of yours. You wit' that?"

"That depends on you. But I'll tell you what. I don't have all night to talk so whatchu spending?"

"I hear ya. Get in."

"How much you spending?"

"How much you cost?"

"Look, you wanna do this or not? I ain't quoting you shit. You look like a cop. How much you spending?"

Genesis could feel the lady was about to stop walking and turn in the other direction. He shook his head as he thought about how badly Prodigy had messed up his night. He was tempted to call up one of his old freak partners, but then he remembered last week when he got all giddy with Terri and called all of his old sex partners and informed them that he was off the market and to never call him again. He even deleted all of their numbers from his PalmPilot.

"I got a twenty-spot for you."

The lady stopped, put her hand on her hip, and stared at Genesis as if to say, "You must be kidding."

"Okay, I'll give you thirty but you better make that thing do some tricks."

The lady smiled as an unmarked police car swerved in front of Genesis's truck and two police officers in black jackets with the letters TASK jumped out with guns drawn.

"Get outta the car with your hands up. Move, move, move," the white officer said as he approached the driver-side door.

Genesis stepped out of his truck with his hands slightly raised. He felt his heart trying to burst through his chest.

"Oh, this is fucked up. Damn, damn, damn, ah damn. I can't believe this is happening," Genesis cursed to himself.

"Toss me your keys, lover boy," the black officer said as he peeked in the passenger side with a flashlight. "And put your hands back on the hood."

Genesis did as he was told and didn't say a word. He didn't know if he was in shock or just plain busted, but he knew words no longer meant anything.

This was the first time Genesis had ever been arrested, and he didn't like the way those cold steel handcuffs felt around his wrists.

"Do you have any identification on you?" the white officer asked.

"In my suit jacket."

"Do you have any needles or anything that might stick me in your pockets?"

"Nah." Genesis's tone was just above a whisper. He felt broken. Helpless. His promise to Terri was all he could think about.

The officer reached in Genesis's pocket and retrieved his wallet. He removed his driver's license and smirked at his name.

"With a name like Genesis you must've been out here trying to save this pretty lady from herself," the white officer said. "Have you ever heard of HIV or AIDS? That's some pretty powerful stuff. It's killing people right and left."

Genesis nodded.

"Mr. Genesis Styles, you are under arrest for soliciting a prostitute. You have the right to remain silent. If you give up that right, anything that you say can and will be used against you in a court of law. You have the right to an attorney. If you cannot afford an attorney one will be appointed to you by the courts. Do you understand your rights?" the white officer asked.

Genesis nodded as they placed him in the back of the white patrol car that had pulled up.

"That ain't fair, Trish. All that ass hanging out. I might've got caught up out here tonight myself," the black officer said as he stared openly at the undercover officer's ample assets.

"You still have time for a sexual harassment charge, or do you wanna shut up and get back in position? I could use the down time it would take to write you up—these heels are killing me," Trish said as she sashayed away in a very convincing hooker's strut.

Genesis sat in the back of the police car trying to figure out a way to get out of this mess. "Ah, do you know Phyllis Olsen?"

"Yeah, what about her?" the driving officer asked.

"That's my sister. You think you can cut me some slack?" Genesis said, praying that the officer would extend some kind of family courtesy.

"Why should I? She doesn't cut anyone else any slack. I can't stand your mean-ass sister. Now be quiet."

Genesis shook his head. He was disgusted with himself, so he sat silent for the short trip to the Atlanta Police Department. His hand-cuffs were on too tight, and he was extremely uncomfortable. His thoughts drifted to Prodigy. *If his ass wasn't trying to run my life I wouldn't be in this position. I ain't fucking with him no more,* he thought.

"Can I make a phone call?" Genesis asked once he was inside a glass-and-steel room.

"In a minute. You have to be processed," the desk sergeant said without looking up.

"How long does that take?"

"A few hours. What is it, eleven o'clock? You'll be able to use the phone by two. That's if you stop talking to me and let me do my job."

An officer led Genesis through the long process of fingerprints, mug shots, and the taking of his personal items. After all of that business was done, he was given an orange jumpsuit and a pair of white flip-flops to wear and placed in a holding cell.

"My man, you think you gonna be making bail tonight?" an older officer asked Genesis.

"Yeah, if y'all stop fucking around and let me use the phone," Genesis snapped.

"Look, son. You're the one that has yourself in a bind. I'm trying to help you. I'm a Christian man. A God-fearing man and I like to give people the benefit of the doubt. Now if you can find it in your heart to apologize to me for your use of profanity, then I might be so inclined to ask the officers to leave you down here. Because if they decide to take you upstairs, you won't be issued a bond until some-time late tomorrow. I'm waiting," the old man said in his soft voice.

"My bad, dog."

"No, no. That's not an apology and do I look like a four-legged animal? One last chance."

"I'm sorry," Genesis said.

"That's better. Use that phone over there. Wait until I turn it on." The officer pointed to a black phone in the corner.

Genesis looked at the clock on the wall and sure enough it was 2:45 in the A.M. "Damn, I hope Prodigy is home," Genesis said as he dialed Prodigy's number.

"Hello," Nina answered sleepily.

"You have a collect call from an inmate at the Atlanta detention center. Caller, state your name," the automated voice system said.

"Genesis."

"Will you accept?"

"Yes."

"Nina, is Prodigy home yet?"

"Yeah, are you okay?"

"Yeah, I left my driver's license home and they locked me up for that. Can you believe that?" Genesis stomped his foot and frowned up. He knew that was a lame lie. He had been so focused on getting a phone call that he didn't think about what he would say if Nina answered.

"Hold on. Prodigy, it's Genesis. He's in jail."

"Jail." Prodigy took the phone. "Hello."

"What's up, man? I need you to come get me out."

"Where are you?"

"Downtown. At the detention center."

"All right, I'm on the way." Prodigy hung up the telephone and got dressed.

AFTER PRODIGY LEFT, Nina picked up the phone and called Terri.

"Hey, girl. I don't know what's going on, but Genesis just called here from jail."

"Jail? What's he doing in jail?"

"He said something about a driver's license. I just thought I'd give you a call to let you know what was up."

"A driver's license. They lock you up for that? He didn't go to the bachelor party?"

"I don't think he showed up. I heard Prodigy talking on the phone to one of their friends and he said something about Genesis being mad about not having strippers or something. I don't know the whole story so don't quote me."

"Okay, girl. Thanks for the call. Anyway, which jail is he in, do you know?"

"Atlanta City, I think. Yeah, that's it," Nina said as she checked the caller ID.

"Okay, thanks for letting me know. That boy is gonna drive me crazy yet."

"A'right, girl. If you need anything, call me, okay?"

"Okay, thanks, Nina."

"No problem. Bye-bye."

" 'Bye." Terri hung up the phone and picked it right back up and called information to get the number to the Atlanta detention center. She pressed 1 to be automatically connected.

"Hello, I'm calling about a Genesis Styles. Is he there?" Terri asked.

"Hold on a minute." The female went away for a few minutes then came back. "Yeah, he's here."

"What's the charge?"

"Umm, just a second. Looks like he was arrested for solicitation."

"Solicitation?" Terri felt her heart drop a thousand feet.

"Yeah, soliciting a prostitute. Are you calling from a bonding company?"

Terri hung up the phone without answering the lady. She didn't know what to think. "That lying-ass freak." Terri placed her hands over her face and cried. She knew something was up with Genesis but she was hurt just the same. She picked up the phone and called Nina.

"Hello," Nina answered.

"He wasn't arrested for no damn license. He was arrested for trying to pick up a nasty-ass prostitute. Do you believe that?"

"Oh, my goodness. Are you okay?"

"I thought he was going to his bachelor party. He's out there trying to stick his little … I don't know. I don't know what to do. We're through. Done!"

"Well, don't do anything until you've had a chance to calm down. Maybe this was all a misunderstanding." Nina took a shot in the dark. She knew she was pushing it, but her best friend's feelings were at stake, and she wanted to project as much hope into the situation as possible.

"Nina, my wedding is in one week, and he goes out and does some dumb shit like this. Oh, I'm not marrying him. I don't even want to see him."

"Terri, try to calm down. Do you want me to come over?"

"Who's going to watch Blake?" Terri asked. She was trying hard not to cry.

"Prodigy's mother is here. Give me about twenty minutes, okay?" Nina said.

"Nah, I want to see what lie he tells when he gets here. I'm going to let him dig a hole big enough for him to crawl his wormy ass in."

"If you need me, call, okay, and don't do anything to get yourself in trouble. No one's worth that."

"Nina, can you believe this crap?"

"Hey, give him a chance to tell his side of the story before you go jumping to conclusions. This might be some sick premarital joke by one of his friends." Nina was still trying, hoping for the best. She really liked Genesis and, for his sake, was praying for a miracle.

"Yeah, I'm going to see just what this lying ass has to say. I'll call you tomorrow."

"Okay, hang on in there, girl."

"I'll talk to you later." Terri hung up and started pacing. She couldn't remember ever being this upset. "You know, God, I prayed for You to send me a sign letting me know if this marriage was the right thing to do. I guess this is Your sign to me, huh?" Terri said, talking to herself as she sat on the side of the bed. Gabrielle started crying, and Terri walked over to her and picked her up. "Well, thank God for you, little lady. I hope you never have to deal with a deceitful, conniving, unfaithful, disrespectful, lying man." Terri cried as she held Gabrielle. She changed her diaper, fed her, then placed her back in her bassinet. Another hour went by before she heard the front door ease open.

eighteen

SINS OF DADDY

G race sat at her mother's bedside in a reclining chair with a million and one thoughts going through her head. Her mother had recovered enough to carry on a half-decent conversation. Her speech was a little impaired, and she suffered from some short-term memory loss, but she was functioning at about eighty percent of her normal capacity.

"Baby, you asleep?" Mrs. Styles said in just above a whisper.

"No, ma'am."

"Genesis told me about Jalen. God is good, ain't He?"

"Yes, He is. All the time."

"You a'right? You look worried."

"I'm just thinking."

"Well, what you thinkin' about?"

"A lot of things, but mostly Daddy."

"What about your daddy?" Mrs. Styles did her best to sit up in the bed.

"Momma, Phyllis told me that Daddy was not her father. Why didn't you tell us?"

"What difference would it have made?"

"I don't know, but don't you think that's something that we needed to know?"

"No! If I thought that y'all needed to know, then I would've told you," Mrs. Styles said and lay back down in a manner that told Grace that she didn't want to talk about the matter anymore.

"So that's it. You want me to just leave it at that?" Grace asked, reading her mother's body language.

"Yeah, chile, you need to let sleeping dogs lie. Didn't Phyllis have a good daddy? Well then." Momma Styles answered her own question.

"Momma, I don't want you to get upset, so I'll shut up."

"I ain't upset. Why would I be upset about God blessing me with a good man after the first one ran out and left me with a child to raise?"

"Okay, Momma," Grace said as she twisted her lips.

"Why you lookin' like that? You got something else on your mind? I mean, let's get all your little questions answered. Ain't no telling how long God got for me to be here."

Grace was contemplating whether to ask her mother about the molestation incident with Phyllis, but she decided that she better leave that alone.

"I see you and Phyllis been talking. That's good, but y'all need to let your father rest. He was a good man. You should be proud to have had a daddy like Grover. Ain't many chillun can say they had a daddy that bent over backwards for them to have the best of everything."

Grace frowned and shook her head. She thought her mother had to be the most naive woman she ever met. But she relaxed when she realized that she, too, once thought that her father could do no wrong.

"Momma, stop. Daddy was a good provider, and I'll give him that, but he wasn't a good husband. He—"

"Now you wait just a minute, little lady. What me and my husband did was none of y'all's business. That's always been your problem, you always got ya nose meddlin' in somebody else's troubles. That's why you don't have a husband now."

Grace sat silent for a moment to let her mother's words sink in.

"When you can keep a man for more than a week then you can start judging me. I kept mine for twenty years before the good Lord took him home," Mrs. Styles continued. She couldn't believe the audacity of her youngest daughter, bringing up her marital business, especially while she was lying up in the hospital bed.

Grace could tell she was upsetting her mother, but she didn't like how she was being attacked.

"Momma, I'm just trying to get some closure."

"Well, close your damn mouth. Don't know why you wanna be scandalizing your daddy's name anyway."

"I'm not trying to scandalize his name, but what's wrong with me asking? You just said I could ask you."

"That was before you started asking stuff that ain't none of your business."

"Okay, Momma. I'm through. You just try to get some rest," Grace said as she stood up and walked toward the door.

"Where you going?"

"I'm going to the snack room. I'll be right back."

"Come here. Sit down." Mrs. Styles's tone had softened.

Grace did as she was told and sat back down in the recliner chair.

"Your daddy wasn't perfect but he was a good man. You hear me? He had a good heart, and he always loved his kids. And I mean Phyllis, too, when I say his kids. Now I know you trynna get at his running around with different women. But I realized a long time ago that we all have our own crosses to bear. That was his, not mine. Now why you so worried about your father right now is beyond me."

"Momma, do you know why I don't have a man? It's not because I talk too much, that may be true, but that's not the reason. It's because I cannot trust men because of the things I saw my daddy do with my own two eyes. Things that ... even at a young age I knew was wrong."

"What kind of things?" Mrs. Styles asked, almost daring Grace to speak.

"He use to take us with him while he visited his different women. We would play outside with whatever kids were around, but one day I had to use the bathroom so I went into the house, and I saw Daddy in the bed with this lady. He saw me and told me to go back outside and play. He acted like he wasn't doing anything wrong. He didn't even bother to tell me not to tell you," Grace said.

Mrs. Styles sat silent for a moment, absorbing what she had known for years. "What you gonna do about it? Baby, I don't mean to sound evil, but what can you do about it? Even if your father was still living, there is nothing you can do about it. The past is just that, the past. You have to live your life for you. Stop judging every man you meet on what your father did. You think I'm dumb? I ain't ever been dumb, blind either. I knew what he was doing. But there are times when you gotta put your family first and let a man be a man."

"That's not being a real man, Momma."

"Hush your mouth. You can't tell me nothing about what a man is. If you shut your mouth sometime you'll learn something. Some-times you have to put your family first. I don't have an education like none of y'all, so I put my feelings aside and thought about my kids. If your daddy wanted to run all around the country spreading his business all over, I couldn't have cared less. My joy came from knowing my kids had food in their stomachs and clothes on their backs and a place to call home. So no, I didn't put up no fuss with your father about his frolicking. Seeing y'all now I have mixed feel-ings. Sometimes I'm real proud of y'all but there are times when I peel the onion back a little deeper. That's when I wished I would've taken y'all and ran like the wind. All of y'all got a lot of your daddy's ways. Grover handles his problems the same way his daddy did. He turns to the bottle." Mrs. Styles never did accept the fact that Grover was using more than alcohol.

"Genesis is running around here about to get married and knowing he ain't ready to settle down. He got that from his daddy. Phyllis." Mrs. Styles shook her head. "My poor child. If she could get out of that skin of hers, she would. She's been through so much. Things I would never wish on anybody, nevertheless my own child." Mrs. Styles took a breath. She looked as if she wanted to cry when some memories of her eleven-year-old Phyllis came back. Mrs. Styles took a moment to fight off the anger and rage she felt when she found out that some man had touched her child improperly.

"Momma, Phyllis told me what happened. She wanted Daddy to be there for her."

Mrs. Styles closed her eyes and slowly shook her head. "Go on and get that snack, baby."

Grace sat silent for a moment, unable to move. Somehow she found the strength to stand and take her mother's advice.

GRACE WENT INTO the snack room and picked up the phone to call Phyllis.

"Hey, did I wake you up?"

"No, I'm sitting up here going over some cases. How's Momma doing?"

"She's fine. We just had a talk."

"About?"

"Daddy."

"And what did you discover about your daddy dearest?"

"She knew all about him," Grace said, still not believing that her mother could stay with a man she knew was cheating on her.

"Grace, you have to understand Momma. She is one of those

women who felt like she had to have a man. She felt incomplete without one. So she would always turn a blind eye to any kind of conflict just for the sake of having a man."

"I don't know. I just can't see staying in an emotionally neglected relationship just to say I have a man."

"Women do it every day. I did it. It gets a lot easier when you have a kid. But we have to learn to let the negative things in our life go, or we'll just repeat the cycle or live a very unfulfilling life. I'm finally learning that."

"Yeah, we were just talking about how Grover and Genesis are just like Daddy but in different ways. I don't know."

"It wasn't just them, it was us too. Did the evening doctor come by yet?" Phyllis asked, changing the subject.

"Yeah, he said she might be going home in a day or so."

"Good. Well, I gotta get some work done." The phone beeped. "Wait a minute. Who is this calling me at this time of night?"

"Must be Nathan," Grace teased.

"No, because he's here." Phyllis smiled. "Hold on."

"All right then. No, you go and grab your line. I'll talk to you tomorrow," Grace said.

"Okay, 'bye." Phyllis clicked over to the other line. "Hello."

"Mrs. Phyllis Olsen. This is Sherry Martin. I hate to call you this time of night but I'm desperate."

"Sherry Martin?" Phyllis didn't know the lady, but it was obvious the lady knew her. "What can I do for you, Mrs. Martin?"

"My son is in jail. He's a good boy, and if he goes to prison our whole family is gonna suffer."

"Who is your son?" Phyllis asked to be sure. She had been looking over the case file of Joey Martin since Prodigy had called, but still hadn't changed her mind about his sentencing request.

"His name is Joey Martin."

"I'm looking at his file. He's committed a serious crime. What do you suggest I do?" Phyllis had plenty of experience dealing with irate and irrational family members who didn't care what the accused had done. All they wanted was for their folks to come home. But when she asked those same family members what they would do, most stammered.

"I don't know. He's a good boy and his sister done 'bout gone crazy without him around. Hold on. Do I look like I got money for a damn TV? You see I'm on the phone," Mrs. Martin yelled at someone in the background.

"Mrs. Martin, this may not be my place, but what's your status? Are you working?"

"Not right now, but I'm looking."

"Are you using drugs?"

"What that got to do with my son?"

"It has everything to do with your son. He's a minor, and if he doesn't have a stable home life then we're just delaying the inevitable. Jail time for him is a definite possibility. Now, if you aren't willing to make changes in your life then you might be losing more than your son."

"Oh, fuck you. You high-and-mighty bitch. You let my son outta that damn jail," Mrs. Martin yelled as she lost all of her patience. "I hate niggers like you, sitting back judging my baby. You cracker wanna-be. When was the last time you ever came to where we live?"

"If this is your way of asking for a favor, then you need to work on your people skills. Mrs. Martin, you have a good night." Phyllis hung up and tried to calm herself. Lately she'd been feeling the same way about herself as Mrs. Martin thought. The last thing she ever wanted to be was a person who turned her back on those who needed her. That was the very reason she went into law. But now she was starting to realize that her people needed her in a different way.

"Are you all right?" Nathan asked. He sat in a nearby chair and couldn't help but overhear her conversation.

"Yeah. I'm fine. Why is it that people think that their kids can commit a crime and not have to suffer the consequences?"

"Joey Martin?"

"Yeah, that was his mother. I know she's upset but she called me all sorts of foul names."

"You've been practicing law long enough to know how parents are about their kids," Nathan said, as he was interrupted by the telephone.

"Hello," Phyllis said.

"Mrs. Olsen, I'm sorry about the way I acted and what I said to you. It's just that almost everybody in my family is in prison or dead. We ain't got nobody left. I just got out of prison after doing five years. Prison ain't done nothin' for me but made me worse. I don't want that to happen to my baby. I'm trying to get myself together, it's just hard," Sherry Martin said.

Phyllis thought she heard her sniffle but she knew that had to be a cold. Phyllis had become acutely aware of the sound of hopelessness and despair. Phyllis could tell Sherry Martin was barely hanging on, and her children were her lifelines. No, there would be no tears falling from the eyes of a woman who had obviously witnessed more than her share of pain.

"Mrs. Martin, do you know where my office is?"

"I got the paperwork at home. Is the address on there to where you is?"

"Yes, it is. I want you to come and see me on Monday morning, and we'll see if we can't get you some help. I'm not interested in putting a Band-Aid over the problem. Your son committed a serious offense but I'll make sure that he doesn't do any prison time, if you promise me you'll commit to an in-house twelve-step program. That's the only deal I'm offering. Take it or leave it."

"Lady, if I was near you, I'd kiss you and I ain't even freaky like that. I love my babies and I'll do a fifty-step program if that means my boy coming home. God bless you."

"Monday morning and God bless you too."

"Guess what I just did?"

"What's that?"

"I just broke my pipe."

"I'm sorry to hear that," Phyllis said, confused.

"No, I meant to do it. It's a crack pipe. I'm gonna beat this thing and get my family back."

"Well, I have all the confidence that you will. Good night, Mrs. Martin."

"'Bye, Mrs. Olsen, and thanks for speaking with me again after all of the nasty things I said to you."

"Not a problem, I've been called worse. You just be there on Monday morning."

"I'll be there, my family is depending on it."

"Hey. Mrs. Martin? How did you get my home phone number?"

"Lady, when a girl's back is against the wall, you find a way."

"I'll remember that."

nineteen

FACE THE MUSIC

Genesis paced back and forth in the holding cell, waiting on his name to be called. Prodigy should've been there by now. *He picks a fine damn time to run late,* Genesis thought, frowning.

"Hey, big man, you got a smoke?" an old man asked Genesis.

Genesis ignored the old man, just as he had the last fifty times the same man asked him that question.

"Ain't no need to be mad. You got caught. Do ya time like a man. I bet you done called somebody to come pick you up, didn't ya?" the old man said.

"Man, will you shut the hell up?" Genesis said, clearly frustrated with the old man and his entire situation.

"No, I won't shut the hell up. Time goes by faster when I talk. What they get you for?" the man asked, as if he were talking to a longtime friend.

Genesis didn't respond. He gave the toothless old man with the scraggly beard his best "leave me alone" expression.

"Well, young blood, I already know what you in for. I know everything. You one of them pretty boys. One might think that you didn't have to buy no pussycat, but then again you're probably spoiled as hell. Use to having your way. Well, I bet you 'bout shit in

your pants when them Red-Dogs jumped out on you. Didn't you?"
The old man laughed.

Genesis shook his head and let out a slight chuckle at the sight
of the old man having a good time at his expense. Then he heard his
name being called over the intercom.

"There ya go, young blood. You gotta laugh at this shit. Funky-
ass police gonna lock somebody up for spending their own
money on somebody else's pussycat. That don't make no sense,
huh? Seems like you ought to be able to sell ya own ass if ya
wanna."

Genesis waited for the deputy to come down and let him out of
the holding cell. He didn't respond to the old man, but somehow he
had struck a nerve when he called him spoiled.

Genesis did all the things he needed to do in order to be out-
processed. He was given back his personal items and made to sign a
few papers before he was on his way.

"Damn, man, what took you so long?" Genesis snapped at
Prodigy as they walked out to Prodigy's truck.

"What you think I had to do? Say I was here for you and they
would let you out? I've been down here for two hours trynna get
your punk ass out."

"Well, good. Cuz it's your fault. If you wasn't trying to preach
and change me every five minutes I wouldn't be in this shit."

"Man, I should punch you in your damn mouth," Prodigy said
with a stern face. "You got to be the most self-centered asshole I've
ever met. Nothing is ever your fault. When will you learn that the
world doesn't revolve around you? I gotta get up out of my bed and
leave my family to come and pick you up and you screaming it's my
fault." Prodigy took a deep breath and tried to regain some compo-
sure. "I was playing with you about not having strippers at your
bachelor party."

"Man, why you play so much?" Genesis really felt like a fool then.

Something told him that Prodigy was joking, but that was right when he saw the undercover prostitute.

"Look man, we gotta roll. I gotta get home cuz Blake's asthma is acting up and I still gotta run by the store to get him a pump. You better come on or you gonna have to walk to the impound."

"Whoa, whoa, you can't take a minute? I need to talk to you about some things," Genesis said as he jumped in the passenger seat and closed the door.

"What you wanna talk about?"

"Man, I messed up for real this time. How am I gonna keep this from Terri? I know Nina got on the phone and called her as soon as I hung up," Genesis said.

"Yeah, she sure did. I heard her on the phone when I was walking out. So whatchu gonna do?" Prodigy asked as he pulled behind the building where Genesis's truck had been stored since it was impounded.

"I don't know. I've been trying to come up with something good to tell her but I keep coming up short. I pick a fine time to run short on lies."

"Well, I'm done giving advice. You gotta make your own call on this one, my man. But I am sorry that you got locked up because of one of my jokes," Prodigy said.

"Nah, it wasn't your fault. Look, dog, I'mma holla at you later. Thanks for getting me out of there," Genesis said. He got out of the truck and leaned on the door. "Listen for the phone. I might need a place to stay tonight. Knowing Terri, all my things will be across the lawn if I can't come up with a good lie."

"I'll be listening. But you'll be a'right."

"I hope so, but you still listen in case she puts my ass out. Ain't that something, I'm scared of being put out of my own damn house," Genesis said, shaking his head.

"I thought I told you that wasn't your house anymore—it's Terri's. You go on and get outta here. I'll holla at you later."

Prodigy stayed and waited until Genesis picked up his truck. They flashed their lights at each other and pulled off in different directions. Prodigy went home to his family and Genesis headed home to face the drama he'd created.

As Genesis drove his truck home he couldn't shake the feeling he was having in the pit of his stomach. He hadn't felt this sinking sensation since he lost his father. His thoughts were on Terri—what would she do? While he was in jail, he thought of a million lies to tell her to cover for his absence, but Prodigy and the old man's words rang in his ears. *Spoiled, self-centered. Damn,* he thought. *Everybody can't be lying on me.*

Genesis drove home as slowly as possible. He was glad to be free, but he didn't know what awaited him behind the walls of his once-peaceful home. The uncertainty was killing him. He pulled up in his driveway and slowly stepped out of his truck. The light was on in the house. He stepped up on the porch and slid his key into the door lock, but couldn't bring himself to turn the handle.

Genesis stepped away from the door and took a deep breath. Jail had been his absolute lowest point. And all for a piece of booty that wouldn't have meant a thing to him, even if he did get it.

Jail had also given him time to do a little soul searching, and everything came back to Terri. She was his world and he had to admit that he didn't keep it real with her. Prodigy's words were starting to take effect. How could he treat a woman who meant so much like she was worthless? Genesis closed his eyes and fell to his knees, and for the first time in more than ten years he prayed. It had been so long since he had had a conversation with God that he didn't really know what to say or where to start. But somehow he found a few words.

"God, please forgive me for straying from You. I was raised on Your word but I let the Devil have his way with me. Please forgive me. Will You take me back and watch over me? God, I'm sorry for everything. I really don't wanna lose Terri. She means so much to me. Please take my selfishness away and replace it with whatever You'd like for me to be. And God, please watch over my momma, make her well again. God, I don't wanna be married but still looking, so if You can find it in Your heart to let Terri forgive me, I give You my word that I'll never do her wrong." Genesis stood and turned around just in time to see Terri's shadow walk away from the window.

Genesis walked into the house and called Terri's name. She walked into the living room.

"Where's Jalen?" Genesis asked nervously.

"Phyllis came and picked him up. He's spending the night with Zachary."

"What? Not Phyllis." Genesis was surprised at his older sister's actions, but Terri's expression told him now was not the time for small talk.

"I'm sorry," Genesis said, trying his best to gain some sympathy.

"You took the words right out of my mouth because you're about the sorriest man I've ever laid eyes on."

"Terri, I screwed up," Genesis pleaded.

"Yeah, you did," Terri screamed. "We're suppose to get married in one week, and you're out there trying to have sex with some hooker. You didn't think about what God-awful disease you could've brought home to me, did you? No, cuz all you think about is having sex. Doesn't matter the consequence, just as long as you get some, huh? You think you're so slick, don't you? Well, I'll tell you what. I'm not marrying your slick ass. Fuck you," Terri said, and stormed back into the bedroom and slammed the door.

Genesis knew to leave her alone and not push it. He sat on the couch and tried to make sense of this evening that was supposed to be a send-off from his closest friends into married life.

Now the wedding was off and he had spent the first night in his twenty-nine years on earth in jail. How did it come to this? The old man's words came back. *Spoiled.* What was there about him that made a total stranger see right through him? Genesis had a million questions going through his head, and only he knew the answers. He would have to do a little more soul searching.

TERRI WENT INTO her bedroom and cried her eyes out. She picked up the phone and called her mother.

"Perrins' residence."

"Momma, it's me," Terri said through tears.

"Hey, honey, are you all right?"

"Momma, the wedding is off. Genesis was arrested tonight for trying to pick up a prostitute."

"A prostitute? Well, my, my. Well, honey, I don't know what to tell you. What was Genesis thinking about?"

"That's just it. He wasn't thinking. At least he wasn't thinking about me."

"Well, what did he say?"

"Ol', he's just trying to do what he always does when he screws up. He's so sorry now. Well, he should've thought about that before he did what he did."

"Well, baby, I'm gonna surprise you. You know I've never been a Genesis fan but I think you should try and work through this. That's what relationships are about, ups and downs. This is just one of the downs. Sometimes it takes something like this for people to realize what they have. You've done things that you're not proud of. Well, this is one of those times for him. At least he has owned up to his mistake. That should count for something."

"But Momma, how can I see past the disrespect? He blatantly looked beyond me like I didn't exist. How can you recover from that?"

"Ol', my child, the heart will surprise you. It breaks but it heals. You just have to give yourself permission to let it. This will never happen again if he's truly sorry, and you know if he is. Like I said, I never really liked him but I've been running your life since you were born. I realize that now. You're a grown woman, and whether I want to or not, I have to let you go. Do you love him?" Terri's mother was on the other line, shaking her head. She said the words that she thought she needed to say in order to let Terri know that she was backing off, but inside she was thinking, *God, please let my daughter realize that Genesis is a no-good dog.*

"Yeah, but Momma, I don't know. I know everything is not going to be perfect but this is just plain ridiculous."

"Get you some rest. Go to sleep, and when you wake up in the morning, try talking about it again."

"Okay. Good night, Momma."

"You pray about it. God will put it on your heart what to do," Mrs. Perrin said, saying her own prayer that Terri would pack up her things and run for the hills.

"I know. I'll call you tomorrow. I love you."

"I love you too."

Terri hung up the phone and cried some more.

twenty

SOUL SEARCHING

G enesis leaned back on the sofa and ran his hand through his hair. He was contemplating his next move when the telephone rang.

"Hello," Genesis said, lifting up the phone on the first ring.

"Yo, man, you up?" Grover said.

"Yeah, I'm up. What's happening?"

"Did Terri tell you that I called?"

"Nah, I just got in."

"Look here, I know it's late and I ain't supposed to be on the phone anyway. But I need to see ya."

"When?"

"Soon as possible, can you make it up here around nine?"

"Is everything a'right?"

"Yeah, I just got a few things I need to talk to you about."

"That's cool. How you getting along at the place?"

"Man, Phyllis got me up in this bougie-ass place with a bunch of bougie-drunks and drug heads. How you gonna be bougie and you strung out? Anyway, how was the party?"

"Everything was cool, I'll see you at nine, I'm tired," Genesis said, too embarrassed to tell anyone about his incarceration.

"Okay, tell Jalen I said hi. I know you think I don't care about my little dude, but I do. Anyway, we'll talk a little later."

"I'll give Jalen your message."

"Peace out."

"Later."

Genesis stood and headed for the shower. After the night he'd had, all he wanted to do was wash all his sins away. He looked at the clock. It read 5:06. That gave him a few hours to try and sleep before he had to go and visit Grover.

Genesis eased open the door to the master bedroom and noticed that Terri was still up and thumbing through a magazine. She made a disgusted face when they made eye contact and went back to her magazine. Genesis tried to see if Terri was reading a wedding magazine, figuring if it was, there was still some hope, but as he walked over to his underwear drawer and got a better view he saw that it was a *Black Enterprise*.

Genesis didn't say a word as he retrieved his underclothes and a towel. He figured Terri didn't want to hear anything that he had to say right about now, and it would be in his best interest to give her all the space she needed.

Genesis couldn't put a finger on it but something told him that things weren't over between the two of them. He grabbed the rest of his things and walked into the bathroom, gently closing the door behind him.

After his shower, Genesis cuddled up on the sofa and set the alarm on his watch for eight o'clock. Little did he know, he wouldn't need the alarm. For the rest of the dark hours, all Genesis had coming to him was a lot of tossing and turning. He brainstormed and tried to figure out why his life was spiraling out of control.

Genesis's thoughts drifted back to his prewedding counseling session with Dr. Ben and how women raised their daughters to take care of themselves and to put themselves in a position where no man could control their lives. He thought about himself and what he was taught. All of his life, people made him feel like he was something special because of the number of ladies who were attracted to him. He remembered his father sitting at their kitchen table with all his drinking buddies on Saturday mornings, bragging on how many women he had been with. His daddy didn't seem to care if his mother overheard him talking up his conquests or not. Genesis reflected on one particular morning that changed his perspective on women. He was only eight years old but the lesson he learned set the tone for the rest of his life.

"Genesis, come here, boy," Grover Senior had called out to his youngest son.

"Yes, Daddy," the eight-year-old Genesis answered.

"What's this I hear about you crying over some girl at school?"

Genesis just lowered his head. He knew that one of his friends must have sold him out. Genesis made a mental note to find out which one told his secret and kick his butt.

"I wasn't crying," Genesis lied.

"That's not what I heard. Listen here, son. You don't ever let a woman make you cry. And the way you do that is to never get too close to them. Part of being a man is being in control. If you feel yourself falling in love with one, get you another one, that way your little girlfriends will know that you don't need 'em. When a woman controls your emotions she controls you, and a man without control ain't a man. Little girls are just like grown women. They always want what they can't have. So if you keep your heart from 'em, then you'll always have the upper hand. Falling in love is for old folks. You have all the fun you want while you're young. Now go and play, but always remember what I told you," Grover Senior said as he slapped his son on his back. "How many lil ladies you got anyway?"

"Two," Genesis lied, figuring that's what his father wanted to hear.

"Boy, you're a Styles and I know you can do better than that. You got to be nickel slick. Get you some more, but the trick is, you gotta let all of 'em think they're number one. You need at least five, one for every day of the week. You can rest on the weekends." Grover Senior was joking with his son and laughed with his friends when the young Genesis said he'd get three more with no problem. Little did Grover Senior know, but the young Genesis took his father's word as the gospel.

Genesis soaked up every line that ever left his father's mouth and studied his actions to a tee. When Grover Senior went for his Sunday drives, Genesis would always be there with him. He would visit all the ladies that his father was seeing outside of his mother. Genesis never felt bad for his mother; he was too busy feeling proud of his father.

But now, as he lay on the sofa, wallowing in his own pity, he asked himself, why did the double standard exist? How *would* he act if Terri was arrested for trying to buy a man for a few minutes of pleasure? He shook his head at the thought and tried to wipe the mental scene of Terri being with another man out of his mind. Genesis wanted to get up and beg Terri to forgive him, but his pride stood in the way of him ever leaving the sofa.

AFTER THE NIGHT from hell, Genesis was happy to see the daylight creep through the miniblinds in the den where he'd mentally abused himself all night. He sat up on the sofa and shook his head. *I hope today is a better day,* he thought as he stood and walked back to his bedroom. He peeked his head in on Terri. She sat up when she heard the door open.

"I'm going to see Grover and coming right back. You or Gabrielle need anything?" Genesis said, trying to be as nice as possible.

"What are you gonna bring me back? AIDS, herpes, syphilis—or maybe I'll get lucky and just get the clap. No, I don't want anything from you," Terri shot back as she tried to hold in the tears. She could've sworn that she cried all of them out last night. She looked over in the baby bassinet to check on Gabrielle and lay back down.

"Terri, I'm sorry. What can I do to fix this?" Genesis asked as he looked hard to see if Terri was receptive to talking.

Terri ignored his apology, so Genesis eased the door shut and leaned on the wall in the hallway outside their bedroom. He didn't know which way to turn or what to do. He was truly sorry for his behavior and knew in his heart that if Terri gave him another chance, he'd never cheat again.

Genesis walked out of the house and sat in his truck. As he headed out to the highway, he couldn't shake that sinking feeling in the pit of his stomach. Never in his life had he ever felt so lost as when he thought about Terri leaving him. For the first time in the two years he and Terri had been dating, he realized the true meaning of love. He didn't want to be without Terri, and now he had to do everything within his power to convince her of that.

Genesis pulled up at the rehabilitation center where Grover was being treated and stepped out of his truck.

"I'm here to see Grover Styles Junior."

"Please sign this log and take the elevator to the third floor. He's in 302."

"Thank you." Genesis signed the log and walked over to the elevator.

Just as he pressed the up arrow, he was tapped on the shoulder.

"Hey, boy, what you doing here so early?" Grace asked.

"Me, what you doing here?"

"I was just over there seeing Momma and decided to stop by here before I went home. You got bags under your eyes. I guess I don't need to know how the party went, huh?" Grace said, looking at Genesis with accusatory eyes.

"Come here." Genesis walked with Grace over to the seating area and sat down. "I had a bad night last night."

"Did you sleep with one of them strippers?" Grace asked.

"No. I did something worse than that."

"What did you do?" Grace asked as she sat up in her chair.

"Grace, now, I wouldn't tell you this if I wanted to hear a lecture, so could you try not to be Momma and go back to being my sister for a minute?"

Grace relaxed her posture and nodded.

"Last night I think I made the biggest mistake in my life. No, I know I did. I got arrested."

"Arrested!" Grace almost screamed before catching herself. "Arrested for what, Genesis?"

"Soliciting a prostitute."

Disappointment was all over Grace's face and it seemed as if all of the life rushed out her body. "Why did you do that?"

"I wasn't trying to get arrested, damn. It was this undercover sting and I just got caught up."

"No, I mean why did you even go out trying to get a hooker? You're about to get married."

"*Was* about to get married. Terri found out about it."

"Oh, Genesis, this is bad. This is really bad. What are you gonna do?"

"I don't know. She won't talk to me. I wanna let her know that I would never do anything like that again, but she ain't trynna hear nothing I got to say."

"I can't say I blame her. The wedding is next week. Dag, Genesis."

"What can I do?"

"Unless you're really ready to make a total commitment to Terri, I wouldn't do a thing. She doesn't deserve to be treated like you're treating her. I'm not trying to sound like Momma. I'm trying to be a friend."

"But I am ready. I just don't know what to do."

"Genesis, Terri loves you but she's not a fool. If you want this relationship to work, then you'll have to get out your kneepads, big brah, and do whatever you gotta do to let her know that it's all about her. She's probably devastated. I know I would be if I was about to get married and found out some mess like this."

"Yeah, I know, I know, I know." Genesis fell back in his chair and put his hands over his eyes. He wiped his tears away and spoke with eyes closed. "But Grace, people make mistakes. I'm sorry, but what can I do if she's not trying to hear anything I got to say?"

"You have to make her listen—not physically make her, but do whatever you have to do. The love she has for you didn't just up and disappear. It's still there."

"Well, let me go see this boy. He called me about four o'clock this morning saying he had something he wanted to talk about."

"Yeah, he told me all about it last night. That's why I dropped by here this morning to tell him I love him. He's about to blow your mind."

"Damn, is that bad or good?"

"Just go on upstairs and talk to him. Call me if you need anything. Tell Grover I'll check back with him later," Grace said as she reached up and hugged Genesis. "Good luck with Terri."

"You know I prayed last night for the first time since I don't know when."

"Praise God." Grace looked surprised. "You must really be sorry. Keep praying. It'll all work out. I'll see ya."

" 'Bye, Grace," Genesis said as he pressed the button again.

Genesis stepped off the elevator and tried to locate Grover's room. After a few turns here and there, he found himself tapping at Room 302.

"Come in," Grover said as he sat on the edge of the bed in his navy blue pajamas.

"Hey there, man. How you doing?"

"Good, good."

"Grace said hello. She was downstairs but she went on home."

"Okay, tell her hi. How's Jalen doing?"

"Good, I guess. He spent the night with Phyllis."

"Yeah, that's right. Terri told me. My mind is getting bad. I think they taking me off one drug just to put me on another one. Goddamn government's way of getting in on the profits of the drug game. They figure if you're gonna use drugs you might as well get it from them."

"I see you been thinking up here," Genesis said as he took a seat in a chair by the window.

"Nothing else to do."

"So what's up? What do you have to talk about so bad that you got to call me at four in the morning?"

Grover walked over to the window and stared out at the tall trees and pretty grass.

"You know, life is crazy. Here I am thirty-five years old and don't have a pot to piss in but I feel blessed. It did something to me, seeing Momma in the hospital like that. We already lost Daddy, and I don't know what I'd do if we lost Momma. Ya know I miss those days when you and me were tight. When we were all tight."

"Yeah, me too," Genesis said, nodding slowly.

"I've been clean for what, five days, and I feel like I'm about to die. Man, withdrawal symptoms are a muthafucka. You know, the funny thing about crack is that it keeps you chasing something that you can never have. Ever since I took my first drag from that pipe more than ten years ago, I've been searching for that same high that I got the first time, and I can't seem to get it. And you know what? I won't *ever* get it."

"What happened to you, Grover? I mean, why did you ever try crack?"

"That's why I called you here, baby brah. I gotta get this out in the open with the folks I care about. You know they say talking helps ease the pain, but every time I think about the things I need to say, I wanna get high," Grover said as he let out a slight chuckle and walked over to the other side of the room.

"Back before Jalen was born, I was working at this job doing construction in Chicago. That's where I went when I left. I just needed to do my own thing. Ya know, be my own man. Anyway, they laid us off. Man, I must've looked for another job for about three, four months straight. Then I met Jalen's mom. She was a teacher, believe it or not. Anyway, something happened at her job, and she ended up leaving. So she was jobless, and whatever it was that she got fired for she couldn't work in the Chicago school system for a minute. So now both of our asses were out of work.

"Then one day Sara came home with a bundle of crack. She said that we were going to sell it until we could get back on our feet. Well, everything was all good for a minute but then I guess Sara's curiosity got the best of her. I guess she just had to see what was so good about that little piece of rock that had people willing to sell their mommas. In a matter of a few weeks, Sara went from this beautiful woman to a walking demon. She stopped combing her hair, stopped washing. She didn't care about anything but that pipe.

"To make matters worse, she was about six months pregnant with Jalen. I did everything possible to hold us together. I went back to work, but every day when I came home, it was like walking into hell. Folks were banging on my door talking about Sara sold them a package of soap and they were gonna kill her. Ah, man, it was bad. But that ain't the worst part.

"I came home from work one day and saw all of this blood all over the carpet and in the bathtub. I thought this dumb broad done killed herself and the baby. I banged on the next-door neighbor's door, and they told me she went to the hospital. I get to the hospital, and she'd already had the baby, and of course he was addicted to crack. Up to this point I'd never smoked crack a day in my life. Anyway the hospital checked Sara into involuntary rehab. I told the people that I was the father, and I'd take care of Jalen. They didn't care one way or the other. They damn near threw Jalen at me when they took him off all those machines. Man, all he did was cry. That boy cried all day and night. He cried and cried and cried some more." Grover smiled at the memory as if those were the pleasant times.

"His body was looking for that cocaine," Genesis added as he listened intently.

"Right. That's why I just blocked it out. I would hold him all night long until I fell asleep. After a while the crying didn't bother me. I would wake up in the morning, take him to the old lady that lived next door, and go to work. One day when I showed up to pick Jalen up after I got off work, the old lady looked at me like I was crazy. She told me that Sara came and picked him up. Man, I damn near broke my leg running down them stairs trying to find my son.

"It didn't take long to find them. She was at this place the drug addicts called the Space Needle, a crack house. I walked over to the place and went inside and damn near threw up from the stench. It smelled like the worst combination of human funk and human waste that you could ever think of and in the middle of all these drug heads and crack dealers was Sara. She was on her knees giving some guy a blow job while he held Jalen. I lost it. It took every inch of control I could muster not to kill everyone in that house. But for some reason, I remained cool enough to walk over and grab Jalen. That's when the shit hit the fan.

"The dealer that was getting a blow job pulled out his gun and pointed it at me. He told me that Sara had sold Jalen for a fifty-dollar slab of rocks and a blow job. I told him that he would have to shoot me if he thought that he was getting my son. And he did. He shot me right here." Grover held up his shirt and pointed to his side, where he showed Genesis a bullet scar. "I heard the shot, then I felt this hot sensation on my side. All I could think about was not letting go of my son. But I passed out. When I woke up I was laying in my own blood in an alley behind the Space Needle. I crawled out onto the sidewalk and somebody called an ambulance. I stayed in the hospital for about a week.

"After I got out I went looking for Jalen. Everyone knew me on the street as a stand-up kind of guy, and they pointed me right to the nut that had my son. I found out that Jalen was with this big-time drug dealer that had a sexual preference for kids. Freaky bastard!" Grover said as if he was talking to the drug dealer himself.

"Anyway, I found out where the dude was staying and just kicked his door in. I probably would be dead today but I surprised his ass. I beat the living shit out of him. I kept hitting this fool until I ran out of breath. I hit him until his face was a bloody mess." Grover stopped talking as the memories of that day came back in full view. He closed his eyes and looked up in the sky. "Man, I killed the dude. I didn't mean to kill him, I just couldn't stop hitting him. When I heard Jalen crying I followed his sound and man, my son was in the fucking dryer. I guess the dude was trying to muffle the sound of his cries. When I picked Jalen up and put him on my chest he stopped crying. I guess he knew everything was okay."

"Hold up. Why didn't you call the police after dude shot you?" Genesis asked.

"Brah, the police on the South Side of Chicago ain't about to come into no crack house. Them dudes so burned out that they don't wanna hear about a country dude that got involved with a crackhead. When I got shot, do you think I got a visit from one of them investigating the shooting? Hell no."

"That's foul. What about for killing that man, did the police ever come looking for you?"

"This drug dealer was not the kind of guy that anyone would spend much time looking for his killer. I probably did society a favor. Like I said, he was a child molester. The younger they were the more he liked them."

"There are some evil folks in this world," Genesis said, still stunned at what his brother had just told him.

"Well, I stayed in Chicago for about another two or three weeks. You would think that after all the pain that crack had caused me I would've run from the sight of it, but after what I did to old dude, I wanted to die myself. I ain't no killer. I couldn't get over the fact that I had taken a man's life. So I tried to push that pain away by grabbing that damn pipe."

"Yeah, but look what kind of man he was. He was hurting kids. I truly don't think the world will be missing another pedophile," Genesis said, trying to legitimize Grover's actions.

"Genesis, I'm not God. I don't have the right to say who's fit to live or die. But I acted like God that day, and I've been paying for it ever since. Some days I get mad with Jalen for even being born. I never heard from Sara again. I just told Jalen that she was dead. Hell, as far as I'm concerned, she is dead."

Genesis stood and walked over to his brother and gave him a true hug. For the first time since they were very small he felt the bond between them.

"You think I'll get out of here before the wedding?" Grover said as he eased out of his younger brother's tight embrace.

"Ah, man,' Genesis said, walking away. "Might not be a wedding. I got locked up last night."

"You what? I bet you got locked up over some woman, didn't you?"

Genesis stared at Grover. *How in the hell does everyone know me but me?* he thought.

"I knew it. Just like Daddy. He was a ho too. You better get outta here and go and make things right with your girl. A woman like Terri only comes around once in a lifetime."

"Yeah, you right. I'm sorry to hear about what happened in Chicago, but that was a long time ago. You can't keep punishing yourself for that. You've suffered enough. Hell, even if you would've went to jail you would've been out by now. Let that go."

"I'm trying, little brah. Now you go and beg Terri to forgive you. I gotta do whatever it takes to get myself together for my son."

Genesis walked over to Grover and shook his hand. Then his cell phone rang. It was Terri.

twenty one

A NEW DAY

Phyllis lay in Nathan's arms with her head resting gently on his chest, feeling like a new woman. It had been more than two years since she had been sexually active with Carl and even then it wasn't worth her time. She wrinkled her nose when she thought about how bad life with Carl had been. But that wrinkle turned into a girlish smile when she thought about how the past few months had been with Nathan.

He'd made her feel whole again. She felt needed and wanted. He held her in a way a woman needed to be held after she returned from ecstasy. She replayed the night's events in her mind, just for the hell of it. Phyllis had dropped Zachary and Jalen off at the youth center because Prodigy and Genesis were taking the kids to Six Flags. When Phyllis made it home, she prepared an exquisite meal for Nathan. She roasted a duck and followed Patti Labelle's recipe to the tee for candied yams and macaroni with cheese. Phyllis snuck in a can of Glory collard greens because after tasting them she swore to never go back to homemade. For dessert she baked a chess pie with a whipped-cream topping. They would top the evening off with a toast to the drastic change in her life that would soon take place.

After dinner and wine, Phyllis dropped a movie into the DVD

player and sat down on the sofa beside Nathan. Nathan extended his arms, and Phyllis snuggled in close to him. Before the previews of the upcoming attractions had finished, Nathan turned to face Phyllis and without a word he slid his tongue into her mouth and passionately kissed her. Phyllis surprised herself and responded to his advances.

Before they knew it they were affectionately caught up in a tongue tango. Then without a word being said, they both stood and headed upstairs into Phyllis's bedroom. Nathan slowly disrobed Phyllis, and she reciprocated. They slid under the covers and started again where they left off downstairs on the sofa. Nathan paused the action for a moment, leaned over the side of the bed, reached into his pants pocket, and removed a small box of condoms. He tore one from the package of three and unrolled the latex over his manhood.

Nathan rolled on top of Phyllis and told her how much she meant to him. How everything between the two of them felt so natural. Phyllis nodded in agreement as a tear rolled down her cheek. Nathan rubbed his hand across Phyllis's face to wipe the tear away and used the other hand to guide himself into her.

When Nathan's manhood entered Phyllis, he looked down into her teary eyes and knew that they were intimately connected with each other forever.

Nathan had been asking and asking—damn near begging—Phyllis to open up to him and allow herself to trust a man.

Phyllis tried to hold off on getting too close to Nathan because she was still officially married to Carl. But once she finally confronted her fears and realized that she was cheating herself of true love by holding on to a relationship that never meant anything to her, she loosened up. Now she felt closer to Nathan than she had ever felt to any man. Feeling what she felt now, she realized that all Carl ever was was a convenience. Phyllis realized that she never loved Carl, and now it was time for her to experience true love.

"So how do you feel?" Nathan asked.

Phyllis hesitated as if trying to find the right words. "I feel free. I can't explain it but I feel uninhibited."

"I know what you mean."

Phyllis leaned up on her elbow. "You know, I thought that I'd feel guilty, but I don't."

"Good. I don't want you to have any regrets. I have some strong feelings for you. I know this seems fast but this kind of thing happens when you know what you're looking for in a woman."

"Or a man. Thank you, Nathan. If you were to get up right now and walk out of my life forever, I'd still be grateful for the way you made me feel while we were together."

"You don't ever have to worry about me doing that."

Phyllis got out of bed and walked into the bathroom. She returned and handed Nathan a warm washcloth. She wrapped herself in a bathrobe and went downstairs to get a glass of water. When she came back, Nathan was sitting on the edge of the bed. Phyllis handed him the water and kissed him on the lips.

"Hey, how did it go with the lady that called you the other night? The one with the son in jail?"

"Mrs. Martin? It went great. She showed up just like she said she would. And I dropped the charges just like I said I would. We talked for a while. You know, the more I talked to Mrs. Martin, the more I realized that I could do more. I'm going to put in my letter of resignation to the District Attorney's Office in a few days."

"You're kidding me."

"No, I've contacted an old law school buddy about an offer that was extended to me a few years back to come over to his firm."

"Really? So you're going to do a little defending now?"

"Yeah, the more I think about it, the more I realize that's where I'm meant to be. The way this system has been treating my people, I can't just sit back and do nothing about it." Phyllis smiled when she said "my people." Now Nathan, a black man, was in her life and showing her every day that he was a man she could depend on. He always stood by his word and he was developing a wonderful relationship with Zachary. Even though Phyllis found it hard to forgive the men who had harmed her in her past, she was ready to move on.

"You know, Nathan, what's going on in the criminal judicial system is nothing short of modern-day slavery. And just think, I thought I was a part of the solution when all the while I was part of the problem. A black man will get twenty years for something that a white man will get probation for. I feel so bad for my part in that injustice."

"No, you had to go through everything you went through in order to know the system. God works like that. You'll never know until you know. Know what I mean?"

"Yeah, I know what you mean. For my time remaining with the DA's office, I'm going to be looking at my cases with a fine-tooth comb, which is what I've always done, but this time I'll be looking for reasons to give a lot of them another chance. Especially since so many of them were born with not much of a chance to function in this society."

"Well, be careful, if your superiors get wind of this change of heart, they might pull your cases."

"I know, that's why I haven't told anyone what my plans are so they won't be suspecting me of doing anything out of character. Even though I don't plan on any foul play, I know those guys only look for the conviction. Sometimes it doesn't matter how they get it."

Nathan leaned over and kissed Phyllis on the forehead. "I'm proud of you. You might not make a huge dent in this antiquated justice system but you'll definitely make a dent in the lives of the ones you help. I knew you had it in you."

"Well, thank you, honey. Now let's get up so my mom can finally meet you."

"Well, well, well. I must be special. After all of this time I thought I'd never get to meet the woman that gave life to such a beautiful lady."

"Oh, cut it out. She's been evil as a snake since she got out of the hospital, so disregard anything that she says out of the ordinary," Phyllis said as she stood and walked into the shower with Nathan on her heels.

"I like the ladies in my life to be a little snappy. I'm with you, aren't I?"

"I'm gonna spank you."

"Promises, promises."

twenty-two

DRAMA IN THE ATL!

"Prodigy's been shot," Terri said.

"What! What do you mean he was shot?" Genesis asked as he stood in Grover's room by the door.

"Someone shot him a little while ago outside the youth center. He's at Dekalb Medical Center in the ER. I'm on my way up there right now."

"Okay, 'bye." Genesis hung up the phone and told Grover what he had just heard. He slapped his brother's hand and rushed out to his truck.

Genesis drove like a madman until he reached Dekalb Medical Center. All he could think about was whether Prodigy would live or die. He bit his fingernails and starting talking to God.

"God, it's me again, and it's not about me this time. I'm calling on you to save one of your angels you got down here. Watch over him, God," Genesis said as he ran one red light after another before pulling into the Emergency Room parking lot.

When Genesis walked into the Emergency Room, he spotted Nina standing by the wall talking on a cell phone. Just as he walked over to her, Terri appeared on the other side of the doorway.

"Hey. Y'all heard anything yet?" Genesis asked Terri, barely holding back his tears. Prodigy was his best friend. They were closer than he and his own brother were, and all he could think of was life without him around.

"Not yet. We just got here," Terri said.

"Where's Gabrielle?"

"Grace took her to the mall," Terri said flatly. She was still a little standoffish with Genesis, but couldn't bring herself to sit back and not comfort him during this obvious time of stress. She reached up and hugged him. Terri led Genesis over to the waiting area and sat down beside him. Her hands never left his body.

"Did they find out who did it yet?"

"No, not yet. The police were here when we got here. They asked Nina a bunch of questions but the doctors wouldn't let them see Prodigy yet."

"Come on, dog, hold on," Genesis said as he looked up at the ceiling as if he was trying to will Prodigy to make it.

"Hi, Genesis," Nina said, wiping tears from her eyes as she took a seat beside Terri.

"Hey, you okay?"

"I don't know. I just got off the phone with Prodigy's mother, and she's hysterical. Oh, my God. Why did this happen to my husband? All he ever does is help people, and now somebody ..." Nina cried uncontrollably again. Terri let go of Genesis and hugged Nina.

Genesis tried to think of anyone who would want to harm Prodigy. His mind raced to the kids at the center. On occasion Prodigy would have to kick someone out for disobeying the rules, but he would usually let them back in after a few days. But with this new generation of kids with no respect for human life, a simple decision like that could be fatal. Or maybe it was one of the women from his past. *Hell hath no fury like a woman scorned,* he thought. The list had to be a small one because Prodigy didn't have any enemies that Genesis knew of.

A tall white man who looked to be in his late seventies came out and asked for Nina. She stood and talked with the man for a few minutes, then disappeared through a set of swinging doors.

Genesis placed his head in the palms of his hands. He started rocking back and forth, mumbling something under his breath. He looked to be praying. Terri rubbed his back and said a silent prayer of her own.

"He'll be fine, baby," Terri said, trying to comfort her man. She had decided that she was going to try and work through this little problem of theirs. She realized that she couldn't just up and run the first time they were faced with some trouble. The little trip that Genesis made to the county jail for solicitation would definitely put a damper on the honeymoon, but she still loved him and she was willing to make it work.

"I don't know. Things have been so bad lately. Anything that I seem to be involved in turns out bad. I don't know, Terri. I just don't know," Genesis said as he wiped a tear from his face. He wasn't sure if he was crying because of Prodigy or for the fact that he and Terri might be history. Either way the combination was too much for him to take. His mother had just cheated death, and now he wasn't sure if his best friend was going to be as lucky.

"Everything's not as bad as it seems."

"How do you know? My dog is up in here with I don't how many bullet holes in him and you saying things ain't that bad."

"Well, let me rephrase that. All is not lost with us. I mean, I still wanna marry you."

"Huh? Oh, you do?" Genesis said, surprised. He let out a sigh of relief and reached over and hugged Terri tighter than he'd ever hugged her before.

"You better let me go before you kill me. And you still make me sick," Terri said as she punched Genesis in the arm. "Why you do that?"

"I'm sorry, baby. I don't know what I was thinking."

"Well, Genesis, I can't take any more disappointment from you. My tolerance for heartache has never been too high in the first place. So if you can't deal with having just one woman and treating me with some respect, then let me know now. Because the next time that I even think you're doing something foul, I'm gone. And you have no idea how serious I am," Terri said without blinking.

"I'm never going to act up again. I swear to God."

"Look, I've decided to go to my mother's house for a little while."

"You pushing the wedding back?" Genesis asked.

"No, it's still on for next week. I just need a few days to myself. I'm taking Gabrielle with me. My mom wants to meet her. You think you can behave while I'm gone?"

"Please, after almost losing you, all I'm doing is going to church."

The sliding doors opened, and two uniformed police officers walked in with a tall black man in handcuffs. Genesis looked at the guy and did a double take. The guy looked familiar.

"Terri, does that guy over there look like somebody you know?"

Terri looked at the man and strained her eyes as if she was trying to recall the face. "Oh, my God. That's James."

"Who the hell is James?"

"Blake's father. What in the world is he doing here?" Terri stared over in the direction of the officer who had James hemmed up.

"Oh, he's probably the one that shot Prodigy," Genesis said as he stood and headed over toward James, but Terri stopped him.

"Let the police handle this, Genesis."

Just as Genesis calmed down, Nina came back out into the waiting room and caught sight of the man who left her when he found out that she was six weeks pregnant with Blake. It didn't take her long to put two and two together. Her husband just got shot and now he was lying in the hospital bed with IVs stuck all over the place, James calling the house, and now he was at the very same hospital in handcuffs. Nina lost it. She ran over to James and reached up and slapped him before the police officer could react.

"You sorry bastard. You shot my husband." Nina drove her fingernails into James's eyes as far as she could. James squealed like a pig before Terri and Genesis rushed over to pull Nina off of him.

"That's my seed. Ain't nobody gonna tell me I can't see him. Fuck yo punk-ass husband," James shouted back between screams.

"No, fuck you, James. Prodigy is Blake's father, and if you ever come around us again, he'll be raising Blake alone because I swear on my grandmother's grave that I'll kill you myself," Nina yelled before Terri pulled her away.

James yelled out obscenities at Nina. Then it got dark for him. Genesis let Nina go with Terri and walked over to James and hit him in the nose with a right hand that would've staggered Tyson. Blood gushed out of James's nose, and he slumped down against his own weight. A police officer ran over and handcuffed Genesis and rushed him outside. Terri helped Nina to her chair and went to see about her man.

"Officer, where are you taking him?" Terri asked.

"Get back," the officer said as he placed Genesis in the back of his police car.

"Please, Officer, let him go. That guy in there shot his best friend."

"I'm not taking him to jail, but he has to calm down. And you do too. Now go back inside, or I'll have to do the same thing to you."

"Can I just wait out here with him?"

"No, back inside. I told you I'm not taking him to jail."

Terri looked at Genesis, who motioned with his head for her to go back inside like she was told, and she did.

When Terri walked back inside Nina was talking to the same old white doctor that she spoke with before. James was gone.

Nina walked over to Terri and said that Prodigy was going to be fine, but they needed to run a few more tests. One bullet had grazed his skull and the other was in his leg. They were in the process of removing the bullet from his leg and stitching up his scalp.

The police informed her that a few kids from the youth center had pointed out James's car to a police officer who rode by a few seconds after James and his driver had sped off from shooting Prodigy. They didn't even make it two blocks before they were arrested on weapons possession, but with a positive identification from Prodigy, the police was sure to add on an attempted murder charge.

The police officers ushered Nina and Terri to the side and they brought James back out into the waiting area. He had regained consciousness and was back talking shit.

"You tell that tall, skinny nigga that snuck me, he's next. I don't give a shit about jail. I can reach any nigga anytime. That nigga gon' die," James managed to say before an officer jabbed him in his side with a stick, making him shut up.

"Ma'am, your husband won't say if that's the man that shot him or not, so we'll be needing to speak with him again. Here's my card. And if you'll go with the officer over there, she'll get some more information from you," the lead officer said.

"I'll release your husband in a minute," one of the officers said to Terri. "I probably would've done the exact same thing. These thugs don't have any respect for anybody anymore. I know Prodigy, and he's a good man. That one there has a lot of mouth but he can't seem to take a punch that well, huh?" Another officer laughed as he pointed for Terri to go outside and get Genesis.

twenty-three

GOOD VERSUS EVIL

Genesis sat in Prodigy's hospital room trying to convince his best friend that the police would handle James. Genesis was witnessing a side of his best friend's personality that he'd never seen before. It was as if someone had come in the middle of the night and stolen the peace-loving black man and replaced him with a diabolical twin. Prodigy was definitely hell-bent on revenge, and Genesis knew this was his time to be a true friend and talk some sense into Prodigy. But the look in Prodigy's eyes almost made Genesis afraid for his own safety.

"Man, you gonna have to calm down. Look at what you have to lose. This guy's just not worth it," Genesis pleaded.

"Now would be a good time for you to leave," Prodigy said, growing tired of Genesis's pleading.

"I ain't going nowhere."

"Well then, sit your ass down and shut up."

"Why you got to cuss?"

Prodigy looked at Genesis, sighed, and shook his head.

"Prodigy, what good would come from you killing this guy?"

"Look at my head. If I wouldn't have ducked down when I did, you'd be talking to a dead man. He will not get a second chance at me. Fuck that."

"Man, you just have too much to lose. Think, Prodigy, think."

"Genesis, you really need to raise your little narrow behind up outta here. Cuz I ain't trynna hear that shit you talking. You're right I got a lot to lose and guess what? A bullet damn near took all I have away. So I repeat, he will not get a second chance."

"Well, if you just absolutely have to ride on this guy, then damn it, I'm going too," Genesis said as he took a seat in the chair beside Prodigy's bed.

Prodigy chuckled and shook his head. "Genesis, do you even know how to shoot a gun?"

"Hell no, I said I'll ride. I ain't said nothing about shooting nobody."

"I have to do this. James threatened everything that I live for. Do you think that I can just sit back and let this slide? No can do. I'm not from that part of town where you let things like this roll off."

"Man, but what would it prove? And who you trynna prove something to?"

"If you slap me, I'mma slap you back. That's just who I am."

"Man, P, that's not you anymore. Man, you thirty-one years old. You sound like one of the kids at the center. Think past your anger. If you kill this guy, guess who loses. Not your ignorant ass, and definitely not James, he ain't worth the toilet paper it takes to wipe his butt with. But Blake, Nina, your daughter, your mother, and all two hundred and fifty of those kids that can't wait to see your bald head walk through those doors every day at the center."

The mere mention of the people that Prodigy cared the most about calmed him down. It was as if he took a tranquilizer. He laid his head back on the pillow and took a deep breath.

"Ah, man. Why this cat trynna pull me in this water?" Prodigy asked himself. The streets of Philadelphia where Prodigy was raised would call for swift retaliation. But like Genesis said, that would be childish. Now Prodigy struggled with the thought of what might have already happened.

"Well, it's a good thing he's locked up. Hopefully all of that revenge will be out of your system by the time he gets out."

Prodigy grunted and shook his head. "Genesis, go home, you're about the slowest man I know."

Genesis stared at Prodigy, confused. Where did that come from? He was about to ask Prodigy what did he miss when Prodigy's cousin Jermaine walked through the hospital door.

Jermaine was a true thug. He looked just like Allen Iverson but a shade darker. He had so many tattoos that you couldn't even see the true color of his arms. He wore his hair in cornrows and had on enough platinum jewelry to take care of a small country.

"What's up, big baby?" Jermaine said to Prodigy as he walked over to the bed and shook his cousin's hand.

"I'm straight. What about you?"

"Maintaining! What's up, Genesis?" Jermaine said as he walked over to give Genesis a handshake and a brother-like hug.

"I can't call it, Jermaine. How's Philly?"

"Still the same, my man." Jermaine turned and walked back over to Prodigy's bed and whispered in his ear, "Yo, P, I got this old lady to bail that girl James out. We got him tied up in the trunk outside."

Prodigy's face didn't give away his feelings. He knew his cousin would think he was crazy for what he was about to say.

"Man, I swear I don't want to say this, but we gonna have to let him go. I can't risk the repercussions. I'm sorry you came all the way down here, but I wasn't thinking straight when I called you with that kidnap and torture foolishness."

"Man, you too late."

"What you mean, I'm too late? Jermaine, tell me that you didn't kill this fool," Prodigy said as he rose up on his elbows.

"Ah, we ain't kill that punk even though we should've, the world would've been a better place. See, P, I know you better than you know yourself. That gangsta just not in you anymore. Hell, it never really was, you just adapted to your environment. You done been out the streets too long, baby. So I knew you were gonna pull that Martin Luther King shit. But, see, you my hero. That's why that nigga can't get a pass. And that's why his ass is beat beyond recognition outside in the trunk. Nigga so bloody the duct tape kept slipping off."

Prodigy had mixed emotions. "How bad is he?"

"Bad damnit," Jermaine said. "What difference does it make? He's gonna live, but I tried to paralyze his ass. But I promise you that he won't ever come around you, Blake, or Nina again. He got a self-imposed restraining order. We drove him down one of them long backwoods Georgia roads and kicked his ass severely. Every time he acted like he wanted to say something I'd hit him in his mouth with my sneaker. Got blood all over my Air Force Ones. I had to go and buy some new kicks. You owe me a hundred dollars too."

"We? Who you got with you?"

"Stop asking questions. Who the hell are you, the police? Anyway, we took him to this cornfield or something. His punk ass started crying and begging. 'Please, please, please. Don't kill me, I didn't mean to shoot him, I just wanted to scare him.' Man, we literally beat the shit out of him. I kept asking him why did he want to kill the man that was taking care of his son? Especially when *he* wasn't man enough to do it."

"What did he say?" Genesis asked.

"Ah, man, that boy was so scared he would've said anything to stop these knuckles from landing all over his face. I think we broke all his damn ribs," Jermaine said as he rubbed his hand.

"So he's out in the trunk right now?" Prodigy asked.

"Yep. And he boo-booed on hisself. Good thing we stole a car."

"You got a stolen car out in front of a hospital?"

"Yeah, we stole it in Philly," Jermaine said, as if what he did wasn't a problem.

"Boy, you still crazy hell," Prodigy said, laughing. "Damn criminal."

"Ah, you use to steal cars. So shut up. Enough of that. Guess what? I'm getting married."

Prodigy and Genesis both broke out laughing.

"What's so funny?" Jermaine said, as if he were offended. "Genesis, yo hoing ass getting married. And Prodigy, if you can stay married, then anybody can do it."

"Jermaine, ask Genesis about his iron vacation," Prodigy said, ignoring his cousin's announcement.

"Oh no, Genesis, what you doing locked up?"

"Prodigy, go to hell," Genesis said, not wanting to talk about his trip to jail.

"Man, you like family. Spit it out."

"They got me for solicitation."

"Solicitation? Damn, boy, times that hard?"

"Whatever," Genesis said, tired of the topic.

"I bet you was up in there crying."

"So you about ready to stop running with all them sisters and set-tle down, huh?" Prodigy asked Jermaine, because he knew Jermaine would've stayed on Genesis all night.

"Who said I had to stop running my hos? I just can't get caught like this one here." Jermaine nodded in Genesis's direction.

"You sound just like that one there," Prodigy said, pointing at Genesis.

"Did you know that a man is not meant to be faithful? That's why in a lot of countries a man can have as many wives as he can afford. You ain't ever heard of a country where a woman can have ten hus-bands, have you? Hell no."

"We don't live in those countries. So you need to stop trying to justify living foul."

"Oh hell, a minute ago you was trynna kill somebody, now you wanna preach. Let me go and toss this asshole in an alley some-where. I gotta be back in Philly tomorrow to take my blood test, cuz me and my boo gon' do this. Then I gotta come right back down here next week for your wedding. Did your girl find out about your little trip to the can?"

"Yeah, but the wedding is still on," Genesis said proudly.

"Ah, Genesis think he's a pimp. Look here, don't tell anybody I was down here. I'll see y'all next week," Jermaine said as he walked over to Prodigy's bed and shook his hand.

"Genesis, you be easy, baby." Jermaine slapped Genesis's hand and walked out the door.

"Man, do you think Jermaine would've killed James if you told him to?"

Prodigy gave Genesis a look that answered his question.

"Man, damn. What's up with the love? Why can't we just all get along?"

"Okay, Rodney King. That line is played. So you ready for your big day?"

"Man, next week can't get here soon enough. I keep thinking Terri's gonna change her mind."

"Oh, you'll be straight. Just treat her right."

"Jermaine did have a point about other countries letting men have all them wives, huh?"

"Don't you even start thinking about it. Unless you plan on moving to Africa or someplace, you better let that go."

"You right. But why do you think we have such a hard time staying faithful?"

"Greed. Man, women have spoiled us. They make it so easy for us to cheat. A woman can know that you're married and she'll still be down for sex. But then we don't make it any better. We always out there looking for the next piece of booty. Believe it or not, it's hard for me to be faithful sometimes. I had to release myself to the higher power. If my faith in God wasn't so strong, I would've strayed. You gotta find something greater than your testicles to believe in, dog."

"I feel ya. But never before in my life have I wanted something as bad as I want a good marriage with Terri. After that trip to jail, my eyes have seen the light. If her name ain't Terri, then I don't want it."

"There you go. Now you starting to sound like a real man," Prodigy said as he laid his head down.

"Well, I'm going to let you get some sleep. You getting out tomorrow, right?"

"I think so. I'll give you a call when I get home. Kiss Terri and the baby for me."

"I'll do that. You take care and I'm glad that you didn't sanction that murder."

"Yeah, yeah, yeah. I'll call you tomorrow. And try not to pick up any hookers on the way home." Prodigy laughed.

"Man, when you gonna leave that alone?"

"Never. Hit the light on your way out."

twenty-four

THE WEDDING

Genesis was pacing back and forth like a caged tiger. He had never been this nervous in his life. His wedding day had finally arrived and now that he was in the church looking at all of his tuxedo-wearing groomsmen, he couldn't sit still. He must have straightened the tie on his own tuxedo about a hundred times.

"You got the ring?" Genesis asked Grover.

"Yes, I got the ring. Calm down, dog," Grover said, smiling and shaking his head at his little brother.

Prodigy smiled as he walked over with a slight limp and tried to calm his friend.

"Let me see it," Genesis asked.

Grover reached in his tuxedo coat pocket and came up empty. Then he reached in his pants pocket, still nothing. "Oh shit." He put his hand over his mouth as he tried to stop another profanity from slipping from his lips on the church premises.

"Man, where's the ring?" Genesis said, clearly nervous.

"I just had it. Where in the ..." Grover said, as he slapped at all of his pockets frantically.

"Man, you better stop playing with me," Genesis said as he balled his fist.

"Oh, man, get your panties out your butt," Grover said as he pulled out the sparkling diamond and smiled.

"Man, stop playing so much," Genesis almost yelled. "Do not play with me today."

"Oh, calm down, dog," Prodigy added.

"Calm down, nothing. Y'all need to stop playing."

"Man, you got on one blue and one black sock," Prodigy said as he looked down at Genesis's legs and held his side laughing.

"You wanna get shot again? Cuz I'm tired of y'all playing so much. Now stop fucking with me," Genesis yelled, frustrated with his crew of wanna-be comedians.

"I ain't playing, man. Look."

Prodigy, Grover, and the rest of the groomsmen had been getting a good laugh at Genesis's expense all morning. And once again the entire room of guys cracked up laughing when they looked down at Genesis's mismatched socks.

Genesis looked down at his feet when all of the guys started laughing uncontrollably. "Ah, damn! Grover, let me borrow one of your socks?"

"No, sir. I ain't gonna be walking around here looking like a clown, clown," Grover said, as he slid his legs away from Genesis.

"Prodigy, let me borrow a sock."

"No, my brother, you gotta get your own."

"I don't have time to get my own. Man, somebody give me a got-damn sock," Genesis said as he stood as if he was about to hit somebody.

All of the guys in the office were laughing so hard at Genesis that it looked like Bernie Mac had stood in the middle of the floor and given a free concert. Finally Genesis joined in on the fun and cracked a smile.

"Y'all some sorry-ass friends. Oh, excuse me, God, but I swear y'all foul."

"Don't be asking for forgiveness now, you been cursing all morning," Jermaine said.

"Man, why you call me at five o'clock this morning?" one of the groomsmen asked.

"Yeah, why you do that, man, when the wedding ain't until four? We still got an hour to go," Grover said, looking at his watch.

"I thought I was the only one that got a call," Prodigy said, as he took his shoe off and handed Genesis a black sock.

"Cuz I know how y'all are," Genesis said. "I wanted to make sure everybody got here on time. Thank you, P." He smelled the sock before he took off his own shoe. "Gotta watch you, I'll mess around and catch athlete's feet."

"You can give it back, you ungrateful punk," Prodigy said.

"When was the last time you been to sleep, boy?" Grover asked Genesis. Grover was almost back to his old self, but he was still afraid. Over the last ten years he had been "clean" more than twenty times. Yet sitting in there in that church, he felt there was something different about this time.

"I don't know, why?" Genesis answered.

"Cuz you acting silly. I hope you don't sleep through the consummation."

"Oh, don't you worry about that. I might fall asleep right after but I'll be good and alert until then." Genesis slapped everyone a high five.

Part of Genesis's anxiety stemmed from him not seeing Terri but twice in the last week. She had left to stay with her mother on the night that Prodigy was shot. She came back home the day before yesterday just in time for the rehearsal, but right after the rehearsal dinner she left again. Terri was superstitious and thought that the bride shouldn't see the groom before the wedding, so she grabbed a big suitcase, kissed Genesis good-bye, and headed over to Nina and Prodigy's.

Prodigy limped over to Genesis and motioned for him to step out-side the office to the balcony.

"You a'right?" Prodigy asked in a serious tone.

"Yeah, man, a little nervous but I'm cool."

"Why you so nervous?" Prodigy asked calmly.

"Man, I'm just scared of the whole process."

"What, you think you gonna cheat?"

"Nah, I've been praying about that, and there is no doubt in my mind that Terri's the only one for me. I'm lucky that she still wants to marry me after all of the ignorant shi . . . stuff I did," Genesis said as he looked around as if he would be struck down by lightning for almost cursing.

"I'm glad that you've found God. Trust me when I say that He makes a difference when you start getting a little weak. If you know what I mean."

"Yeah, I think I do, but I'm not afraid of getting weak. I just want to be able to give Terri all the things she deserves. I don't wanna ever let her down again, man. That's my heart, and I want to provide her with the best of everything."

"Don't worry about giving her the best material things. One of the good things about love is that you can work together. Let that ego of yours go. You're in a partnership now. Y'all can get anything y'all want if you work together. All you have to do is show her unconditional love and let her know that she's your world. Y'all will be just like Ossie Davis and Ruby Dee." Prodigy laughed.

"Yeah, she's an angel, man." Genesis stared off into space. "I can't believe how I was treating her."

"Yeah, but she's forgiven you. Just don't make her regret that decision."

"Oh, I'm so far away from doing her wrong. I know what you meant now when you were talking about Nina being your best friend and you not cheating on her. Man, I realize that I've been running from something real because I was so used to dealing with the fake. Trust me when I say, ain't no way I messing this up."

"That's good to hear, dog." Prodigy was quiet for a minute. "You know when I got shot, my life flashed before my eyes. All I could see was my family. Nina, Blake, and Arielle. As a man, you have obligations to God, your family, and your people. You got a family now and I'm happy to see that you got your priorities straight." Prodigy shook Genesis's hand.

"Yeah, I'm about to get married, man. Can you believe that?"

"Yeah, I can. Marriage is a beautiful thing but don't think for one minute that she ain't gonna get on the last nerve in your body, but it's all good. Congratulations, dog." Prodigy slapped Genesis on his back.

"Speaking of family, how's little Gabrielle doing?" Prodigy asked.

"She's my doll baby. That's the sweetest little girl in the world," Genesis said, smiling.

"How's that adoption thing going?"

"I don't know, man, that's Terri's thing. I don't think she's done anything else. I think she's afraid that old girl might come back and try to claim her."

"And you don't know who Gabrielle's mother is? Me and Nina been trynna figure out who she is but Terri has so much help coming through that store that it's hard to tell."

"She said it was someone named Yolanda, but I don't remember her. I'm just happy we could help out," Genesis said.

"Look at you, sounding like a family man already. I'm proud of you, boy," Prodigy said, rubbing Genesis's head like he was a child.

"Prodigy, get your hands off of me. Just cuz you can't grow no hair don't try to mess up mine."

"Stop crying. So how's the daddy life been going?"

"I feel like a daddy when I'm around Gabrielle. I can see how you stepped up to the plate with Blake. Kids are something else."

Grace knocked on the door to the office with Jalen and Blake in their little tuxedos and told the groomsmen that it was time for everyone to take their places. Grover stuck his head out on the balcony and summoned Genesis and Prodigy.

AS JOVIAL AS the men's room was, the ladies' room was just the opposite. It was total chaos. Shanice, Terri's pessimistic friend, was running around trying to get everyone's hair looking good and complaining about bad perms. Nina had just gotten off the phone with Terri, who sounded like she was about to lose her mind because the limousine driver hadn't shown up to take her to the church. Not to mention the fact that she still had to ride by her store to get Genesis's ring out of her safe. Nina had informed Terri that the limousine driver called and said that he was waiting in front of Terri's house, but was now en route to pick her up at Nina and Prodigy's place and that everything was fine.

THE CHURCH WAS beautifully decorated with expensive floral arrangements, bouquets, and candles. The male quartet was humming an a cappella version of "Ribbon in the Sky." The pastor stood in the center of the pulpit as Genesis, Grover, and Jalen stood to his left. Genesis smiled at his mother and sisters.

Each groomsman walked halfway down the aisle and waited for his respective bridesmaid. Once the bridesmaid reached the groomsman, he bowed, handed her a single rose, and held out his arm to escort her the rest of the way down the aisle. Once they reached the pulpit, the groomsman walked the bridesmaid to her spot, then continued on to his side.

Once the last person was in place, everyone waited for the queen of the day. All eyes were on the back of the church. When Terri appeared, "Ohh"s and "Ahh"s went throughout the whole audience. Genesis looked like his heart was about beat out of his chest. His legs got weak. He had to do everything in his power to remain composed.

Terri walked down the aisle, eyeing Genesis with every step she took. A steady stream of tears forced her black eyeliner down her almond-colored cheeks. Genesis stood motionless as Terri approached wearing a black warm-up suit and tennis shoes. She handed him Gabrielle and a picture of Yolanda.

"Does this jar your memory? Because this is the mother of your child. I've had enough, Genesis." Terri struggled through her tears.

"Wait a minute. Terri, what are you talking about . . . ?" Genesis stopped in mid-sentence when he looked at the picture of Yolanda. He was speechless and he was caught.

"It's very obvious that you don't respect women. Maybe you can learn to respect this one." Terri reached in her pocket and handed Genesis the letter that Yolanda had stuck in the door of her bookstore before turning and walking away.

Genesis looked down at Gabrielle, who was in a peaceful sleep, and didn't know what to think. He looked up and caught a glimpse of Terri before she exited the chapel door. He found his legs and handed Gabrielle to Grover before running after Terri. When he made it outside, Terri was just stepping inside the limo. Genesis ran over to her and grabbed her arm. She didn't pull away or protest.

"Terri, wait," Genesis said, "I didn't know about Gabrielle. I made a mistake. That was a long time ago."

"Yeah, I'm sure," Terri said. "You seem to make a lot of those." She looked away as Genesis pleaded.

"I can make this right, Terri, please don't do this."

"How? What are you going to do about it? Make that little girl disappear? No, you're the one that should disappear. Let my arm go."

"Terri, please, are you just going to throw all that we have away?"

"All of what? If we had anything then we'd be in that church right now. But look at us. You screwed up again, so yes. I'll throw this half-ass relationship away because it never meant a thing to you in the first place. Let my arm go, you poor excuse for a man," Terri screamed as the tears rushed down her cheeks. She could no longer play the cool role.

"How do you even know she's telling the truth?" Genesis took a shot in the dark. In his heart, he knew Gabrielle was his child.

Terri looked at Genesis as if she was insulted. "Don't you dare! That 'child' that you laid down with wasn't lying. You're the liar. Now get your damn hands off of me before I throw up. You make me sick, you selfish bastard." Terri swung around with her free arm and smacked Genesis as hard as she could in the eye. Genesis tried to cover his face with his free hand but Terri would not be denied her justice. She kept swinging and Genesis kept getting hit until he released her arm. Once she was free, Terri got in the limo and slammed the door. The last thing Genesis heard was the automatic locks slamming shut.

Genesis sat down on the sidewalk and read the letter that broke Terri's heart and ruined his wedding.

Dear Terri,

I hope this letter finds you in time to save you from making a big mistake. I'm sorry for my part in ruining your life but you need to know the truth. I admire you so much, a little too much. I wanted to be just like you. I know there is nothing I can do to take back what I've done but I feel I must tell you the truth. Genesis is Gabrielle's father. He doesn't know it because we were only together once. He didn't force himself on me or anything like that. As a matter of fact, I was the one that initiated the whole thing. It was my eighteenth birthday and I wanted to celebrate. You were out of town, and I asked him if he could take me out. Being with him made me feel like

you. Then one thing led to another, and I'll spare you the details. I
know you may never forgive me for what I did but I thought that
Gabrielle should know at least one of her parents. I'm in no position
to take care of her and I love her enough to want the best for her.

                                        Yolanda "Yogi" Smith

Oh my God. Yogi is Yolanda? Genesis crushed the letter and looked
up toward the sky and asked God why him, but in his heart he knew
the answer to his question. You reap what you sow. Genesis rubbed
his hands over his face. He looked back at the church and all the
people who had congregated outside to be nosy and shook his head.
All of a sudden a certain peace came over him. He really did love
Terri and he didn't want to hurt her any more than he had already.
So Genesis came to the staggering realization that if the ceremony
had gone on as planned, he would've been married but still looking.

GENESIS'S REVELATION

One year later

The last year has brought about a lot of changes for everyone, including me.

Momma's health improved and I'm pleased to say Mrs. Virginia Styles is doing well. Phyllis did leave the DA's office and was working on becoming a partner in her law firm. Her first major victory came when she defended a high-profile Muslim leader who was accused of murdering a white police officer. She finally got a divorce from Carl and he finally got his head out of his butt long enough to try and make things right with Zachary. But now he's complaining about Phyllis and Nathan's relationship. I don't know about that relationship myself. It happened too fast if you ask me but since nobody asked me, I'll just be happy for my sister. At least she got a brother this time. I *think* he's a brother but that ain't my business either. If Zachary likes it, I love it.

Grover's still clean and sober. Prodigy gave him my old position at the youth center, which I left to take a coaching job with the Georgia State University men's basketball team. He's done a full 180-degree turn with Jalen. He's finally acting like a real father. When Jalen has to travel out of state to write songs for his little hip-hop artists, Grover's right there to keep him in line.

Grace was called to preach the word of God at a huge church in

Atlanta. She finally allowed herself to leave the past in the past and is now dating a fellow pastor.

Prodigy, Nina, and Blake have been riding around Atlanta for the last two months looking for a bigger home to make room for the new addition to their family. Nina recently found out that she is pregnant. Prodigy and Blake are hoping for a boy, while Nina prays for a little girl to help balance out their testosterone-driven house.

Terri ... Damn, I miss my baby. I asked everyone that I could think of how she was doing but most people just told me that she was fine. Her little funky-ass friend Shanice told me that she's dating some doctor dude. I didn't believe her, though. I can't believe she could just go on with her life like we never had anything. If she is dating, I hope she's happy. I'm lying; I hope she's miserable and can't stop thinking about me; that way we'll be on the same page. I finally kicked my dad's foolish rhetoric aside and cried my heart out. I've never cried so much in my life, hell, I'm about to cry now just thinking about her. You'd think I'd be over her by now, but I still love that woman. Because every day since she left me outside of that church on what would've been our wedding day, not an hour has gone by without me thinking about her. Grace usually gives me bits and pieces of Terri's world. She told me that Terri finally added on that coffee and bagel shop she had been talking about. She created a Sunday-night social club where she allowed poets and self-published authors to come out and introduce their works to her patrons. I went one Sunday night but she saw me sitting in the audience and had a police officer come over and ask me to leave. I was gonna read my heart out. It took me about a month to write that poem. Prodigy said my poem was corny anyway but he's always been jealous of my skills so he's just hating on a brother. Anyway, I guess it wasn't meant to be.

I took a blood test just to make sure that Gabrielle was mine but I'd already made up my mind that no matter what the outcome was,

I was going to do right by my daughter. That's why I never went up there to get the results. I wasted my damn money. My mom and my sisters help me out from time to time but I try not to ask them for much. Gabrielle's mine and I finally realized that life is no longer about me. Dr. Ben has this saying that has kept me sane. "You got to go through some things to get to some things."

Guess what else, y'all? I've been practicing celibacy since Terri left. Well, a little bit before that cuz y'all know she wasn't giving me any. I haven't been with anyone sexually in over a year. Ain't that something? I just can't bring myself to think about another woman, let alone touch one. I bet y'all asking yourselves why couldn't I do that when Terri was around? Well, I ask myself that same question every day. But time changes people. For me it took losing everything before I could realize and appreciate what I had. I feel like a damn fool. But I realized that I had to release my sex addiction to a higher power. And once I allowed God into my world, my perspective on life changed. I'm no longer interested in self-gratification—I'm only interested in providing a positive example for my daughter and my two nephews.

Guess what else? I joined the church where Grace is a pastor. I tried to join the choir but they keep talking about how I sing off-key. Everybody's sleeping on my skills. Anyway, last Sunday when I sat down in my normal seat, Gabrielle started to cry. Just as I was about to get up and take my baby out of the sanctuary a familiar voice sailed over my shoulder and said, "Give her here, she probably misses her Terri."

Watch out now, I might be back up in there.

READING GROUP GUIDE

The questions and discussion topics that follow are intended to enhance your group's reading of Travis Hunter's *Married but Still Looking*. We hope they will provide new insights and ways of looking at this fast-paced, entertaining novel.

1. Genesis decides that Terri is the woman he wants to spend the rest of his life with, and he asks her to marry him. Why does Genesis almost immediately begin cheating on Terri after their engagement? Do you think that Terri is aware that Genesis is cheating on her? Why would Genesis ask Terri to marry him if he isn't done sleeping with other women? Is it all right to sleep with other people as long as you stop once you say "I do"?

2. When Yolanda leaves Gabrielle in Terri's store, Terri instantly bonds with the baby and considers keeping her to raise. Why does Terri feel such a strong connection with Yolanda's baby? Should Terri be angry that Yolanda left this child and took off on a bus? Is Terri right to consider keeping the baby, or should she turn the baby over to the authorities as an abandoned child? Is it fair of Terri to introduce a new baby into Genesis's life?

3. Once Terri and Nina start planning the wedding, Genesis and Prodigy complain about how wrapped up women get in the

whole procedure. Are they right to complain? Do women get too wrapped up in the material part of a wedding and lose sight of the emotional commitment involved in marriage? Is Terri too wrapped up in planning her wedding? Does this prevent her from realizing what Genesis is doing behind her back? Have you ever been involved in planning a wedding? If so, what was the experience like?

4. Genesis resents his brother, Grover, very much. He feels that Grover is not a father to his son, Jalen, and that he funnels all of his money into drugs and alcohol. Should Genesis be more compassionate toward Grover, or has he already given his brother enough chances? Can a drug and alcohol addict ever be a good parent? Is Grover a good father to Jalen? Do you think that one day he will be capable of being a good father to his son?

5. Throughout her life, Phyllis never dated black men. Was this a conscious decision for her? If so, why would she decide not to date black men? Phyllis's mother says that if Phyllis could slip out of her skin, she would. Is this true? Is Phyllis unhappy that she's black? Have you ever wished that you were born a different color? In what ways do you think that your life would be different?

6. When he was a child, Genesis always saw his father with lots of women, and Genesis truly believed his father when he told him to date lots of women and always have at least two girlfriends. At what point in his life should Genesis have understood that this was bad advice? What do you think was going through Grover Sr.'s head when he gave Genesis advice about women? Is it possible to sleep with lots of women and still lead a fulfilling life? Do you know people who are content to sleep around and not pursue any serious relationships?

7. In the weeks before their wedding, Terri is in a much more comfortable financial position than Genesis. While Genesis is strug-

gling to make ends meet now that his basketball money has run out, Terri is planning an addition to her store. Is Terri uncomfortable with her current financial situation? Is Genesis uncomfortable with his? Why do you think Genesis doesn't tell Terri that he's a little short on cash because of all the wedding expenses? Would it be acceptable for Terri to help pay for the wedding? Is it important to keep separate accounts after getting married, or is it better to have a joint account?

8. Before Genesis heads off to his bachelor party, Prodigy calls him and says that there won't be any strippers at the party. Does Genesis have a right to get angry about this? Are strippers a necessary element of a bachelor party? Is it OK that Prodigy teases Genesis, knowing what a tough time his friend is having? Is the lack of strippers enough to explain why Genesis would solicit a prostitute? Is there ever an acceptable reason for soliciting a prostitute?

9. After Terri finds out about the incident with Genesis and the prostitute, she tells Genesis that the wedding is off. Then Terri's mother tells her to try to work through this with Genesis. Who has the right impulse, Terri or her mother? Is it possible for Terri to forgive Genesis after finding out that he solicited a prostitute? Should she believe Genesis when he tells her that he'll change? Would you agree to marry a man after you found out that he had solicited a prostitute a week before your wedding?

10. When Prodigy is shot by James, he reverts to his old ways and calls in his cousin from Philadelphia. He asks his cousin to kidnap and torture James, and then to kill him. Why does Prodigy go back to his old ways so fast? Does James deserve to be killed after all that he did to Prodigy's family? Does Genesis get Prodigy to change his mind, or does Prodigy come to that decision on his own? Do you think Prodigy would have been able to live with himself if he had had James killed? If someone hurts you, should you exact revenge?

11. When Terri walks down the aisle at her wedding, she's holding
    Gabrielle and a picture of Yolanda. She tells Genesis that Gab-
    rielle is his daughter. Until that moment, does Genesis know that
    Gabrielle is his child? Should Genesis have come clean with Terri
    about everything before the wedding? Would Terri still have
    agreed to marry him? Are there some secrets that husbands and
    wives should keep from each other, or is it better to be upfront
    and honest about everything?

An excerpt from bestselling author
Travis Hunter's latest novel,

Trouble Man

Growing up on Philadelphia's gritty streets, Jermaine Banks always managed to get by. Now, nearly thirty years old, he figures he can't escape the law or the street forever. When his best friend is gunned down after a drug deal gone wrong, Jermaine knows it's time to move on. But with a pregnant girlfriend and a son, Jermaine needs to find a legitimate business fast. One thing he is sure of is that he will never become like his own irresponsible father, who abandoned him and his mother after his birth and, except for the occasional check, has had little to do with them.

Jermaine Banks sat on the side of the bathtub as his three-year-old son, Khalil, played in the sudsy water with a green and white plastic boat. The boat was one of the few toys that remained from Jermaine's own childhood. Khalil loved it and wouldn't take a bath without it. As Jermaine watched his child's carefree smile, he felt uneasy. He knew that, in order to keep that smile on his son's face, he was going to have to make some drastic changes in his life. But how? He was almost thirty years old with only a high school education and absolutely no work experience. Just as he got lost in his thoughts he looked up to see his pregnant girlfriend, Erin, in the doorway.

"Are you guys almost done?" Erin whined, crossing her arms.

"We just got in, Erin. Give us a minute," Jermaine said, shaking his head.

That girl wants everything on her time, he thought.

"I'm just checking, no need for the attitude," Erin said as she turned and stomped down the stairs to the living room.

Jermaine shook his head again and went back to washing his son. For the most part he loved Erin and she was a good woman. She had her ways, but who didn't? They had been together through a lot of thick and thin. Even when Jermaine had stepped out on her and got Khalil's mother, Amani, pregnant while Erin was completing her undergraduate work at Morgan State University down in Baltimore. But then again, that forgiveness had come with a price, and now that Jermaine was trying to take a more active role in Khalil's life, he was starting to notice that Erin was pretty ambivalent about her feelings toward his son. Sometimes she went overboard, trying to act as if Khalil were her best friend, like making sure he had a bedroom at her place, but whenever she was upset with Jermaine, her true feelings about Khalil surfaced.

The last few months had been pretty stressful for both of them: Erin getting used to the idea of being a *real* mom and Jermaine with the burden of becoming a daddy for the second time with no real plans for his future. Rightfully so, Jermaine seemed to be getting it the worst; it seemed as if every day someone was on his case about getting a real job and leaving his hustling days behind him. But just the thought of wearing one of those fast food uniforms turned Jermaine's stomach. As far as he was concerned, those kinds of jobs were for high school kids and grown-up losers. Plus, he didn't see anything wrong with his current "job"—selling weed. As a matter of fact, he felt like he was doing Philadelphians a favor by providing a natural herb that helped folks calm the hell down.

"Jermaine. Jermaine," Khalil called out, with his arms outstretched toward his father.

"What's up, lil guy?"

"I'm ready to get out of the bathtub."

"Okay." Jermaine pulled the stopper and lifted his son onto the toilet seat. He toweled him dry, rubbed lotion all over his already soft skin, and helped him into his favorite Superman pajamas. The kind with the feet attached.

"You're all set, my man."

"Will you sleep with me?"

"You scared?"

"Yep," Khalil said with no shame.

"Man, how you gonna be a tough guy all day and a big baby at night?"

"I am tough." Khalil flexed his muscles for his father to examine. "But I still want you to sleep with me. Please." Khalil smiled.

Jermaine smiled too. He placed his hands on both sides of Khalil's face and looked down at his son. Khalil looked like a miniature version of himself. They shared the same caramel complexion and the same big brown eyes. Khalil even wore his hair in cornrow braids like his father.

As Jermaine stared into his child's eyes, he wondered if he had what it took to raise Khalil the way he deserved to be reared. An overwhelming fear came over him. Nothing else on God's green earth scared him like letting his son down.

"Yeah, I guess I can lay down with you for a minute. But you know what? I want you to stop calling me Jermaine and call me Daddy. Is that a'ight with you?"

"Yep," Khalil said, unaware of the powerful responsibility the word carried for his father.

Jermaine turned around and let Khalil jump on his back. He walked with him into his bedroom and laid him down on his bed.

"Jermaine, I mean Daddy. Miss Erin said I need to say my prayers."

"And Miss Erin is right. Let's do it."

They both got down on their knees and thanked God for his blessings. Once they were done, Jermaine lay down beside his son, and before a good five minutes were up, Khalil was snoring. Jermaine eased out of the bed and made the dreaded trip downstairs to have the same old tired conversation with Erin.

"So is he off to sleep?" Erin asked as she reached for the remote control to turn the television off.

"Sure is," Jermaine said, plopping down in the love seat across from her. "And I wish I could join him." Jermaine sighed, rubbing his temples.

"You can join him but you're going to have to face the truth about yourself one day, Jermaine."

"What truth?" Jermaine asked wearily. "I already know the truth about me, Erin. I live it every day. But what I don't need is for you to sit around all day figuring out ways to judge me."

"Nobody's judging you. But you need to get it together because we are having a baby and I'm not about to let you have my child around your drug-dealing friends while I'm at work. Now, you've let it be known that I can't tell you what to do when it comes to Khalil, but that line won't fly when the baby gets here because this child will be *my* responsibility."

"Baby, baby, baby. That's all you ever talk about. That and me turning into some kind of nerd. This pregnancy is still suspect."

"Suspect? What is that suppose to mean?"

"All of a sudden Erin just has to have a baby. For the life of me I can't understand why you feel like you need to compete with Amani."

"Compete with Amani?" Erin frowned. "Please! Trust me when I say that hood rat is no competition for me."

"Look at you. Always putting yourself up on some pedestal. If you were as high and mighty as you think you are, you wouldn't be trying to trap me with a baby."

Erin started laughing. Laughing so hard she had to hold her side.

"You must've fell and bumped your head. Jermaine, what is there about you that would make me want to trap you? You don't have a job. You got major baby-momma drama and there's a new police report out on you every month. Please! Now *you* need to come down off of your pedestal. If there's anybody that should be doing the trapping it's you."

"You crazy! Your family's got you thinking you're some kind of prize."

"Here we go," Erin said, huffing, leaning back against the sofa with her arms crossed.

"That's right, here we go. You didn't have a problem with where my money was coming from when it was paying for those expensive books that you needed for your bachelor's *and* your master's, which you only got so your mother could brag to her corny-ass friends, but that's another subject."

"Leave my mother out of this," Erin shot back.

"Whatever," Jermaine said, knowing how sensitive Erin was about her family. "Let's talk about that new car that you had to have, that brand-new Acura TL that my dirty money paid for, or what about when that dirty money paid your rent and all your other bills for two whole years so you could concentrate on school? But now you're straight and I'm the bad guy."

"I never told you or encouraged you to sell one dime bag. As a matter of fact, I begged you to stop and get a real job."

"Yeah, after you got everything you needed. Damn hypocrite!"

"That still doesn't change the fact that you need a job. And I can do without the name calling."

"What kind of job do you want me to get? You want me to throw on a suit and tie and head down to Center City and walk up in one of those high-rises? Maybe then I'll be good enough for you, huh? You don't have a problem spending my dough but you got a problem with where it comes from."

"You know what, Jermaine? You are right. I didn't always have a problem with how you made your money, but I've grown up and you haven't. When are you going to grow up? You're still doing the same things you did when we were in high school. The only difference is you went from misdemeanors to felonies."

"So now I gotta operate on your schedule?"

"Just get a life," Erin said with a dismissive wave of her hand. She pushed the button on the remote control, letting Jermaine know that their conversation was over.

"You self-centered, arrogant bitch," Jermaine growled.

Erin's eyes widened and her creamy light face turned red as an apple. As thugged out as Jermaine was, he had never used profanity around her, never mind calling her that word.

She stood and screamed, "Get out of my house! Get your child and get out of my house!" Erin pointed toward the door.

Jermaine jumped to his feet and ran upstairs. He couldn't have thought of a better idea for the both of them, because at this point his blood was boiling and he couldn't stand the sight of Erin one more minute. He felt used and betrayed by the one woman he thought had his back. He knew he had his issues but she wasn't the one to talk. Here was a woman who wouldn't know how to cross the street if her mother didn't tell her, trying to tell him how to live his life. He raced into the room where Khalil was sleeping peacefully and quickly gathered his son and all of his belongings.

"Where we going?" Khalil asked sleepily.

"Go back to sleep, man."

He raced back downstairs and slightly bumped Erin as he passed her. She exaggeratedly grabbed her shoulder, acting like it was broken.

"Bye, Miss Erin." Khalil waved as his father carried him out to the street.

Erin sucked her teeth, rolled her eyes, and looked away.

Twenty minutes later, Jermaine parked his black BMW X5 on the street in front of his mother's row house and turned off the ignition. But before he could open his door there was a huge crash and broken glass went flying everywhere. Startled, he ducked down to avoid being hit by whatever else might be coming.

"Get outta this truck," an angry man's voice growled as he reached into the now open window, unlocked and opened the door. He grabbed Jermaine and pulled him to his feet, pushing a gun in his face. "I oughta kill yo' black ass right here, right now," the man growled.

The sound of the glass breaking woke Khalil, who had been sleeping peacefully in the backseat, and he let the entire neighborhood know of his displeasure by crying at the top of his lungs.

Once Jermaine got his bearings, he focused on the face in front of him. The bloodshot eyes, the dark skin with a mole on the tip of a pointed nose, and the eighties-style Jheri curl belonged to none other than Roscoe Jones, Erin's father. The hate subsided a little in Roscoe's red eyes when he heard Khalil's cries.

"You trynna make my baby girl have a miscarriage?" Roscoe whispered in a furious tone.

Slap! Punch! Slap!

"Man," Jermaine said, doubling over in pain. "What's your damn problem?"

"Didn't I tell you the next time you made my baby girl cry, I was gonna kill ya? You don't upset nobody that's pregnant. Babies come out all deformed and shit. Now take that boy in the house and come right back out here."

Jermaine touched his lip and looked at the blood on his hand. "Roscoe, have you lost your mind?"

Slap! "I told you to take that child in the house and bring yo' ass back." Slap! "I ain't playing wit' you," Roscoe said as he put his police-issue gun back into its holster.

Jermaine closed his eyes and took a couple of deep breaths. *I don't believe this broke-lookin' Barry White out here beating my ass,* he thought.

Jermaine walked around his truck and unbuckled Khalil from his car seat. He picked up his son and placed him on his shoulder, which was enough to quiet him.

"Hurry up, son. I ain't got all night," Roscoe said in his country accent, leaning against the hood of Jermaine's SUV.

Jermaine walked into his mother's house and sat Khalil down on the sofa.

"What's going on? Why is the police out there?" Nanette "Nettie" Banks asked her son, turning away from a rerun of *Sanford and Son.* "And why is your lip bleeding?"

"That's Roscoe," Jermaine said, trying to downplay the incident.

"Wait a minute. Roscoe hit you?" Without waiting on an answer Nettie went into a rage. "I don't play nobody puttin' they hands on my child. Who in the hell does Roscoe think he is?" Nettie hurried toward the kitchen, no doubt going for her gun. "I'll show that mother—"

"Hold up, Mom," Jermaine said, grabbing his mother's arm to stop her. He knew he had to come clean with his mother or in a matter of minutes Roscoe would be lying on his stomach in the back of an ambulance as the paramedics tried to remove a few .32-caliber slugs from his gluteus maximus. "Erin's pregnant. That's why he's tripping."

"Pregnant?" Mrs. Banks yelled, then reared back and planted one across Jermaine's face.

Slap!

Jermaine held his face and frowned. *Man, what is this? Slap the shit outta Jermaine day?*

"Boy, what is your problem? You barely can take care of this one here with his cute self." Nettie alternated from ranting to calm just as she always did when Khalil was around. "I'm getting too old to be takin' care of babies all the time."

"Who said you had to take care of my kids?" Jermaine said, still holding his face.

"Who else is going to take care of 'em, Jermaine? Not you. I know how you make your money. You ain't slick. Selling drugs ain't all that dependable, you know? And what makes you think you can get away forever doing something illegal? You need to stop being so damn lazy and get a job."

Here we go again, Jermaine thought.

"You've been getting slaps on the wrist all your life but one day one of those judges is going to put your butt in the penitentiary and I ain't sending you shit," Nettie said.

Jermaine ignored his mother just as he did every time she tried one of her scared-straight tactics. "Erin said she was on the pill."

"Oh, so it's Erin's fault, huh? How far along is she?"

"About three months, I guess."

"Three months?" Nettie yelled. "And when were you going to tell me? When the lil fucka graduated from pre-K?"

"Why you gotta cuss so much?"

"Why you gotta be trifling? Go on back outside. I should come out there and help Roscoe slap some sense into you."

Jermaine looked at his mother. "Mom, I'mma grown man and you're gonna have to figure out another way to get your point across besides hitting me," he said before walking back outside.

"Well, start acting like one then," Nettie said to her son, slamming her front door as he trotted down the steps and out toward the street.

Jermaine walked up to Roscoe, who was sitting on the hood of his truck smoking a cigar.

"Why you get my daughter pregnant without consulting me?" Roscoe asked as Jermaine walked up.

"Huh?" Jermaine frowned at the awkward question.

"You heard me, damn it. And don't make me get up again, cuz I'm tired. I been arresting lil niggas like you all night," Roscoe said, shifting his weight to face Jermaine. "People ask fathers for their daughters' hands in marriage but nobody ask if they can get 'em pregnant. And that's ass backwards if you ask me. You can get a divorce and go on about your business but when a child is involved, ain't no going on about your life. Now, why didn't you ask me before you went and did the nasty with my daughter?"

"What do you want me to say, Roscoe? Me and Erin been together forever, you didn't think we were having sex?"

Roscoe raised his eyebrows and looked as if he'd seen a ghost. "Hell no! Y'all ain't married."

"Come on, Roscoe. As much as you wanna think Erin is a little angel, she's still human," Jermaine said as he walked over beside Roscoe and leaned on the hood. They had never been friends. As a matter of fact, they didn't like each other at all; they simply tolerated each other for Erin's sake.

"Jermaine, you know I don't like you. I can't stand yo' lil skinny ass. You ain't no good for my daughter. You ain't no good for black people in general. When white folks look at us, they think every one of us is like you."

"Roscoe, I couldn't care less what white people think about me."

"Ya see, that's why you ain't got nuttin' now. White people got all the power, boy, and to get a little bit you got to know how to deal with 'em. See, you're a part of that new dumb generation."

"And you are a part of that step-and-fetch-it generation."

"Shut up and listen. Some good people died just so you could have some opportunities in life, but do your ignorant ass take advantage of it? Nah. You and your little wanna-be gangster friends run around here trying y'all best to screw things up worst than they were before."

"Oh, you think so?" Jermaine said, not trying to hear the sermon.

"I know so. Did you know that as a black man, I'm more likely to die at the hands of a nigga than any other natural force in this world? Tornadoes, hurricanes, any of that shit! I'm about nigga'd out."

Jermaine wanted to laugh at Roscoe but the more he thought about it, the more he realized that Roscoe was right. Every act of violence that he ever witnessed or participated in involved another black face.

"When was the last time you had a job?"

"That's not your business," Jermaine said defiantly.

"I'm making it my business. And you need to get a haircut."

"Roscoe, how you figure you can come over here breaking windows, throwing punches, and demanding haircuts? You got some weed in that cigar?"

"I love my wife," Roscoe said, ignoring Jermaine. "I really do. But I was the worst thing that could've ever happened to her. I wasn't worth a dirty nickel. Still ain't much better than I used to be. But she saw something in me and it screwed up her whole life. Before me, she was on the fast track to success. She was in her first year of law school and doing just fine for herself but then here I come trynna get some and she's never been the same. You see what I'm getting at?"

"No."

"You screwing up my daughter's life," Roscoe yelled.

"How you figure?" Jermaine responded calmly. He was getting used to Roscoe's rants.

"Cuz you ain't worth a damn! But you'll learn. Cuz you're taking care of Erin *and* that baby. Now, I got a friend who'll hire you at his car dealership. I already set everything up, all you have to do is go—"

"Hold up! Stop! I haven't said a thing about working at no car dealership. I'm my own man and I can get my own job."

"Either you can take your ass up there and try to make a legitimate buck or I'll have one of my men bust you every time you set a foot on the street. And I'm not mentioning what I'mma do to ya."

"Roscoe, I don't know what makes you think you can handle me like your child, but you need to stop pushing your luck. I'm really trynna to be respectful here because I don't let people put their hands on me."

"Jermaine, shut up."

"Okay, but you better act like you know."

"I don't better nothing but stay black and pay my taxes. Now, before you went and violated my daughter, I could ignore you and just hope you went away. Lord knows I prayed you would go away but since you done *welcomed* yourself into my family, I gotta make sure you live a straight-and-narrow life cuz I don't want my grandchild around any foolishness."

"I guess you got it all figured out, Roscoe," Jermaine said. He knew there was no use arguing with Erin's father. He stood and walked over to the driver's side of his car. "Man, why you break my window?"

Roscoe stood and walked around to survey the damage. "You lucky I didn't break my foot off in yo' ass."

"Roscoe, you used up all of your hit-me-free cards. You raise your hands up again and I'mma knock yo' ass out," Jermaine said with a steely intensity that made Roscoe think twice about how old he really was.

"Okay, tough guy. Use some of your dope money to get your window fixed," Roscoe said as he walked over to his police car. He opened the driver's-side door and sat down, which caused the entire car to tilt to one side.

Who hired him as a police officer? You can walk and outrun him, Jermaine thought. *And how does everybody know I sell weed? I guess I do need to get a job.*

TRAVIS HUNTER is the author of the besteller *The Hearts of Men* and the upcoming *Trouble Man*. He is a motivational speaker and founder of The Hearts of Men Foundation, through which he mentors underprivileged children. For more about Hunter, his books, his tour events, and other news, visit his website, www.travishunter.com.